I0563254

Counting on Midnight

by

Jane Drager

Midnight Sky Series, Book Two

Copyright Notice
This is a work of fiction. Names, characters, places, and incidents are either the product of the author's imagination or are used fictitiously, and any resemblance to actual persons living or dead, business establishments, events, or locales, is entirely coincidental.

Counting on Midnight

COPYRIGHT © 2024 by Jane Drager

All rights reserved. No part of this book may be used or reproduced in any manner whatsoever including the purpose of training artificial intelligence technologies in accordance with Article 4(3) of the Digital Single Market Directive 2019/790, The Wild Rose Press expressly reserves this work from the text and data mining exception. Only brief quotations embodied in critical articles or reviews may be allowed.
Contact Information: info@thewildrosepress.com

Cover Art by *The Wild Rose Press, Inc.*

The Wild Rose Press, Inc.
PO Box 708
Adams Basin, NY 14410-0708
Visit us at www.thewildrosepress.com

Publishing History
First Edition, 2025
Trade Paperback ISBN 978-1-5092-6060-7
Digital ISBN 978-1-5092-6061-4

Midnight Sky Series
Published in the United States of America

Dedication

To Margie, my long-time friend and former classmate.
You left this world too soon. I will truly miss you.

Chapter One

Skylar Dawson winced as she squeezed the trigger on a nine millimeter pistol. She stood in the basement of Monroe Security Solutions in the shooting range she avoided like the plague. Despite ear protection, the blast vibrated her eardrums, and the gun's recoil was enough to jerk her shoulder out of joint. *Ugh*. She hated guns. They were cold and heavy and made far too much noise. *Give me a guy with a knife any day.*

Near the back wall, Logan Greene, ex-cop and firearms instructor, snorted.

The man enjoyed torturing her. Couldn't he have picked a smaller gun, like the kind a gambler slipped from his vest pocket to shoot a cheater? Oh, how she wanted to kick Logan in the shins for talking her into this. He deserved a good pounding...the bedroom kind, but hey, they were at work, and teaching her how to shoot was not what she'd call sexual foreplay.

Stepping inside the three-sided cubical, Logan clamped onto her wrists and pushed a palm against her left elbow. "Hold the wrists tight and lock the elbow, Sky. You'll have more stability." He patted Sky's shoulder. "Not bad for a beginner, though. At least, you held onto the weapon. Try another shot, but this time, keep your eyes open."

She'd rather look at her muscular bedmate rather than some paper target on the wall, especially when he wore T-shirts that outlined the bulges on his chest and arms. His muscular physique caused every woman within eyesight to salivate—herself included—and would be perfect for the cover of a romance novel. She loved brushing her fingers across his solid abs to watch the goose bumps rise.

She and Logan met last year when she came to New Jersey from Chicago. By a twist of fate, she inherited her aunt's estate in Woodstown, and oh my, what an estate. The property included a beautiful boardinghouse and a separate rancher with lots of acreage. Unfortunately, not only did Ginger's Manor house a load of quirky tenants, but it also contained a cold-blooded killer. Logan was a cop on an undercover assignment and rented a room among those tenants. When all this information came to light, she almost hightailed it back to Chicago and said adios to the inheritance. After all, she had no idea how to be a landlord and, even more important, how to catch a killer. She was just an ordinary bartender living an ordinary life who so happened to inherit a multi-million dollar estate from an aunt she never knew. *Talk about a storybook plot.*

Huffing, Sky glanced over her shoulder at her brown-haired lover boy. His copper-colored eyes gazed at her like she might take a swing at his handsome face. She'd never hurt him, but she could handle five men his size without breaking a sweat. "Why is Monroe pushing me to use a gun? He hired me for martial arts and not one of his cloak-and-dagger guys."

"We're not cloak-and-dagger, Sky. We're security. Big difference. The more you know about how to handle a weapon, the better you can disarm." He adjusted his earmuffs.

Well, true. She might have ninja skills, but a bullet was faster. Over the years, she trained with every conceivable weapon created, but Grand Master Li never brought guns onto the mat. At Ginger's Manor, when she discovered her aunt was one of the victims, she had no idea what to do. Logan convinced her they could work as a team, and together, they caught the killer...well, *she* caught the killer. Not because she acquired great skill under Logan's tutelage. She attributed the encounter to being in the wrong place at the wrong time. She faced the killer with a pistol and managed to survive, but she'd rather not repeat the experience, thank you very much. She was perfectly content teaching self-defense to a bunch of ex-cops on the payroll.

Because of how well she handled herself—in other words, she didn't panic or cry her eyes out—she was offered a position at Monroe Security Solutions in Newfield, New Jersey, as their part-time martial arts instructor.

Logan also received an offer but as a full-time agent.

Right now, Logan had her in the basement of the Monroe building surrounded by soundproofing tiles she'd prefer were over her ears, instead of plastered to the walls. Those black foam tiles might work a lot better than the safety ear muffs that were supposed to block out the noise.

Exhaling audibly, Logan shifted on his feet. "Come on, Sky. One more round."

Sure, if she wanted to lose the rest of her hearing. Those three little words belonged in the bedroom, not here in this chilly basement. But over the last few months, she and Logan found their jobs interfering with bedtime activities. Not that she didn't try, but some of his assignments took him away for weeks.

He nudged her arm. "Open your eyes, Sky."

Rats. He caught her. Peering through one eye, she squeezed the trigger.

Logan released a long breath. "I can see you need some practice."

"Hey, I hit the target."

"You hit the edge of the paper. That's like a warning shot off the starboard bow."

Simultaneously, their cell phones chirped with a text message.

Since she assigned special tones for important people, she recognized instantly who called. She slipped the phone from her back pocket and read. "Monroe wants to see me in his office."

"Me, too. Something's up." He swiped his finger across the screen and frowned.

After replacing her phone into her pocket, she grinned. "I hope it's food. I'm hungry." She removed her earmuffs and placed them on the counter against the back wall.

He smirked. "You just had a big lunch. Where do you put all this food?"

"I have a great metabolism." Or was lucky. She wasn't sure which. At five-foot-eight and a hundred and thirty pounds, she couldn't claim to be anywhere close to an hourglass figure. Her martial arts kept her body lean but muscled.

Logan took the gun from her hand. "Monroe's probably calling a meeting."

So, why involve her? For the most part, she had little to do with the day-to-day operations of the company. Thanks to her inheritance, she not only owned a successful business but also her own separate rancher, all free and clear. To be honest, Sky didn't need to work at all, but she wasn't one to sit around and read magazines while munching on a box of chocolates. Teaching self-defense was an excellent way to keep in shape—especially when her students were big, burly men.

Logan pressed the button to release the gun's clip, then chambered the last bullet from the barrel. "You'll eventually learn how to break down a weapon to clean it."

Oh, joy. "Why?"

He narrowed his gaze. "A clean gun is a dependable gun." Opening the cabinet behind him, he placed the weapon and clip on a shelf and locked the door. After removing his ear protection, he slid the muffs alongside hers on the counter. "But before we go—" He clamped onto her arms and crushed her back against the foam tiles.

His mouth hit hers with a hunger that both surprised and thrilled her. He was the one man who roughhoused her and lived to talk afterward. By now, anyone else would be flat on the floor. As her tongue touched his lips, she sighed. Logan always tasted so good. If given a choice, she'd stay lip-locked for hours, but Monroe was waiting. *Like I really care.* She hooked her arms around Logan's neck and deepened the kiss. Well, hell, maybe shooting a weapon *was* foreplay— especially for a guy like Logan.

When he lifted his head, he smiled. "Your mouth is

a temptation I can't ignore."

Returning the smile, she pecked his lips. "You can crush me against these foam tiles anytime." Logan was so different from the men in her past. Their time together wasn't always the wham-bam-thank-you-ma'am stuff. Because of his busier schedule, he leased an apartment near Monroe Security while she lived twenty minutes away in Woodstown. When he came to her place, he stayed the night and prepared breakfast in the morning. He liked to cuddle—yes, cuddle—and they often had long talks while snuggled under the sheets. His gentle ways left her speechless and…loved—or maybe a better word was cherished. Neither of them talked about love or exclusiveness and certainly never discussed marriage with the white picket fence and two point five kids. She might be a closet math whiz, but how could a woman have half a kid?

Nodding toward the door, he released her. "Come on. Let's see what Monroe wants."

She still hoped it was food. And now that she had weak knees, she needed sustenance. Leading the way, she ascended the steps to the main floor. The building also had a second floor with a weight room and several large mats where she enjoyed throwing big men over her shoulder. Since most of the guys were ex-cops and outweighed her by a good hundred pounds, they sauntered onto the mat full of skepticism about her abilities to take them down. Two minutes into their first lesson, they soon learned how her speed and agility earned her three black belts.

Continuing down the hall, she glanced into the conference room. Empty. The next office was Pamela's, their information technology expert with her array of computers—also empty. By process of elimination, the meeting was in Monroe's office at the end of the hall. Since hardly anyone buzzed around the office today, that left her, Logan, and Vittoria Carbone, the office manager, for this meeting—unless Monroe called in the gang.

All right, so she was curious.

She had to congratulate Robert Monroe on his foresight. He started his security firm before he retired from the New Jersey State Police and went from working in a shabby office with state budget constraints to one boasting of success. When she and Logan entered through the opened door, as expected, the six-foot-four man with his notorious crew cut and sharp gray eyes sat behind his large mahogany desk with its beautifully carved corners. On the wall behind him, framed awards and photos hung, along with degrees and certifications. A plush sofa of soft leather rested against one wall, and on the opposite side of the room was a mini-bar full with some of the finest liquor money could buy.

A man in a dark gray suit lounged on one of two plush high-back chairs in front of the desk. Glancing over the high-back, he stood and turned with an expression about as readable as a mask.

Confusion flooded her. As the martial arts instructor, she never met any clients except in passing, and this man most definitely appeared like a client. Monroe's services weren't cheap, and if she wasn't mistaken, the man wore an off-the-rack suit. He also studied her, as if she were some kind of puzzle. She glanced at Logan.

He merely shrugged his broad shoulders.

Her lover boy was of no help whatsoever.

"Sky, Logan, come in and have a seat." Standing, Monroe waved toward the sofa. "This is Dominic Pasquale from the United States Treasury Department in Washington, D.C. Dom, meet Skylar Dawson and Logan Greene."

Dominic Pasquale certainly fit the tall, dark, and handsome description. With his dark, curly hair, brown eyes, and full lips, he was as swoon-worthy as a movie star. He looked about Monroe's age, maybe early fifties, but wow, if the man smiled, he might melt her into a pile of goo.

Logan coughed. Catching her gaze, he cocked a brow.

Ah, so he noticed her ogling the man. *Too bad.* She appreciated fine art when she saw it. Smiling, she waggled her eyebrows, then turned to Dominic and extended a hand. The treasury guy shook with a weak grip without a smile or a grunt, but he watched her with his gaze a tad too scrutinizing, which confused her even more.

After shaking his hand, Logan cleared his throat. "Let's sit, Sky."

Yeah, because she had the strangest feeling she wouldn't like anything about this meeting. From the way Monroe acted by standing to the side, he had something up his sleeve, and her gut churned. Granted, she had a beef burrito for lunch, but the recipe wasn't too spicy. Lowering onto the sofa, she perched herself on one side while Logan filled the other end.

Strolling to the front of his desk, Monroe slipped his butt onto the corner. "I suppose you two are wondering why I called you here. Way back when, Dominic and I worked Vice in and around Elizabeth, and he's presented us with an unusual case. It's a deviation from our normal security details. So, listen carefully. Go ahead, Dom."

Sky raised a hand. "Who's Elizabeth?"

Gaze twinkling, Monroe quirked his lips. "It's a city in North Jersey."

"Oh...sorry." Her knowledge of New Jersey could be described on one tiny slip of paper. She moved east less than a year ago and still struggled to find places in South Jersey, let alone any town north. Adventurous she was not, and right now, she fought like mad not to stomp like a petulant child and scream, "Why am I here?"

The treasury guy stuffed his hands into his trouser pockets. "For several years, we have followed the trail of money disappearing from some high-income men. The amount is always the same and always in cash—two hundred and fifty grand." He shot a quick glance between Sky and Logan. "As per banking regulations, the amount triggers an alert to the treasury department with a similar alert issued when the money is deposited, but a deposit never happens. Either the person receiving the money deposits the cash in small increments into several banks over a period of time, or the money is buried in a backyard somewhere." Pursing his lips, he strolled around the room.

"It took more than a year to pinpoint the common denominator linking all these men. Our records showed withdrawals from banks in New York and northern New Jersey and two from Pennsylvania. By luck, one gentleman transferred his money from his hometown bank in Brooklyn to a branch in Atlantic City where he withdrew the cash. From there, our investigation tracked his steps to the Whirlwind Casino on the boardwalk." Pausing, he again shifted his gaze from Logan to Sky. "Then, he disappeared." He continued his leisurely stroll.

"As we proceeded with the investigation, we uncovered some viable reasons why these men vanished. Background checks revealed three were escaping the clutches of a divorce gone bad. One was involved in a lawsuit with his own children, and two wanted out of a marriage where divorce wasn't an option. Once we cleared the casino of any wrongdoing, we studied the security footage and found several of the men in question sitting at the second-floor bar near the high-roller tables. This bar became our starting point for our undercover operative." Pausing again, he jiggled the change in his pocket and faced Sky and Logan.

"Since our operative was already divorced, he used the ex-wife angle and was approached by the bar manager, Johnny Dee. For two hundred and fifty grand, Johnny guaranteed to make anyone disappear. He claimed he had the ability to create false IDs and passports and provided whatever the client desired. So, our operative met Johnny with marked money at a house not too far from the casino. The money and operative have yet to surface."

Sky shivered. The agent's story didn't sound good at all, and again, she wondered why she sat here. She shot a quick glance at Logan to see his eyes bright with interest. Yeah, he would be. Like any man, he thrived on action. She, on the other hand, would rather hop on her motorcycle and return to her cute little rancher.

Logan leaned forward. "You think your operative is dead?"

Exhaling a long breath, Pasquale met Logan's gaze. "We don't know. As far as we can tell, he had no reason to disappear. Yet, where did he go?" He sighed. "To track his movements, we secured a homing device to his body. Once he entered the house, his signal disappeared. It never reappeared on our computer screen."

Sitting back, Logan crossed an ankle over his knee. "Maybe he took the money and defected. He can give a foreign government a lot of intel about our treasury department."

Keeping his right hand inside his pocket, Pasquale rubbed the nape of his neck with his left. "We arrived at that assumption and changed all access codes. He's virtually locked out of the system." He replaced his left hand into his pocket and continued his slow stroll. "If any information was downloaded prior to his disappearance, our IT techs would have discovered it." He stopped alongside Monroe. "We have other agents willing to go undercover, but with so many unanswered questions, we needed a different approach." He smiled at Monroe. "Bob and I often discuss our puzzling cases. When everything comes to a standstill, it helps to get a fresh perspective, and he suggested some intriguing ideas." He cleared his throat. "Your turn, Bob."

"Right." Crossing his arms over his massive chest, Monroe lifted his lips into a half-smile. "Since the entire case centers around the Whirlwind's second-floor lounge, what we need is to place someone behind the bar." He locked his gaze onto Sky.

Her stomach rolled. *Oh, holy hell…no!*

Chapter Two

Monroe was joking, right? She had zero training as an agent and had absolutely no interest in becoming one. Sure, back in Chicago, she was a darn good bartender and earned enough tips to spread among the other employees, but really, Monroe was out of his mind. *No way, no how.* Frowning at Monroe but shifting her gaze to the treasury guy, she fought to keep her voice steady. "Why don't you just go into the house where your operative disappeared?"

With a snort, Pasquale shook his head. "If we did that, we'd blow the entire undercover operation. Even if we performed a little B and E, we'd be spotted on the exterior cameras."

Arching a brow, Sky looked at Logan. "What's B and E?"

Jerking his head back, Logan stared. "Breaking and Entering."

See? She couldn't speak cop legalese either. Monroe was making a big mistake here.

Pasquale held up a finger. "The exterior of the house is covered by cameras. We have no idea what might be inside, but we assume more cameras." He crossed his arms over his chest. "For two solid weeks, we kept the house under twenty-four-hour surveillance. No one came or went."

Logan dropped his foot to the floor. "Surely, you

wired your man with more than a homing device."

The agent shook his head. "We couldn't take the chance. Casino security is tight. We have no idea how many people are involved or who. Our operative only met the bar manager. However, it's possible someone was already waiting inside the house." He dropped his arms. "Phone records show multiple calls from disposable phones and never the same number more than twice. Since our operative was not instructed to use a disposable phone, then Johnny Dee must have a partner." He rubbed his forehead, then shifted his gaze between Logan and Sky. "You can see the dilemma we face. If we barge in with a warrant, we'll destroy years of work." Dropping his hand, he smirked. "We'd never get a warrant, anyway. Johnny's clients pay for a service. Is it illegal? Technically, no—except for the false IDs. He isn't aiding and abetting criminals. His clientele happens to be rich men wanting to escape a personal crisis."

Yeah, rich men who believe they can buy anything. What a bunch of wimps! Instead of facing the problem, they paid a huge sum of money to run and hide. Whatever happened to having a little backbone? She could think of a hundred better uses for so much cash. Averting her gaze, she lifted an ankle onto her knee and tugged on the pants hem.

Monroe cleared his throat. "We studied Johnny's finances. He is not a rich man. Deposits into his account come from his casino paycheck. He lives alone in a modest condo, has been married twice, and pays no alimony. So, where is the money he earns with every disappearance?"

"A vault," Logan suggested.

Pasquale tapped the side of his nose. "Exactly. We're guessing the money is stuffed inside a safe somewhere and possibly inside that house."

Slipping off the desk, Monroe stepped alongside his friend. "Here's the kicker, Sky. In the past three years, two bartenders disappeared from Johnny's bar. These were ordinary women who seemingly vanished off the face of the earth. From what we uncovered so far, Johnny prefers female bartenders. So, we suspect he uses them as lures to get the men talking."

Oh, swell. What more could he say to make her want to jump up and run? *Put me on a hook and dangle me as bait*. Maybe she should quit while she was ahead. She glared at Monroe.

Crossing his arms over his chest, Pasquale stared with half-veiled eyes.

His scrutiny was a bit unnerving. If he had doubts about her ability to work this case, he should express them now. She could use all the negative comments to her advantage.

The treasury guy shifted his gaze to Logan. "We don't know how long this operation has been in existence. We could be talking about dozens of clients. What we need to know is if Johnny Dee is funding a drug cartel or a terrorist organization or even a foreign government hostile to the United States." Frowning, he met her gaze. "We are not forcing you into this, Ms. Dawson, but we don't have a female agent on staff who tended bar nor do we have the time to train one to be convincing enough to fool Johnny Dee. Should you decide not to participate, you have the right. We will work out something else. As per Bob's stipulation for taking the case, Bob will be in control from here on out.

I'll be a phone call away with whatever help he needs. Good luck." He turned to Monroe and shook his hand. With a nod toward Logan and then Skylar, he left the office.

Well, this wasn't fun. Throwing a big guy over her shoulder and slamming him onto a mat was fun. How could Monroe think she'd agree to go? Yes, all right, from day one, he pushed her to be more than his martial arts instructor, but she wasn't an ex-cop like some of the other agents. Her noteworthy skill consisted of mixing cocktails from memory.

She sighed. Her whole life, people pushed her to better herself. First, her high school counselors encouraged her to enroll in more difficult courses. With her IQ nearing the genius level, she heard one counselor after another list reasons why she should accept the challenge of higher education. She laughed at their suggestions. She had no desire to attend college. Sure, her parents were disappointed, but she hated school and couldn't wait to graduate.

Next, Grand Master Li pushed her to compete in mixed martial arts. He said she could become a world-class champion. Maybe so, but why would she fight for a living? She'd met a few MMA competitors. They were covered with scars. *No, thank you.*

Now, Monroe nudged her to be an agent, and she didn't like the push one bit. Why was it so hard for people to understand she hadn't an ambitious bone in her body?

She should thumb her nose at Monroe and go home to eat dinner with the gang at the manor. While she was technically their landlord, she enjoyed the family atmosphere and soaked in all the love and support they offered, and they made a great sounding board. Normally, she'd talk to Logan, but in this case, she'd waste her time. The man thrived on this covert stuff, and judging from the glow in his eyes, he couldn't wait to get started. She, on the other hand, wanted to go home and take a nap. Frowning at Monroe, she shook her head. "I'm not interested."

Monroe held up a hand, palm outward. "Before you continue, let me explain the plan." Turning, he lifted one of the large leather chairs to the front of his desk and placed it to face her and Logan.

The man was powerfully built. He handled the high-back like it was an aluminum beach chair. She'd need to place those little sliding thingies under the chair's feet just to turn it. And his hands…*Lord Almighty*. They were the size of bear claws. Too bad, he never married. Those hands would make a woman very happy.

As he took his seat, he unbuttoned his suit jacket.

Ever since she'd known him, the man dressed in a suit. When he worked for the state police, he always wore a tie, but as the head of Monroe Security, he was sans tie now. He appeared a lot more relaxed without a noose around his thick neck.

He shot his gaze from her to Logan. "We already know our primary target is Johnny Dee. Thanks to the reports filed by the operative, we know the regulars who frequent the bar and the staff. We also know the house where the clients disappeared. So, we have a lot of intel to begin."

Sitting forward, Logan leaned both elbows on his knees. "Our primary objective is to discover what's inside the house. Can't we jam all the security cameras?"

Monroe shook his head. "Pamela completed her recon and said the system is sophisticated enough to have safeguards in place—like remote access and battery backup. The only way to disable it is wherever the main control is. Pam's guess is a computer inside the house. So—" He sat back. "My plan is to place Sky as the bartender. She will be the eyes and ears for all the bar activity. Logan will enter as the disgruntled chief executive officer going through a bad divorce. All money for this case will come from the treasury department."

Feeling as if she might explode, Sky slammed a foot to the floor and leaned forward. "Why me, Bob? I'm not trained for this stuff."

Monroe gave a soft smile. "Listen, Sky, you're sharp and beautiful. Those are two major pluses for this case to succeed. You also have years of tending bar under your belt, which is something Johnny will see."

"But I don't have a New Jersey license."

"Yeah, well—" He coughed. "New Jersey doesn't require a bartender license, per se, but most of the towns demand certification. For Atlantic City, I've already put your application on the fast track. As per our own security protocols, your name has been changed to your code name, Midnight Sky. Logan will also be under a false name." With his gaze intent on her face, he leaned forward. "I know you can take care of yourself, but Logan will always be nearby. He will be Johnny's main focus. You will be in a position to listen and supplement Logan's story. You'll both watch each other's back. We don't know how many people are involved, and that's what we need to uncover."

Logan huffed. "What about Johnny's phone records? Did Pam have a go at them?"

Monroe sat back. "Pam took a good look at what the Feds uncovered. The records show a long stretch in time from one disposable phone to the next. Each coincided with a client's disappearance. This fact alone tells me Johnny communicates with his partner whenever a client comes into the picture."

Logan frowned. "In other words, we need to go through the entire process in order to get our answers. But that's what the Feds did."

"Yes, we will be especially vigilant, but it's safe to say the plan hinges on Sky and what she hears and sees." Meeting her gaze, Monroe held up a finger. "I'm still working on details. As far as the two missing bartenders, the records show two men paid double. It's safe to assume they asked the women to tag along, and Johnny demanded payment."

Snorting, Sky pressed against the sofa's back cushion and folded her arms across her chest. "I haven't agreed to this yet, Bob." She might not agree at all, but something told her Bob had no other option. If that were the case, he wouldn't surrender easily. She rubbed her forehead. "Maybe I should make out a will."

"Hey." Rotating to face her, Logan touched her arm. "With what you inherited, you should have one."

Oh, sure. What thirty-one-year-old woman thought about all that legal stuff? But he was right. She owned a nice chunk of real estate, and without family... She met his gaze. He looked at her as if she had a screw loose. Could she help it if she hated all that legal mumbo jumbo? Curling one side of her mouth, she nodded. "Yes, all right. I'll make an appointment with a lawyer."

Monroe cleared his throat. "I can't force you into this, Skylar, but I can assure you we won't move forward without a firm plan in place. While we have no idea what's inside the house, I will work with assumptions. As we proceed and uncover more information, I will make deviations to the plan, and that's all part of keeping my agents safe." Gaze twinkling, he leaned forward. "If it helps with your decision, the casino employees wear black T-shirts with black trousers. Right up your alley."

Oh, good grief. As if wardrobe would be key to her decision. Come to think of it, yes, he could be right. She wore black—period—save for the diamond-studded wristwatch from her late father. Her hair—while short-cropped and shaved close to the neck—was naturally black. In fact, her two bursts of color consisted of tanned skin and crystal-blue eyes. Even her big-ass motorcycle was black, along with boots and jacket. Her great-aunt left her a white sedan, though. She should trade it in.

Monroe slapped his knees and stood. "I have work to do. In a few days, I'll call everyone involved for a briefing. Logan, talk to her." He tugged off his suit jacket. "Now, you two get out of here and have some fun."

Fun? Was that what bosses told their agents before sending them to face who knew what?

Halfway down the hall, Logan slid an arm around her shoulders. "You okay?"

The man still shot sparks across her skin. She'd known him for ten months, and over time, those sparks intensified into bolts of lightning. She half-expected her hair to stand on end. She glanced his way. He had a cute smile that turned her insides into mush. From day one, his light brown hair and copper-colored eyes drew her in like some magnet, and his woodsy cologne was embedded into her memory forever. The man was just too handsome. She huffed out a breath. "I'm not sure about this. Monroe has more confidence in me than I have in myself."

"As an employee for the casino, you'd be in a prime position to eavesdrop on the bar patrons. One of them could be Johnny's partner. In fact, anyone acquainted with Johnny could be a potential accomplish."

"Or Johnny could be by himself with no partner whatsoever." She headed for the lunch room near the stairwell to the second floor.

He followed. "Truthfully, Sky, I'm leery about you getting involved. Not because you can't handle yourself, but because cases can go in all sorts of directions."

Gaze narrowed, she whirled to face him and clamped onto the front of his T-shirt. "Did you have any idea about this assignment? Is that why you practically dragged me to the shooting range?"

He raised his hands, palms outward. "No to both questions. But if the case hinges on a bartender, you are the most qualified. The best part is we'll be working together again." He dropped his hands. "I like the idea."

Logan as a partner was a plus, even if his presence failed to help her confidence. She humphed, but before releasing his shirt, she pecked his lips. Entering the lunch room, she aimed straight for the coffee machine on the far counter.

Leaning against the counter, Logan crossed his arms over his chest. "If you remember, you didn't want to solve your aunt's murder, but you performed beyond expectations."

"Pfft. My involvement catching the manor killer was entirely by accident, and you know it. Besides, I felt a certain obligation. Aunt Ginger left me so much, and I owed her. I don't owe anyone this time." Scanning the selection of coffee pods, she chose a French vanilla roast and popped it into the holder. All these wonderful flavors made her time at the office worthwhile. Coffee at home was…coffee. Here, she had a selection for whatever fancied her. After pressing the On button, she faced Logan. "I'll admit I'm a little intrigued about Johnny Dee's operation. He must meet some desperate people if disappearance is their only option."

"Desperation is the hook." He tugged on his ear. "Bob talked about expanding the business into different areas. Missing people seems like a place to start."

Pushing away from the counter, he strolled to the refrigerator and extracted a bottle of water. After a long pull, he smacked his lips.

She always liked his longish, light brown hair. The wavy strands slipped through her fingers like silk. Would he need a haircut for this assignment, maybe something more stylish for a man with money? She hoped not, but as long as he avoided a crew cut like Monroe's, she'd live with the change. Hair could grow back.

"I won't lie to you, Sky. No assignment is a piece of cake. After being an undercover cop for the state police, I can tell you with each case, I had no idea the

21

level of danger until I faced it full on. You expect the worse, and when it doesn't happen, you're pleasantly surprised." He sipped his water, then pointed the bottle her way. "The one important aspect I learned working for Monroe Security is Bob's projects are planned to the letter. He's meticulous and will do everything in his power to minimize the danger."

He'd need to be super thorough with a complete novice at the helm. With her coffee done, she took a sniff. French vanilla. *Yum.* For an extra treat, she added a lot of sugar and cream. She could afford her own coffee pods at home, but then, coffee at work wouldn't be special.

Logan smiled. "Wait for the briefing and make your decision then. I know he's counting on the quick-thinking Midnight Sky. If he had doubts, he wouldn't have involved you."

Well, she sure had a load of doubts. After the arrest of the manor's killer, not once had she itched to repeat the danger of her first encounter with death. So, why was she considering it now?

Chapter Three

As the days passed, Skylar hemmed and hawed over what to do. She stayed locked in her rancher and paced, slept little, and ate even less. On several occasions, she called Monroe with a list of questions, and he soothed over whatever doubts she had, but she hated how the entire case hinged on her participation. The man was crazy for thinking she could pull this off. She had zero experience with secret agent stuff. What if she said or did something wrong? She could jeopardize Monroe's hard-won reputation for being one of the rising security firms in the business.

Logan was no help. He came over to stay one night. They talked. They cuddled. As usual, sex was amazing. But Logan had more preparations for his assignment—namely, a new wardrobe. He would be playing a wealthy CEO and had to look the part. But could she let him go on this assignment alone or worse, with another woman? No, she couldn't. On the flip side of the coin, she was the only qualified person to handle a busy bar. Really, though, she could do the job with her eyes closed. A decision made, she called Monroe and agreed to be the undercover bartender. *Shoot me now*.

When she, Logan, and several others gathered for the final briefing, she again questioned her sanity. Serious pros sat in this conference room who, thankfully, didn't look at her like a bug smear on the wall. Monroe emphasized her pivotal role. Yet, in the next breath, he stressed how the case could go in any direction. Why did he have to say that? She was not a seasoned agent and would lean heavily on Logan's experience. Of course, leaning on her favorite guy was not the worst part through all this, but for the first two weeks, she would be on her own. That little tidbit of information kept her nerves on edge. Per Monroe's plan, she had to get her foot in the door and establish her presence. Somehow, Monroe's reassuring words were not so…reassuring.

Being home surrounded by her extended family helped keep her anxiety in check. The old calm-before-the-storm sort of thing. Despite being the landlord, she had a bunch of people who looked out for her. She couldn't disappear for a month or however long the case lasted without telling them. So, no more putting off the inevitable.

The next morning, Skylar stepped from her rancher into the bright April sun and stopped. Almost every single day, the awe hit her at the size of the property her great-aunt bequeathed. Sky would have been happy with just the rancher, but Lord Almighty, the boardinghouse was something else. The converted mini-mansion consisted of twelve small apartments, two large sitting rooms, and one enormous kitchen. Her separate rancher and the manor sat on five acres surrounded by a four-foot hedgerow, and beyond the hedge, a farmer rented a twenty-acre field for crops.

The income generated from both the field and rooms allowed her the freedom to work at Monroe Security whenever the mood hit. Plus, her aunt left sizable bank accounts and investments. How lucky could one girl get? And on this beautiful spring morning with a warm sun overhead, yet with a nip in the air, she felt light and carefree—to a point…if she could keep the nervous energy to a minimum.

"Skylar!"

Startled to hear her name come out of nowhere, she turned toward the parking lot in time to see Philip Santini slam the door on his red sports coupe. She never understood how he fit into such a small vehicle. He was over six feet. Maybe he liked driving with his knees up to his chin. She waved. "Hey! What are you doing here?"

The guy was handsome and knew it. Tall and nicely tailored in a gray suit, he epitomized the image of a successful lawyer. They met when his mom resided at the manor. Unfortunately, he and Logan were always at odds—over her, of course. Not that she encouraged them, but their feud sure helped her ego.

"I'm delivering your legal documents." He raised his briefcase. "Can we talk privately?"

"Sure. Come into my office." She always sounded so important whenever she mentioned *her* office. She understood nothing about business, but with the help of her late aunt's best friend and housekeeper, Fay Bartleson, Sky learned a detail or two. The woman kept the manor running like a well-oiled machine, and to make her a partner turned into the smartest decision Skylar Dawson ever made. Philip handled the legal aspects of their business association, but today, Philip's visit had nothing to do with manor business. Sky finally got her butt in gear and devised a will.

Leading the way into the office—which was

nothing more than the rancher's converted front porch—she waved toward the chair alongside the desk. "Have a seat."

"No, thanks. This won't take long." He rested his briefcase on the desk and clicked the metal locks. After lifting the lid, he grabbed a packet and held it out. "It's all in there. Your will, power of attorney, and advanced directive with detailed medical instructions."

"Thanks." She fingered the fat packet, then smiled. "You shouldn't have come all the way here. I would have been glad to return to your office. I'm totally out of your way now." He'd recently left the Salem County Public Defender's office for a well-known firm in Cherry Hill. Being new to New Jersey, she hadn't a clue where Cherry Hill was. Up north somewhere, she guessed.

"Are you still with Logan?" He closed his briefcase and snapped the latches.

Well, *that* question was coming. Every time he visited, he asked, and her answer was always the same. She chuckled. "Yeah, Philip, still together."

With a raised brow, he cocked his head. "And not serious?"

So predictable. She shook her head. "Not serious." *Poor guy.* He'd like nothing more than to hear Logan left the state. She opened the packet with one of those string thingies to tie the flap. She skimmed the documents.

"You should read them carefully, Sky, and let me know if you have any questions. The language is straightforward without too much legalese. If you'd like, we can discuss any questions over lunch." He waggled a brow.

The man never gave up. Smiling, she touched his arm. "You know my answer."

He harrumphed. "Right. Anyway, I've stored a copy in the firm's safe."

"Thank you, Philip." She wished he would find someone special. He deserved a nice woman. After she waved goodbye, she put the packet in her bedroom for later reading, then returned to her original task of informing Fay. After hopping onto the manor's rear patio, she entered the kitchen through the back door.

As usual, the aromas of bacon, eggs, and coffee filled the air. Three tenants lounged at one of the two large tables with mugs of coffee in their hands. Since the room rent included meals, two tables plus sixteen chairs accommodated all the tenants. The kitchen was huge, and she always felt as if she walked into a banquet hall that so happened to include appliances. But the tenants were her family now, and three of her favorites looked up as she entered.

Anthony Powers, a retired engineer, was the oldest tenant at eighty-something. Next to him sat Tyrone Houser, a retired maintenance man in his seventies. Tyrone, a black man, always made Anthony look a little pale whenever they stood side by side. But the two elderly men were inseparable. If one entered a room, the other followed.

The third man was Too-Tall Joe Ryan. The tenants gave him the nickname because he needed an extra-long bed. Joe still worked as a bartender and was a bit peculiar with his strange Bible quotes, but something about the man was likable. Too bad, he wasn't younger and female. Monroe could have used him as his bartender.

At the sink, Fay Bartleson, in her ever-present waist apron, rinsed dishes before placing them into the dishwasher. A woman in her fifties and widowed, she fussed over Sky like some mother hen. She would be the one to send out the army if Sky failed to tell her about her new assignment.

Fay turned and smiled. "Good morning. Did you eat?"

The woman always acted like Sky hadn't an ounce of food in the rancher. But a warm feeling spread inside her chest to know someone cared. Sky's parents were long gone from this earth, and the feeling of family with Fay and the tenants was the main factor that prompted her move from Chicago. Sky shot Fay a quick grin. "Yes, thank you, and good morning to everyone."

She immediately headed for the coffeemaker and poured herself a cup. Coffee was her go-to beverage. She never started a day without a shot of caffeine. This was her second cup this morning and probably not her last. After a sip, she pulled out the chair next to Joe and lowered onto the seat. Shifting her gaze from one man to the next, she felt an unease settle within her gut. These three guys loved her as much as she loved them, and her news would not be welcomed. She swallowed a gulp and nearly burned her tongue.

Anthony peered his sharp, brown eyes over his glasses. "What's the matter? You break your coffee machine again?"

Flashing a set of beautiful white teeth, Tyrone chuckled. "More likely, she ran out of coffee."

These two guys were always a big tease. She wasn't their only target, but she suspected they enjoyed pulling her chain. Snorting, she put on her best indignant face, which didn't work. Her lips had a mind of its own, and she fought to hide a smile. "I'll have you know it's none of the above. I'm being sociable."

While wiping her hands on her waist apron, Fay walked over. Her speckled eyeglasses had slipped halfway down her nose. She used a finger to push them up. "You usually come in at dinnertime, not breakfast. You must have something on your mind."

Busted. "All right, yes. I came in to tell you something."

With a gnarled finger, Anthony tapped the table. "Well, spit it out, woman. We ain't getting any younger over here."

The tenants nicknamed Anthony Mister Grumpy, but Sky always liked him. He had a way of lightening the mood. Between him and Tyrone, they always made her laugh. "Have a seat, Fay."

"Uh-oh. Sounds serious." Fay pulled out a chair opposite Sky and flopped onto the seat. "What's up?"

Raising her cup to her mouth, she avoided eye contact. "I'll be going away for a while, and I don't know how long." She sipped.

Joe lowered his cup to the table. "Where ya going?"

"Not far, but I can't give you any details."

Behind her glasses, Fay narrowed her gaze. "Does this have anything to do with Monroe Security?"

"Yes." Sky swore Fay was a mind reader. The woman had this uncanny ability to put facts together before explanations were given. On the plus side, she saved Sky a lot of time.

Tyrone gave her a one-eyed stare. "This is more than you being a martial arts instructor, isn't it?"

She swallowed a sip. "Yes." She hated to keep secrets, especially from people she loved. She cleared her throat and turned to the housekeeper. "Fay, if you don't mind, keep an eye on the food in my refrigerator. I'm hoping to be home before anything expires."

With a pinched face, she huffed. "Okay, but I don't like it. What Logan did was dangerous enough. I don't fancy you following in his footsteps."

Joe wagged a finger. " 'Bread of deceit is sweet to a man; but afterward, his mouth shall be filled with gravel.' "

Well, duh. Another strange quote that made no sense. The man must have the Bible memorized.

Joe crossed his arms over his chest. "If Logan's there to watch over you, we'll feel better."

See? They were a bunch of nice people who cared. "Yes, Logan is on the same assignment. I'll be a bartender again, which is something I can deal with." Wincing, she tugged on her right ear. "Truthfully, I don't know if I'm cut out to do this covert stuff."

Anthony grunted. "If you're working behind a bar, it doesn't sound too covert."

Fay patted Sky's arm. "You can do anything you set your mind to, honey. Just don't let Monroe push."

"He didn't. He gave me enough time to think." She sipped her coffee. The liquid was getting cold, but it still tasted good. "I'll leave in a few days. I've some packing to do. You can text with any problems but keep it to a minimum, and don't expect me to answer right away." She gulped the last of her coffee and stood.

Fay also stood and wrapped Sky in a tight hug. "You be careful. If anything happens to you, I'll ream Monroe's ass." She dropped her arms and grinned. "We all will."

The woman was always so warm and welcoming, and Sky's heart swelled. Fay's mother hen title fit like a glove. "So you know, I went to Philip Santini and wrote out a will. It was long overdue."

Joe chuckled. "I'm glad Philip pushed the lead out of his ass and joined a real law firm. He can't pay for his mother's upkeep on a public defender's salary."

Anthony grunted. "Too bad, the old battle-ax is in la-la land and doesn't know how much he's doing for her."

No one missed Maria Santini—Sky included. The woman was downright crazy. With nothing more to say, Sky moved toward the back door and, turning to face them, sucked in a calming breath. "Wish me luck." What she really needed was a whole lot of courage.

****

Logan paced Monroe's spacious office. Luckily, a plush carpet covered the floor, so his boots wouldn't echo with every step. Damn, he had a strong urge to kick something. With all this nervous energy, he acted like some trapped lab rat. He should be upstairs punching like hell on one of the bags in the workout area. Not because he was angry. Frustrated would be the word—no, more like anxious. Before joining Monroe Security, he'd been an undercover cop for years and understood the dangers involved. "I don't like it, Bob."

Sighing, Monroe swiveled in his chair. "We've had this argument already. Give her a chance. She listened to the briefing and didn't bolt."

"Hell, I know she'll do okay. I'm concerned about you counting on Sky too much."

"Who else do we know who's worked behind a bar for five years?" He held up a finger. "I know you're thinking of Joe Ryan, but a woman is vital for success. Sky is an excellent choice. She's smart, beautiful, and has killer ninja skills. If necessary, she can defend herself."

The woman had the potential to be a world-class MMA champion but chose not to compete. Thank God for small favors. He'd hate to see a scar on her gorgeous face. "I'm worried we're stepping into something way beyond her skills."

"I won't dispute that, Logan, and I've already talked to her about possible scenarios. We can't have weapons on this assignment. Security at the casino will stop you in your tracks. Sky's weapons can't be confiscated."

Not unless some crazy bastard chopped off her arms and legs. He jammed his fingers through his hair. "I'd like it better if we watched the bar from the camera room."

Monroe shook his head. "Anyone hanging around the casino is a potential partner, Logan, and suppose the partner is watching from a cozy chair in the control room? The Feds couldn't clear them all, so how could I? Besides, we need to hear conversations. You can't eavesdrop from watching a bunch of cameras—unless you read lips, and I don't have anyone on staff with that skill." He picked up a pen and scribbled on a notepad. Shooting a glance at Logan, he grinned. "I'll look for someone who can read lips." He threw the pen on the desk. "No, Logan, we go this route with Sky planted to observe and listen. She's sharp. I don't believe for one second she'd walk into something without being on full alert."

Vittoria Carbone, Monroe's office manager, walked through the open office door.

The fifty-plus-year-old grandmother of seven ran a tight ship and kept everyone on their toes. Her brown eyes peered through gold-framed glasses, and she studied Logan like he was standing in the middle of the room wearing dirty underwear. She was round and short with brown hair always in a beehive. "To give me height," she claimed. Logan suspected bees lived in her old-fashioned hairdo and would be unleashed at any moment with a flick of her finger.

She placed some papers on Monroe's desk. "You don't give our pretty Skylar much credit, Logan. Coming alone to Jersey from Chicago to start a new life took a lot of guts."

Logan stopped pacing and thrust his hands into his jeans pockets. "I don't want anything to happen to her." Monroe always planned with meticulous care. What the hell was he worried about?

Monroe leaned forward to inspect the papers. "Thanks, Vicki. Has Pasquale made the money transfer?"

"Yup, all set and deposited into Logan's CEO account." She turned to Logan. "Your fashion stylist will be here in an hour. Don't give her a hard time."

He harrumphed. "She's taking me to some swanky men's store for a complete makeover." He shuddered.

"Just relax and enjoy it." Stepping toward him, she tapped a finger on his chest. "You should tell Skylar how you feel."

He dropped his jaw and stared. "What are you talking about? I worry about all my colleagues."

With a cock of her head, she smirked. "I seriously doubt you'd pull your hair out over Tank or any of the other guys."

"Sure I would." What a friggin' liar. He wouldn't pace the floor, either.

"I call bullshit, young man. You like her." She grinned. "Maybe more than like her. Tell her."

Did his heart rate just skyrocket? *Well, hell, yeah.* He could face a man with a loaded gun and not bat an eye, but to tell a woman how he felt? He'd need to consume a bottle of blood pressure pills. Glaring at Vicki, he shook his head. "She'll think I'm asking for a relationship. She doesn't do relationships, and before we started, we established some ground rules."

She rolled her eyes. "I didn't say ask for her hand in marriage. Just tell her how you feel. She might surprise you." She headed for the door. "Oh, and by the way." She smiled over her shoulder. "You might as well throw out those ground rules. Like it or not, what you two have is called a relationship." She left the office.

What the hell! Why would Vicki make such an asinine comment? He and Sky didn't live together. They didn't date. Those two basic scenarios were the definition of relationship, right? Yet, they were pretty much exclusive. He certainly enjoyed every minute they spent together. Sex was phenomenal, and he preferred her company more than anyone's. Sure, he felt something whenever they were together but always kept the words to himself. Their friends-with-benefits arrangement was a mutual understanding. So, what would be the purpose of discussing feelings? Besides, men avoided *The Talk* about emotions. They'd rather break down a wall with their bare hands.

Monroe coughed. "I won't reinforce what Vicki said. Your personal life is your own business as long as it doesn't interfere with your assignment." Narrowing his gaze, he peered. "Will it?"

Lifting his chin, Logan straightened his back and met Monroe's steady gaze. "No, it won't. I know better."

"Good, because we have a ton of unanswered questions with this case. We won't get any answers until we play the game."

Early on, experience taught Logan how dangerous these games could be. The worse part? Sky was a rookie. Never in his career had he worked with a raw cadet, and the prospect scared the daylights out of him. Why did the newbie have to be the woman who'd become so special?

Chapter Four

D-day had arrived. And oh, boy, was Sky nervous as hell.

With her gut in a knot, Skylar arrived at the Whirlwind Casino and maneuvered around a multitude of slot machines. Somewhere in the middle of this lower level were the escalators leading to the second-floor lounge. Sure, Monroe showed her a map of what was where, but he never mentioned the noise and people causing so much distraction. How in the world could a person work in such a deafening environment? Every slot machine had its own catchy tune, and some were pretty damn loud. With no desire to linger on the lower level, she scooted around one crowd after another until she found the moving staircase leading to the upper floor. What she needed was a little fortification in the form of a cold beer. She hadn't been this nervous since…well, never.

Pausing at the top of the staircase, she scanned the area. Before starting her assignment, she studied the intel gathered by Monroe. The floor where her bar was situated consisted primarily of high-roller gambling tables. Compared to the lower level, noise was virtually non-existent. In fact, she left the clamor of bells and whistles on the first floor to the quiet of a mausoleum. Up here, people were solemn-faced and focused, like they waited for a funeral procession to pass. Maybe they were. She never understood gambling, but she supposed it took a great deal of concentration not to lose a home to creditors. She entered the second-floor lounge and slipped onto a bar stool.

"What will you have?"

A tall, lanky bartender spoke like he was bored to death. If he expected a tip, he should consider putting on a nicer expression. "Give me your beer on tap, please."

No smile or acknowledgment, not even a slight nod. Then, he delivered a frosty mug with entirely too much foam. She sighed. Her gulp of fortification would have to wait.

When she first moved to New Jersey, she received a slew of suggestions about where to go and what to see. She wasn't one for sightseeing, but the gang at the manor insisted on a trip to Atlantic City. As a born-and-bred Chicago native, she'd never seen an ocean. So, one day, Fay, Anthony, and Tyrone dragged her from the rancher and drove her to the shore to spend a day in the sun with a little gambling on the side.

The entire day turned into one big disappointment. She wasn't sure what she expected, but all the noise and people hawking their merchandise along the boardwalk created an atmosphere more akin to a carnival rather than a place to relax. The ocean, while endless across the horizon, rolled dingy-brown waves onto the sand and not something she'd stick her toe in. When she followed the gang into one of the many casinos, she couldn't help the flood of more disappointment. The majority of the patrons sitting at the one-armed bandits acted like automatons, even when they won a big pot. Some looked annoyed to be interrupted because, *golly gee*, they had to wait for an attendant to hand over their winnings. In fact, the fun and good times seen in casino TV commercials were gross exaggerations. Not once had she witnessed anyone doing a happy little jig.

Now, here she sat, in the Whirlwind Lounge, staring into a beer with too large of a head. If she waited any longer for the foam to dissipate, she could die of thirst, and since her nerves took over the second she stepped through the front entrance, her throat had gone bone-dry. She sipped, then wiped the foam mustache with a napkin. Shifting slightly on the stool, she studied her surroundings.

The entire lounge was built onto a platform with a two-step entrance and a wrought-iron rail to set it apart from the gaming area. Small, round tables with two chairs were lined up against the rail with potted palm trees between them. She wasn't sure the plants were real, but it gave a little ambiance to an otherwise typical lounge. The wooden bar itself was curved but not very long with twelve padded stools with high backs. Hey, she was a bartender. She counted stools.

Being mid-afternoon in the middle of the week, a few people occupied the small tables. One bearded guy, who resembled Santa Claus without the red suit, was actually asleep. Two others played on cell phones. Otherwise, the rest of the tables were empty.

At the bar, a younger man sat three stools away and closer to the wall. He had the bleary-eyed look of a man awake all night and with hair that stood on end, like he tugged its roots one too many times. He played the video poker game built into the bar. Ten bucks a pop. The casino wanted everyone to lose their money as soon as possible. Heaven forbid a gambler took five minutes to breathe.

Two drink servers rushed between the bar and gaming tables. Like Monroe said, they wore black slacks and a black Whirlwind T-shirt. Would she have taken the job if the shirts were fluorescent orange? Hell…oh, well, maybe—provided Monroe paid her double.

Johnny Dee worked behind the bar, grumbling. She wasn't psychic or anything. She simply caught a glimpse at his name tag when he served this too-foamy beer. The missing Fed agent had provided names of the regulars but no descriptions. Really, though, she recognized a manager when she saw one. Like any person in charge, Johnny wasn't used to doing the actual job of his employees. He filled orders the servers needed and was very sloppy about it, too. But his bartender hadn't shown today. So, the man had to get off his butt and work. *Aww.* Having a no-show was no accident. Just one of Monroe's machinations. In another few minutes, a crowd would converge on the small lounge and order a bunch of specialty cocktails—all of which Skylar knew by heart. She strategically took the stool closest to a display case where the mixing guide should be.

Poor Johnny. As planned, he appeared frazzled. If he had any hair on the top of his head, he'd probably pull out every last strand. As it was, little wisps stuck up from a bald dome. The sides were dark brown and trimmed short, and his nose, though straight, was a tad too long. The man was tall and wiry with no muscle whatsoever. His chest barely filled out the white dress shirt, and his tie dangled from his thin neck. He was definitely not the kind of guy a woman noticed.

Logan, with all his muscles, was a feast for any woman's eyes—hers included. Over the weekend, she and her muscle man enjoyed a marathon of sex because she was days away from moving into an efficiency apartment as part of her cover. Without knowing when they would have another chance to get together, she and Logan behaved like two bunnies in a bush.

The chatter of voices drew her attention to the steps leading to the lounge. A group of eight people ambled in dressed like they had money to burn. Sky recognized none of them, but she knew they were ex-cops on Monroe's payroll.

One of the drink servers with blue-and-pink hair combined several tables and rearranged chairs, then took their orders. She hurried to Johnny and handed him the list.

Johnny's brows shot straight into his wispy strands, and he glared at the server. "You've got to be kidding me. I've never heard of these."

The little woman huffed. "I have. You'll find them in the mixing guide." She grabbed a few pretzel and peanut bowls from the bar and returned to the tables.

Cussing, he opened a drawer under a display case, rummaged, then cussed more.

Showtime. "Can I help?"

He whirled. "What?"

The damn man acted like she just plopped onto the stool. For crying out loud, she'd been nursing a beer with too-high foam for the past thirty minutes. "I said, can I help? I'm a bartender, currently unemployed."

He narrowed his gaze. "How much experience?"

"Five years."

He handed her the list. "Can you make these

special cocktails?"

Taking the list, she studied it and then handed it back. "As long as you have the liquor, yes."

Frowning, he bit on his lower lip. "I can't hire someone without a security check."

"Your loss." She sipped her beer. *Damn foam*. She wiped her mouth.

Turning, he again rummaged through the drawer and cursed. After opening another drawer, he cursed louder.

The blue-and-pink-haired server hurried back to the bar. "What's the holdup? They're complaining, and you're ruining my tips."

"I don't have a mixing guide."

Well, that's because Monroe took care of that little problem, too. The man could be a sneaky devil.

Johnny shifted his gaze from Skylar to the large group, then back. He leaned forward. "You got a current certificate?"

"Absolutely—not on me, though. I'm sure you can check online with the city."

Straightening, he hissed. "How about a record?"

Lifting her mug, she frowned at the foam. "No, I don't sing. Lousy voice."

"Dammit, woman, I'm talking warrants and police record."

She loved pulling his chain. "Nope." She sipped.

"What's your name?"

"Midnight Sky."

He jerked back. "You're serious?"

"Yep. Want to see my driver's license?" She returned the mug to the coaster.

"Yes."

She reached into her cargo pants and extracted a wallet, then handed him the card.

Eyes wide, he stared. "Well, I'll be damned."

The server tapped the bar. "You should have called Jackie. She's looking for some overtime."

"Tried. Her line's been busy all day." Johnny slid his gaze between Skylar and the server before settling on Sky. "You're hired. Get behind the bar and get started. I'll put in a security check on you, then order a new mixing guide. Valerie, meet Midnight Sky." He pointed a finger in Sky's face. "If you're pulling my leg…"

She grabbed onto his finger. The urge to bend it backward forced her to pause. Instead, she shook the finger like it was a hand and smiled. "You won't be disappointed." She stood and strolled around the bar to the opening on the other side.

Mission accomplished.

Over the next two weeks, Sky fell into a routine. Casino security had cleared her, of course, and she worked the two to ten p.m. shift. The lounge had one manager, Johnny Dee, and he worked from eight in the morning until eight at night. No other manager shared his office, which Monroe considered a vital piece of information. Smack her alongside the head, but she saw no logic in the statement.

In the staff room at the end of the hall, she was assigned a locker but had very little to place in it. If anything, she hung her jacket since the nights were chilly at the shore. Plus, the jacket had a hood to protect her from the mist blowing off the ocean.

The casino wouldn't allow her to wear her usual cargo pants. "Too many pockets to hide stuff," they claimed. Johnny suggested black jeans or slacks, and purses must be clear vinyl. Since she never carried a purse, she kept her wallet and keys in her locker, but her phone—per Monroe's order—remained in her back pocket. And—oh, yes—Johnny issued her three black T-shirts with the Whirlwind Casino logo on the back.

Every afternoon, she walked the four blocks from her apartment to the casino. She missed her motorcycle, but Monroe said tags could be traced and her real identity revealed. If she needed a ride, someone would be a phone call away. The man was thorough with protecting identities. Before anyone started their first day with his firm, he had Pam delete all social media from the Web. Those who balked were politely shown the door. She didn't care. She never posted anything, anyway.

While her afternoon walk along the boardwalk to the casino was filled with the smell of salt water and the sound of waves crashing on the shore, her evening trek to her apartment was anything but relaxing. She soon learned the Atlantic City boardwalk wasn't the safest route for a nighttime stroll. Twice, assailants confronted her, and twice, they ended up in the hospital. A girl couldn't live a lifetime in Chicago and not learn a few survival tricks about night stalkers. After the second confrontation, she avoided the boardwalk altogether.

Valerie McIntire, the blue-and-pink-haired drink server, entered the lounge and aimed for the bar's counter opening at the far end.

The opening was near the hall leading to Johnny's office and the staff locker room, along with the service elevator and supply rooms. Usually, no one entered Sky's domain unless the drinks were either mugs of tea or coffee. If Sky had the time, she prepared the coffee.

Valerie approached with a smile. "I'm getting some nice tips because of you." She handed Sky a list.

The woman could only be described as a perky little woman. Even at five-foot-one, her bright hair flashed like a neon sign. No one could miss her in a crowd. Taking the paper and reading, Sky smirked. "I don't think I have anything to do with your tips."

"Sure, you do. You're fast. People like that."

Valerie and Carmela Ramone were the two servers on her shift. They hustled between the patrons in the lounge and those at the gaming tables on the casino floor. For the most part, Skylar exclusively served the bar customers, but occasionally, like on a busy night, she served the small tables. Tips weren't pooled like her last job in Chicago where the boss took a cut just for sitting on his butt.

The list complete, Val hefted the heavy tray and headed onto the casino floor.

Two minutes later, Carmela hurried in and slapped a list on the counter.

She was older than Sky and Val, probably in her late thirties or early forties. She wasn't a raving beauty with her dark hair and eyes, but she had curves with an ass that caught a man's attention. Since she'd been here the longest, she covered for Johnny whenever he left the bar.

Carmela yawned and glanced toward the far end. "Jason is fidgeting more than usual today."

Sky glanced at the man she observed on her first day at the bar. "Yeah, I sometimes wonder if he drinks a gallon of coffee before coming in here."

For a guy in his late twenties, Jason Carter

certainly was a Nervous Nelly. With blond hair and blue eyes, he'd look more like a poster boy for a surfer magazine *if* he didn't look like a man who stayed awake all night. The missing Fed agent listed Jason as a regular at the bar. True to form, he sat on the same stool every single day and wore his usual blue jeans and T-shirt. That meant he gambled every single day. Where the hell did these people get all their money?

Sky leaned toward Carmela and kept her voice low. "Every time he sits down, he tells me he lost a bundle. Does he have a job?"

Carmela shrugged. "He's definitely an enigma. All I know is the casino comps his meals and room of which he never uses. I don't think he's rich-rich—if you know what I mean. He's a lousy tipper."

Sky snorted. "Yeah, I noticed." Who in hell left a quarter as a tip? Shaking her head, she finished with Carmela's list and sent the server on her way.

"Hey, beautiful."

Todd Daniels, the security guard working on her shift, had approached on her first night and introduced himself. Like Valerie, the guy was hard to miss. With his tall frame and bright-red hair, he stood out in a crowd. His uniform of gray shirt and black slacks fit a lean body, and his brown eyes and easy smile attracted a lot of women. She smiled. "No excitement tonight?"

He slipped onto a stool. "So far, we have a bunch of subdued gamblers, but don't worry. Someone will eventually have too much to drink." The two-way radio on his belt crackled. He unclipped it and hit the side button. "Daniels."

"Passed-out patron on elevator two. Someone's holding open the doors."

"Received. On my way." He stood and smiled. "Duty calls."

Between Valerie, Carmela, and Todd, the Whirlwind Lounge turned into a decent gig. Everyone got along, and not once had Sky heard a word that would qualify as a backstabbing comment. That, by itself, was unusual. Far too many people fought tooth and nail to get ahead, and they didn't care who they stepped on in the process. Despite the pleasure of working with Val and Carmela, she couldn't forget her real purpose for being here.

Any minute, Logan would arrive under his code name, Logan Grandal. As per protocol, Monroe always kept a part of the operative's real name to avoid any inadvertent slip. Good thing, too. She was a complete novice. But Monroe was smart about one point. Putting Sky behind the bar early gave her a chance to relax in her new environment. She was ready for the next phase of his plan without feeling like her gut swallowed a bag of Mexican jumping beans.

Chapter Five

A little after six in the evening, Logan wandered in.

Sky's heart thumped. Ever since he'd come into her life, he wore nothing but jeans and casual shirts. Here, he wore well-cut trousers with a white silk shirt sporting ruby cuff links. An open collar revealed his strong neck and a sparkling gold chain. His light brown hair was neatly trimmed, and diamond pinky rings sparkled from each hand. The man looked like money and a far cry from the smelly gardener she met a year ago. And oh, boy, did he look hot.

Pausing for a second, he locked those copper-colored eyes onto her, then quickly scanned the rest of the lounge.

Sky always loved his eyes but never told him. She had a strange feeling any mention of love in any context would send him bolting faster than lightning.

Mister Commitment-Phobe only recently left his loner life as an undercover cop to become part of Monroe's team. Last year, when he divulged his connection to the New Jersey State Police, he adamantly defended his solitary lifestyle. She doubted anything changed because he worked for Monroe. She and Logan shared a bed but not their lives. For now, bedtime with Logan was enough.

Logan strolled toward the end of the bar near the opening to the hall and slipped onto a stool.

Her nightly emails to Monroe were filled with inane observations. She never knew what to include, but Monroe asked for details. So, she wrote about everything, including the location of the stools near the bar's opening and the way the hallway amplified voices. Since Johnny's office was a mere ten feet on the other side of the wall, he'd overhear any problems arising, including any pertinent conversations.

After serving another patron, Sky inched her way toward Logan. A long time ago, Logan told her the only way to survive an undercover assignment was to stay locked inside your role. She didn't need to pretend playing a bartender. She was damn good at her job. Case in point, she always had a habit of grabbing empty bottles and glasses whenever she moved down the bar. After dumping her load onto the dishwasher, she faced Logan and smiled. "Welcome to the Whirlwind Lounge. What can I get you?"

"Whatever light ale you have on tap."

"We have several, sir. I can recommend a local brew."

"That's fine." He scrubbed a hand over his face.

She poured his beer and returned. After slipping the cold mug onto a coaster, she smirked. "Bad luck at the tables?"

"Actually, no." He sipped the beer. "I'm sorry I answered my phone."

"Ah, that would do it."

After passing through the bar's opening, Valerie gave Logan a quick scan and then handed Sky her list.

Glancing at the abbreviations, Sky paused. Three beers, a whiskey sour, and a Long Island iced tea. She pointed to the last one. "Someone wants to sleep well?"

Val shrugged. "He's losing at roulette. Maybe he's heading upstairs soon."

Long Island iced tea contained four different types of alcohol and not a drop of tea. Sky only tasted it once. The concoction was way too sweet for her liking. Moving away to prepare the drinks, Sky set to work and placed each glass onto a tray.

After filling two mugs with coffee, Val set them on the tray and leaned close. "Who's the guy?"

Sky prepared for such a question, but dammit, jealousy shot through her veins, anyway. Frowning, she followed Val's gaze. "Never seen him before."

Waggling her brows, the woman stared in Logan's direction. "He's good-looking. I hope he sits at one of my tables." She grabbed her full tray and went out the same way she came in while giving Logan a saucy smile.

Since the thought hadn't entered her mind until now, how would Sky feel about Logan sleeping with another woman to obtain information? While he worked undercover for the state police, he admitted to the tactic on more than one occasion. If Monroe's plan failed to proceed as scheduled, would Logan entice Val or Carmela to his luxury suite?

In all honesty, she couldn't be with a guy who took another woman to his bed—even for the sake of an assignment. She'd terminate any future liaisons, regardless of their friends-with-benefits label. She couldn't handle any sharing.

Mrs. Marian Masterson, a woman in her seventies, stepped into the lounge. The Fed agent's notes listed Marian as a regular who wandered in whenever the mood hit her, and from what Sky determined, the mood was often. The woman had money, as evidenced by the diamond rings sparkling from both hands. She wore expensive clothes and always had her hair coiffed in flyaway style. So far, she buried three husbands, and each one left her wealthier.

On Marian's right arm was Charles Dilly, a man in his late sixties—another regular. Where Marian was, Charles followed. From the way he doted on her, Charles might soon be husband number four.

They slipped onto stools near Logan.

Marian and Charles made an odd couple. Her high-class look contrasted to his middle-income appearance. He wore off-the-rack clothes, had a belly that stuck out like a seven-month pregnant woman, and the top of his head glowed like a shiny dome while the side hairs were on the verge of turning completely gray. His nose was long and straight with a slight hook at the tip, and his lips were a trifle too thin. But as the saying went, for every trash can, there's a lid. Obviously, Marian saw something in Charles that eluded Sky.

After adjusting her dress, Marian smiled. "The usual for both of us, dear."

Skylar poured straight bourbon for Charles and then mixed gin and vermouth with two olives for Marian's martini. Marian loved her martinis just a tad on the dry side. She hated the vodka version, and two olives were a must. Sky placed the glasses on coasters.

From what Sky uncovered so far, the casino comped Marian's room and meals, along with show tickets and appointments at the spa. Charles rarely left her side, but he was a table gambler while Marian enjoyed playing maximum bets on all the penny machines. As a general rule, if the patron gambled, drinks were on the house. Tabs at the bar were usually billed to a patron's room.

On the third evening of his usual six p.m. time, Logan sauntered in wearing a wide smile and slipped onto his stool.

His smile always increased his attractiveness, and she wasn't immune. So, before she melted on the spot and spoiled tonight's script, she placed his standard-order ale in front of him. "You're happy tonight. Has your luck changed?"

"Something even better. I sold my company for a ton of money. All I need now is to disappear so my ex-wife can't sue me for half." He sipped his beer.

Sky raised her brows. "Can she do that? I mean, you're divorced, right?"

"For two years, but technically, I owned the company while we were still married. Since she's sleeping with this hotshot lawyer, she'll come after me—guaranteed."

Using her towel, Sky wiped the bar. "That doesn't seem fair." A movement at the lounge opening caught her eye.

Marian Masterson entered alone.

Sky craned her neck to see if Charles lagged behind but nope, no Charles. "Excuse me. I better get Mrs. Masterson her drink." The poor woman might kill her liver drinking all these martinis.

With a nod toward Logan, Marian slipped onto a stool.

Sky placed her cocktail on a coaster. "Where's Charles?"

She fussed with the skirt on her dress. "He went home. Something to do with business."

"Oh? And where's home?"

"I've no idea."

Maybe Marian wasn't as interested in Charles as assumed. How could she be? They were like night and day.

Mrs. Masterson sipped her martini and sighed. "Very nice, dear. By the way, Harriet's joining me after her bathroom break. She said to pour her usual."

Harriet Jones was another regular. For a woman in her sixties, she fit her tailored pantsuits like a model on a runway. Tall and slim, she carried a wooden cane, which Sky suspected was more a weapon than a crutch. Every time she walked in, she wore a different hat. Tonight, her bright-orange hat with two bouncing daisies made her dark skin glow. The woman claimed to be spending her late husband's retirement money, and her hours at the gaming tables proved the truth in her words. Timing her arrival perfectly, Sky slipped her red wine onto a coaster. "All right, ladies. You let me know when you want a refill." She moved over to Logan. "So, you planning on a trip around the world?"

Shifting his gaze from the other end of the bar, he looked at her and smiled. "I'd love to, but I won't go alone." He swallowed half his beer. "What I need is to drop off the surface of the earth."

She raised both brows. "Just to avoid an ex? That seems awfully drastic."

"Yeah, well, you don't know her like I do." Frowning, he drummed his fingers on the bar, then shot her a one-eyed glare. "I shouldn't talk to you like this. I don't even know your name."

Leaning forward, she pointed to her nameplate. "Midnight." She held out her right hand.

Brows high, he paused with his mug nearly to his lips. "You're serious? It sounds like a nickname."

"Nope."

After returned his drink to the bar, he shook her hand. "Logan." He squeezed before releasing.

"Okay, Logan, congrats on your good news. Do you need a refill?"

"What I need is someone to help me celebrate. How about joining me with a toast?"

Boy, wouldn't she love a drink, but she was a professional. She shook her head. "I never drink on the job."

"Then, how about afterward? What time do you get off?"

Smiling, she grabbed a few lemons and cut them into thin slices. "Sorry, no can do."

Pouting, he sat back. "Why not? You married? I don't see a ring."

Marian leaned over. "You should accept his offer, honey. If he's got money to burn, he might as well include you." Straightening, she sipped her drink. "He's too young for me." She winked at Logan.

Skylar chuckled. "Marian, you are a trip. But the night is still young. I'm sure he'll find someone suitable." Gad, she almost choked on the words.

"Order in!"

The strong voice belonged to Carmela. Skylar swore the woman should be a singer. She wouldn't even need a microphone. After excusing herself, Sky joined the server at the other end of the bar.

Carmela handed over her list, then nodded toward Logan. "The way he's watching you, he's bound to hit you with a proposition."

"He just did. He earned a ton of money selling his company and wants someone to help celebrate." And God help her, she refused because she followed a script. What if Logan deviated and found Carmela too good... No, he wouldn't do that, right? He would follow the plan...she hoped.

"Really?" Gaze twinkling, Carmela adjusted her tight T-shirt. "I wouldn't mind a little celebration."

Approaching, Valerie leaned on the bar and handed Sky a list. "What are we talking about?"

Carmela licked her lips. "That guy down the end hit on Midnight."

"Ooh, nice. About time, too. He's been eyeing her like candy for the past three nights."

Sky grunted. "I'm not interested, so you two can work your magic." *Ouch.* Even those words hurt.

Valerie nudged Carmela. "You haven't been laid for a while. Go give him a shot. Entice him with your boobs."

Oh, God help me. Sad to say, Carmela had a nice rack and was bigger than Valerie and Sky combined. Turning away, Sky studied her two lists. "I'll get your drinks ready."

She couldn't look. Jealousy coursed through her body, and she busied herself mixing drinks. The emotion rose without warning, and she silently chided herself for the reaction. She knew darn well Monroe's plan included pumping others for information, and she wasn't sure how far Logan would go to get it. *See, dammit?* She wasn't cut out for this secret agent stuff.

She stared at Val's list and paused. Then, she burst out laughing. She turned to Val. "Who ordered Sex on the Beach?" Throwing a thumb over her shoulder, Val snickered. "I've got a lady celebrating her ninety-second birthday. Her granddaughter ordered it."

"Oh, my. Then, maybe I should go easy on the booze." She set out a tall glass and grabbed the vodka and peach schnapps. Next came orange juice and ice, then topped with cranberry juice and a garnish of orange slices and cherries. She slipped it onto Val's tray.

Eyes wide, Val stared at the glass. "That's gorgeous!"

"The colors are supposed to resemble a sunset, but the trick is not to stir. Tell her happy birthday for me." She continued with the rest on the lists.

"Egad." Eyes wide, Val gaped. "Carm's practically pressing her chest into his face." She sucked in a breath. "Oh, my God! He's turning her down. What chance do I have?"

"Hey, you're cute and perky." She still couldn't look toward Logan. She finished mixing the drinks and placed them on the proper trays. "Go give him a shot, Val. He might like cute and perky. Was he at one of your tables?"

"Yeah, throwing big bucks at roulette." She wagged a finger. "I might be cute and perky, but you have this bad girl vibe. He probably likes dangerous women."

"Dangerous, eh?" She snorted. She wasn't sure what Val's description meant, but wearing all black didn't make Sky dangerous. People had commented about her badass motorcycle, but her cycle was still parked in the garage at home.

Carmela plodded back and huffed. "He only has eyes for Midnight."

Glancing over her shoulder, Sky laughed. "Then, he's wasting his time. I don't do casual."

Sighing, Valerie grabbed her tray full of drinks. "No sense me trying. I don't have Carmela's curves nor Midnight's mysterious air."

Mysterious? Well, that word never entered her mind. Dangerous *and* mysterious. She liked it.

Carmela cocked her head. "The word fits you, Sky. You're quiet about yourself. You *do* like men, right?"

"Oh, yeah, but I never mix work and pleasure. Been there, done that."

"Now, there's a story I can't wait to hear." Smiling, she grabbed her tray and headed for the gaming area.

Twenty minutes later, Logan threw fifty bucks onto the bar, winked, and left.

Sky wasn't sure why, but she always felt a sense of panic every time he stood to leave. She blamed her inexperience with all this covert stuff. She also blamed Monroe for putting her in a situation she was ill-equipped to handle. Yes, all right, she was a great bartender, but she could still say or do something to spoil Monroe's plan.

Johnny Dee emerged from the hall and glanced around. With a hand gesture, he signaled for Sky to approach.

Slipping the fifty-dollar bill into her pocket, she grabbed a wet rag and strolled over. "What's up?"

He leaned on the bar. "I overheard that Logan guy proposition you. You okay?"

"Why wouldn't I be?" She placed a used mug into the nearby sink. "I get propositioned almost every day."

"What do you know about him?"

"Not much. He sold his company and wants to celebrate. I turned him down." She wiped the counter where a patron spilled his drink.

He pursed his lips. "I heard something about an ex-wife."

Yeah, well, Logan certainly talked loud enough. "Oh, that. He sold his company and doesn't want his ex to get her hooks into the money. He said he'd like to disappear." She rolled her eyes. "Can you imagine something so stupid?"

"No, I can't." He curled one side of his mouth.

Oh, good grief. If he had a handlebar mustache, he'd be twirling the tips. Bad enough his dark eyes glowed with the news. "In this day and age, I don't know how anyone can disappear. Every street corner seems to have a camera mounted on a traffic light."

He waggled a finger. "He can do it, but he must be careful. Let me know if he raises the topic again."

"Will do."

The seed had been planted.

Chapter Six

For the next two nights, as the clock neared the six p.m. time, Sky skimmed the crowds for the arrival of Logan. She forced herself to do discreet glances because she sure as hell couldn't appear too obvious. Her own fault. She liked Logan…a lot. Whenever he entered the lounge, he had a way of releasing all the tension in her shoulders. Even though each day she became more comfortable with the assignment, she'd still prefer knowing he was nearby.

True to form, a few minutes after six, he walked in with a smile and slipped onto his usual stool by the hall.

Sky barely placed his beer onto a coaster when Marian, Harriet, and Charles wandered in.

Valerie followed.

The damn perky drink server stepped behind the bar and flirted with Logan while placing dirty glasses into the dishwasher. Then, she refilled his pretzel and peanut bowls, even though he hadn't touched them. Not to be left out, Carmela hurried in and topped off his beer, which—technically—was Skylar's job. But geez, let the man take a few sips first.

Sky caught Logan's twinkling gaze and frowned. He was enjoying their attention. But all this flirting by Val and Carmela annoyed Sky to no end. She had no idea why. Sure, Logan played the rich guy role to the letter, but why must women fall all over themselves to get into the man's pockets? What happened to self-respect?

Unable to watch all the flirtatious banter, Sky double-checked to see if her customers had what they needed, then headed to the stockroom to grab a few bottles of vermouth and gin. Marian Masterson was like a sponge with her martini intake, but hey, at her age, if her liver held on, so what?

"Midnight?"

She turned to see Johnny standing in the doorway. Naturally, he'd want to know if she dug up any info on Logan. But over the past few nights, talking to Logan took a backseat because of the steady flow of customers entering the lounge. She forced a smile. "You'll need to order more vermouth."

"Huh? Oh, yeah, sure." He tugged on his tie. "Listen, Logan Grandal is dropping some serious bucks at the roulette table. The casino is comping his meals and room. I'm told to kiss his ass."

Well, gee, she liked kissing his cute butt, and she kissed several other parts as well. But, of course, Johnny was using a figure of speech. She had to shake away the visual.

While crossing his arms over his chest, he leaned against the doorjamb. "I need you to find out how serious he is about disappearing."

"You mean before he gambles away his entire fortune?" Grabbing the bottle carrier, she slipped the gin and vermouth into slots. Facing him, she pursed her lips. "How do you expect me to ask such an awkward question? I haven't talked to him since he told me."

"Why not?"

She fought the urge not to strangle him. As if she

had all the time in the world to chitchat with one customer while others waited. *Geez.* She returned to the vermouth shelf. "Because the bar's been busy, and someone is always too close to eavesdrop." Like Marian and Charles. Especially Marian. She always sat one stool away from Logan. Shaking her head, Sky included two more bottles of vermouth and gin in the carrier. Satisfied she had enough liquor for a while, she grabbed onto the handle. "Look, Johnny, if I get a chance, and no one is within earshot, I'll strike up a conversation with Logan and see what he says. Maybe he'll mention his ex-wife, and I can go from there. Okay?"

"That's fine. Just find out as much as you can." He rubbed the back of his neck. "Valerie and Carmela don't usually have a problem getting men to talk, but they aren't asking the right questions."

Whoa. Johnny admitted using his two drink servers to scope out potential clients. Did that mean they were aware of his side business? Damn, she hoped not. She liked the two women and couldn't bear to see them sent to jail for aiding and abetting. Sky rested her heavy load on a nearby box and met Johnny's gaze. "And what are the right questions?"

He shrugged. "The usual stuff. The company he sold and what else he's done to hide from his ex. Whatever you uncover can be helpful. Pump him full of booze and keep him talking."

She narrowed her gaze. "Why?"

Jaw twitching, he chewed on his inner lip while his gaze scrutinized her face.

She could see the wheels turning in his conniving brain. Should he trust her? *Hell, no.* But what choice did he have?

After a minute, Johnny nodded. "I can give him what he wants, Midnight. If I'm satisfied with what you uncover, I'll make it worth your while."

I'm sure you will. Monroe assumed she could act, and from what she observed, undercover work required a whole lot of acting. Roles needed to be played and believed. So, she'd better make this look good, even though she fought like hell not to break a bottle over Johnny's head. Smiling, she cocked her hip. "All right, I'll give it a try, but I can't guarantee success."

"Wonderful. That's all I ask." He slapped the door frame and left.

If she hadn't an inkling about Johnny's motives, she'd tell him to go to Hades. No woman should compromise her self-respect for any man. Even though she itched to send a quick text to Logan, she couldn't chance it. With her luck, someone would be looking over her shoulder and see his name light up the screen. She'd be safer to wait for a face-to-face meeting. Yanking the carrier from its resting spot, she returned to the lounge.

Logan still sat on his stool, nursing his beer. He cocked a brow in her direction.

Marian and Harriet were gone, but Charles sat next to Jason at the far end of the bar, both intent on the video poker game before them.

Leaning toward Logan, she winked. "Don't go anywhere."

Gaze twinkling, he sipped his beer. "I'll be right here."

Approaching the middle of the bar, Valerie plunked down a loaded tray full of used glasses. She yawned. Meeting Sky's gaze, she shrugged. "I lost a whole lot of sleep last night." She waggled her eyebrows, then shot Logan another saucy grin.

Sky tensed and almost flung her carrier at the woman. "With Logan?"

"Lord, no. One of my high-rollers gave me an offer I couldn't refuse." She jerked her head in Logan's direction. "That man has eyes only for you. You should accept his offer."

Sky shot her gaze from Logan to Valerie. "I'm thinking about it."

"Well, don't think too long, honey. The man won't be here forever."

After setting the liquor bottles onto the shelves, Sky slipped the carrier out of the way and grabbed Val's tray.

Johnny rushed from the hall and stopped while scanning the lounge. Within seconds, he locked his gaze onto a buxom blonde carrying a briefcase. Passing a hand over the wisps of hair on the top of his head, he straightened his shoulders and hurried over.

My God, the woman was gorgeous! She had long, golden hair that flowed around her shoulders like a drape. Her makeup was meticulously applied, and her business suit fit an hourglass figure. But holy hell, four-inch stilettos showcased legs toned to perfection. If the woman walked through the casino, she probably had every male drooling. Sky leaned toward Val. "Who's that?"

"I've never seen her before, but she's from the state liquor board. I texted Johnny to say she was here. He hates a surprise visit."

"Oh." Sky checked her watch—nearly seven. What

state employee worked after five o'clock? "Do they always come this late?"

Not removing her gaze from the buxom blonde, Valerie smirked. "We get surprise visits at all hours, not only from the liquor board but from the casino commission and board of health."

Sky scanned for anything out of place behind the bar. Immaculate, as always. She returned her gaze to Val and glanced down at her empty hands. "No list?"

"Not yet." She smiled and, with a new tray in hand, left the lounge.

With Johnny busy and the lounge virtually deserted, Sky ambled over to Jason and Charles. "You guys need a refill?"

Without removing their gazes from the video game, they both shook their heads.

Okay, then. Now was a good time to flirt with Logan. Walking over, she replaced his empty mug with a fresh beer and smiled. "How's your luck tonight?"

He gave a sly smile. "It could be better."

She *did* miss him. When he wasn't on an assignment, he slept in her bed, at least twice a week. With luck, this case would close before her vagina shriveled into a desert wasteland. She cleared a few used glasses from the bar and placed them into the dishwasher. "I'm beginning to think you live here, Logan." Straightening, she met his gaze. "Do you live nearby?"

"New York, where my ex is constantly on my ass. But yes, I am living here temporarily."

"Then, you're hiding. That's not fun." After loading in the soap, she closed the washer and hit the Start button.

"Yeah, don't ever get married. It isn't worth it." He sipped his beer. "I should have seen the dollar signs when we were dating, but—" He shrugged. "I opened my eyes too late. Why are you still single?"

Grabbing a clean glass, she polished it with a towel. "How do you know I am?"

He twisted one corner of his mouth. "I asked around."

She held the glass to the light. "I hate commitments."

"You are a man's dream, Midnight." He leaned forward, gaze intense. "Come to my room tonight."

Ordinarily, she'd jump at the suggestion, but she had to play it cool. Even though old eagle-ears Johnny was busy with the state rep, he needed to hear her conversation with his next target. Considering how the hall acted like an echo chamber, he should overhear some of their confab. She placed the sparkling glass on a shelf. "I don't even know your full name." She grabbed another glass and wiped.

"Logan Grandal. The hotel is comping my meals and room." He sipped his beer. "You can enjoy some of it. Let me feed you."

Well, she shouldn't play *too* hard to get, right? *Listen up, Johnny.* She placed the glass on the shelf and faced Logan. Leaning over the counter and keeping her voice just loud enough for the boss to hear, she smiled. "Tell you what. Order a nice meal and dessert plus two bottles of expensive wine, and I'll join you."

"What time?"

"My shift ends at ten." Still smiling, she straightened.

Reaching across the bar, he grabbed the front of

her T-shirt and closed the distance between them. "Room 1412." He brushed his lips across hers. "I'll be waiting." Releasing his hold, he winked, threw a fifty-dollar bill on the counter, and left.

She glanced down at the money and chuckled. For the first time in her bartender career, she would go to bed with a customer, and she couldn't wait. Even his light brush on her lips got her all tingly. She checked the time on her wristwatch. *Three long hours to go*. The anticipation might kill her. Biting back a smile, she pocketed the fifty and grabbed Logan's empty mug.

Seconds later, Johnny walked from the hall with the buxom blonde and escorted her to the steps leading out of the lounge. Whirling, he hurried to Sky and cocked a brow.

Yup. Despite being busy with the state rep, he overheard every word. Sky shot him a glance. "Everything good?" She placed the dirty mug on a tray for the next wash cycle.

"Depends. With the state liquor board, yes." He leaned over the counter. "I heard you talking to Grandal. Any news?"

She shot him a cocky grin. "Dinner for two on the agenda tonight."

Johnny fist-pumped and returned to his office.

The man was so damn predictable.

As was her habit, whenever a lull occurred, which usually coincided with a show in the auditorium, Sky wiped the bar until the wood sparkled. She took pride in the cleanliness of her workspace, no matter whether a swanky place like this casino or the corner hangout where locals gathered. Another mindless task was polishing liquor bottles, and she started the chore while her gaze wandered over the lounge and gaming tables. She froze. *Holy Mother of God, no*!

Philip Santini, her lawyer and friend, sauntered toward the lounge.

Two equally tall men flanked his sides.

He hadn't spotted her yet, but one of the men with wild, curly hair stared directly at her and smiled. She had the overwhelming urge to run and hide in the stock room. Of all people to head for her bar, why Philip? He knew her real name and where she lived. They even went on a few dates and kissed. The fierce rivalry that developed between him and Logan became an everyday topic of discussion between the tenants. Two handsome men vying for her affections gave a healthy boost to her ego, but that boost was about to kick her in the ass.

Even though Sky and Logan had worked together to catch the manor's killer and grew close in the process, at the conclusion, Logan disappeared. For two months, she heard nothing—no phone calls, text messages, or emails. Assuming he moved on to his next assignment, she agreed to a couple of dinner dates with a very persistent Philip. His kisses were nice enough. His touch was…a touch—no sparks, tingles, or chills. Everything about Philip, she compared to Logan. The poor guy never had a chance. Now, he could blow her cover with a few simple words. What should she do? Johnny was still in his office. Val and Carmela were busy at the tables but could return any second. Logan had come and gone, but Charles and Jason were still sitting at the bar.

With panic tightening her chest, she ransacked her brain for a solution. Monroe was too far away to help. Should she call Logan? With both men always at odds, no way would their meeting end well. Monroe had confidence in her ability to think. Now would be a good time to prove him right. She must not let Philip blow her cover.

As he climbed the two steps into the lounge, Philip met her gaze and did a quick double-take. Gaping, he paused by the small tables while his eyes grew wide as saucers.

Yeah, surprise, surprise. Without giving him time to say a word, she plastered on a smile. "Philip!" She hurried around the bar and toward the tables. Her main objective was to keep him out of earshot to Johnny's office. So, she latched onto him with arms tight around his torso.

Clearly hesitant, he wrapped his arms around her. "Sky?"

She leaned close to his ear and whispered, "Please, follow my lead." She held him at arm's length and met his startled gaze.

His two companions gawked as they stepped into the lounge behind him.

One buddy with the wild, curly hair groaned. "Damn, Phil. We dragged you here to meet the hot bartender, and here you already know her. You've been holding out on us, pal." Grinning, he tugged on his belt. "Introduce us."

Still with a startled look, Philip nodded. "Yes, hmm, we met—"

"Midnight Sky." She held out her right hand to Curly. "Nice to meet you."

The guy smirked. "I'm Jake, and this is Harold. We were here a couple of weeks ago."

"Well, I'm glad you came back." Not like she

remembered their faces. With the number of patrons flowing in and out, she was lucky when she had time to stock the shelves. Smiling, she cocked her head. "Hot, eh?"

Jake grinned. "Damn right. A sight for sore eyes after losing a bundle at craps."

Philip cleared his throat. "Sky, what—"

She interrupted again while hooking onto his arm. "Would you gentlemen mind if I talk to Philip alone? Have a seat at the bar, and I'll be right with you."

Gaze alert, Todd Daniels approached. "Everything okay here?"

The man looked out for her, which she greatly appreciated, but at this moment, she needed him somewhere else. She smiled. "He's an old friend, Todd. We're good." She practically yanked Philip toward the far corner.

After a cursory glance in her direction, Todd wandered over toward Charles and Jason.

Philip jerked his arm. "Sky, what the hell is going on?"

He stiffened under her grip. Not that she could blame him. She was acting like some lunatic. "Shhh. I'll explain, but please, lower your voice. My boss is still here, and I'm not supposed to fraternize with the customers." After releasing his arm, she placed a hand on his chest. He wasn't as muscular as Logan, but he still sported some nice abs. "I'm doing a favor for a friend. For security reasons, my bar name has always been Midnight Sky, and I need you to keep quiet about my real name and where I live."

He widened his eyes. "Okay, I can do that, but why do you need to work? From what I know, the manor is doing well."

"It is. This job is temporary." She shot a furtive glance toward the hall. "Look, female bartenders have a tendency to attract stalkers. We have to be careful."

"Oh, I didn't know." He narrowed his gaze. "Does security escort you to your car at night?"

"Sure." What a damn liar. But no way in hell would she tell him she walked alone to her apartment every night after her shift. Unfortunately, Philip was a lawyer, and questions always flowed from his mouth.

He smiled. "How about if I wait and follow you home?"

Oh, hell. Now, what? She touched his arm. "There's no need. You should enjoy your time with your friends." She smiled, hoping he would take the hint and leave.

"I won't mind waiting for your shift to end."

The man was too damn dense. "No, Philip. You deserve to have some fun. Stay with your friends."

He frowned. "Call when you get home, then."

Dear Lord Almighty. The man tested her patience. She gave him as stern a face as she could muster. "Philip, no."

Hands raised in a gesture of surrender, he sighed. "All right, but be careful."

"Always am." She squeezed his arm. "Thank you for caring. Now, how about I get you and your friends a drink?"

Chapter Seven

Monroe would be proud. Skylar had successfully diverted a potential crisis. Somehow, she convinced Philip and his buddies to visit the nightclub on the first floor where a lot of single women gathered. Naturally, Philip wanted to wait until she finished her shift so he could walk her to the garage. The man was just too damn…kind. She shuddered to think what might have happened if Philip's friends hadn't dragged him away. Maybe she should have told him about the assignment before leaving the manor. No, that wasn't a very bright idea. Knowing him, he'd have wandered in just to check on her.

Fifteen minutes after her shift ended, Skylar knocked on Room 1412. While waiting for the door to open, she inwardly smiled. Johnny Dee had no idea how much she would enjoy this information-gathering liaison. She and Logan hadn't slept together for three weeks, and she was more than ready. With luck, he ordered steak for dinner. For what she had in mind, they'd both need the extra protein.

The door flew open. No sooner had she caught a glimpse of light from his room when Logan swept her into his massive arms. A mouthwatering kiss followed. To say he caught her by surprise would be a gross understatement. Normally, Logan kept his displays of affection on the private side, but to do it in the hall where other guests could see was just…wow. She liked it. Even more important, she missed him.

Still in a lip-lock, he dragged her into his room and kicked the door shut. Lifting his head, he grinned.

She blinked, totally floored by this emotional display. "Hello to you, too." She took an extra minute to feel the muscles under her fingertips. Yeah, she missed him, all right, but then again, reality kicked in. He had a role to play. Patting his chest, she pecked his lips and broke free. "Was that for show, or did you actually miss me?" She straightened her jacket.

"Both. Johnny might be watching the hall cameras."

Figures. She'd forgotten about the security cameras. *Duh.* She should know by now Logan was very good at his job.

Reaching into his rear pocket, he extracted his cell phone. "Here. Listen to this. Pam forwarded the recording about an hour ago." He tapped the screen. "You knew Pam broke into Johnny's cell, right?"

"Monroe mentioned it." Before taking the phone, she removed her jacket and tossed it over a chair.

Thanks to the skills of their IT tech, Pamela planted a spy program into Johnny's cell phone. This allowed Monroe to listen in on his conversations, in particular, to the calls from the burner phones. The taped information was inadmissible in court, but eavesdropping gave Monroe an edge far and above what the Feds could do.

Logan stopped her from starting the recording. "I must warn you. Whoever is on the other line could be using one of those voice-altering apps. I haven't a clue who is talking or whether it's male or female. Johnny's voice, though, comes in nice and clear."

She hovered her fingers over the Play button. She should tell him about tonight's visitor to the lounge. Yes, dammit, she really should. Cringing, she met his gaze. "Just so you know, Philip wandered in with a couple of his buddies."

Jerking, he raised his brows. "Santini?"

She nodded. "I stopped him from mentioning my real name."

"Damn. This isn't good." Stepping away, he passed his fingers through his hair, then glanced her way. "Is he staying overnight?"

"No, but I wouldn't be surprised if he swings by again." She stepped farther into the room. "I told him it was a temporary job, but you know how tenacious he is. He'll go to Fay and dig for information." She stared down at the phone in her hand. Then, she met his gaze. "You should tell Monroe. Philip could waltz in and see you at the bar. I don't know what will happen."

"The case will blow sky-high, that's what would happen, and probably at its most crucial point." Pacing, he hissed.

Grabbing onto his left arm, she stopped him. And because she loved the feel of his rock-hard muscles, she squeezed. "I'm sure Monroe will find a way to distract Philip. Now—" Dropping her hand, she took a large breath and focused on the phone. "Let's hear this recording." She hit the Play button.

Unknown Caller: *"I got your signal. What now?"*

Wow. Logan was right. The app changed the voice into something mechanical—with an accent, even. She had to place the phone's speaker close to her ear to understand.

Johnny: *"We have a potential client."*

UC: *"Who?"*

J: *"Logan Grandal."*

UC: *"Seriously? What do we know about him?"*

J: *"Not much. I have Midnight checking him out. They're having dinner in his suite."*

UC: A loud groan. *"Must we go through that again, Johnny boy? Try not to tell her too much, okay?"*

J: *"I won't. But she'll give me a starting point for an Internet search. Right now, typing in his name isn't giving me a damn thing. If he just sold his company, then I should find some headline somewhere. But I don't know the name of the company."*

UC: *"All right. I'll check back with you tomorrow."*

Sky stopped the recording. "I can't even guess who might be talking to Johnny." She returned his phone. "At least, we got the ball rolling."

Monroe considered it imperative not to send her any recordings, for which she wholeheartedly agreed. With her luck, some busybody would look over her shoulder at the worst possible moment and see information best kept secret. As per Monroe's instructions, she carried her cell with the sound off in her rear pocket. This way, Pam could track the phone's signal via her own special *You Can't Hide* app, should she suddenly disappear. Not that she planned on vanishing any time soon, but knowing someone kept an eye on her gave her comfort.

Logan tossed his phone onto the dresser. "This conversation confirms the existence of a partner. From their short exchange, it's hard to tell who's in charge." With a half-smile touching his lips, he met her gaze. "I ordered room service."

She felt an immediate lift to her mood and smiled. "With two bottles of wine?"

Cocking his head, he wagged a finger. "Of which we will only drink one glass apiece."

"Oh, darn." Moving closer, she leaned against him and fluttered her eyelashes. "I planned to get you wasted, so I can have my way with you."

Wrapping his arms around her, he laughed. "You can do whatever you want, sweetheart. I need to positively glow when I walk into the bar tomorrow. You can't fake the aftermath of great sex."

So true. From day one, she and Logan enjoyed each other's bodies like there was no one else in the universe. Truthfully? He spoiled her for all other men.

With her height of five-foot-eight, plus the extra inch from the heel on her boots, she stood nearly at eye level to Logan's six-two—which she absolutely loved. She could stare into his copper-colored eyes without getting a kinked neck. Slipping her fingers into his hair, she kissed him tenderly while tracing her tongue along his lips. He tasted like beer and peanuts. The salt on his lips reminded her she hadn't eaten since this morning, and her stomach growled. With luck, room service would arrive before she starved to death. Reluctantly, she released herself from his embrace and looked around the room. "Nice."

An understatement. This was luxury at its finest. A large-screen TV hung on the wall with a swivel adapter that could be tilted to face either the bed or a sitting area with its sofa and recliner. A table and two chairs stood by the floor-to-ceiling windows with drapes drawn wide to show a view of the nighttime shoreline.

But she riveted her gaze onto the plush king-size bed. Oh, how she wanted to strip him naked and…well, enjoy him.

From behind, he placed his hands on her shoulders and squeezed. "Wait until you see the whirlpool."

Eyes wide, she hurried to the only other door in the suite. Pausing at the opening, she gasped. *Dear Lord*! The tub was large enough for four people. She counted twelve water jets, six different bubble-bath scents, and four plastic wine glasses. A glass-encased shower stood on the opposite wall, and *dear God in heaven*, the entire bathroom was covered in mirrors.

Logan stepped in the doorway. "Not bad, eh?"

Grinning over her shoulder, she stripped off her T-shirt. "I'm going in."

"Sky—"

The edge to his voice made her giddy. Naturally, he'd seen her black lace underwear many times. He even ripped off a few. She turned the spigots to fill the tub, then shot him a saucy look as she unbuttoned her pants. "After room service arrives, you can join me. I hope you like bubbles." She sniffed a complimentary bottle of lavender, then dumped the entire contents into the water.

He growled. "Room service better get here soon, or the cart will sit in the hall."

A knock sounded on the door. "Room service."

Logan narrowed his gaze. "Get the rest of your clothes off. I'll join you in two minutes."

Oh, yes. This part of her assignment she could repeat over and over again.

****

"Well?"

Oh, for the love of…

Arriving at work the following morning, Skylar barely had a chance to clock in before Johnny burst into the locker room. *Anxious much?* He better not ask for details, because she had a great night. She'd like to bask in the memory for a few more hours, thank you very much. Cocking her head, she smirked at the man waiting in the doorway. "You bug this room?"

He started. "Huh? No, of course, not. I heard you come in." He shifted on his feet. "What did you uncover?"

That Logan didn't bring enough condoms, that's what. She reached into her jacket pocket and handed him a business card. "I took this from his wallet when he was in the shower."

Logan Grandal, CEO and Chairman of the Board
Interactive Technologies, Inc. New York City, NY

She pointed to the card. "This is the company he sold for big bucks. It's a privately held company. You won't find much on the Internet."

Frowning, he shot her a glance. "He told you that?"

"Yeah, he had to explain about the privately held stuff and how he kept the publicity to a minimum, but his ex found out, anyway." She unzipped her jacket. "I asked why he hung around here when he could hide on some exotic beach." After grabbing onto the lock securing her locker, she entered the combination and opened the door.

"What was his answer?"

She removed her jacket and slipped it onto a hook. "His ex has a PI watching his condo. He can't go home to get his passport."

"Surely, the PI can track his credit card. He needs

cash to gamble."

"I threw him that question." During their briefing, Monroe had covered a ton of mind-boggling details. She swore up and down she would never remember half of what he said, but thanks to Logan, he repeated some key questions that might come her way. She shut her locker door. "He said he ditched his old cards when he changed to a new bank. He's using a debit card via his phone."

"Excellent." Johnny rubbed his hands together.

Oh, good grief. He acted like some diabolical scientist about to unleash a deadly contagion onto an unsuspecting population. All he needed to complete the picture was a little more hair on the top of his head, instead of the wisps, and maybe the handlebar mustache she pictured earlier. Wouldn't it be nice to shove her boot up his a-hole to wipe the smile off his face? But she had to be all professional and contain her impulses. Narrowing her gaze, she frowned. "Why does this news make you happy?"

"Because I like helping people. Tonight, I'll talk to him and see how serious he is about avoiding his ex."

Yeah, he helped people for a price. Shaking away the thought, she plastered on a grin and held up a finger. "*If* he comes in. I wore him out. He was still asleep when I left." Not really, but her ego beamed, like she was some super woman who knocked out her men with great sex.

"Good job, Midnight." He patted her shoulder. "You've earned a bonus in your next paycheck." He turned to leave.

"Hey, Johnny, be a little subtle, will you?" She tugged on her T-shirt's hem. "He'll know the information came from me."

Winking, he tapped the side of his nose and left.

So far, so good.

That night, to increase tension, Logan became a no-show.

Every fifteen minutes, Johnny hurried into the lounge, looked around, then paced before returning to his office while muttering a curse.

Sky loved this part of Monroe's plan and got a kick out of watching the bar manager sweat. If she had her way, she'd tell Logan to stay away another night, just to see if Johnny pulled out the rest of his hair.

While staring at Johnny's retreating back, Valerie plunked her tray onto the bar. "What's eating him?"

Biting back a smile, Sky shrugged. "Ants in his pants, I guess."

"He acts like he's waiting for someone." Frowning, she looked around the lounge. "Are we getting another inspection?"

"Not that I heard." Sky grabbed the dirty glasses off Val's tray and slipped them into the dishwasher.

If Sky could take a video of the guy, she'd show it to Monroe and let him gloat. The tension buildup worked and turned Johnny into one big ball of frustration. He repeated the in-and-out activity until he threw his hands in the air and left for the night.

Around the eight-thirty mark, Charles wandered in and sat at the bar.

Smiling, she approached. "How was the show?"

"Not bad, but not my cup of tea. The lead comic sounded like he had a cold." He palmed a handful of peanuts. "Marian enjoyed it, though." He shoved the entire handful into his mouth and chewed.

The more someone spent at the gambling tables, the more freebies they received, and show tickets climbed to the top of the list. Even for a B-rated entertainer, the price for a ticket cost a ridiculous amount of money. She wiped the counter. "Your usual bourbon?"

"Yeah." He threw a thumb over his shoulder. "There's hardly anyone here tonight. Your boyfriend coming back?"

She stared. "What boyfriend?"

"The guy from last night. Him and his pals are lawyers. He seems like a nice catch."

"Meh. We went on a few dates but no spark." She slipped his bourbon onto a coaster. "Where's Marian?"

He huffed. "She said she needed a long bath." He sipped his drink. After placing the glass onto the coaster, he cocked his head. "So, what are your plans for life?"

Sky was in the middle of polishing a glass when the question stopped her. "Plans? I never have plans. I live one day at a time." She held the glass to the light, then placed it on the shelf.

"But don't you want to meet a rich man and live a life of luxury? That's why you're here, right?"

Before grabbing another glass, she stopped and stared. What an odd question. From the look on his face, the man was serious. She puffed out a breath. "I'm here to earn enough to eat and keep a roof over my head. If I can put something in the bank, that's a plus."

Smiling, he raised his glass in a gesture of salute. "Don't take offense. Anyone can see you have your eye on Logan." He sipped, then smacked his lips. "Look, I know women take jobs in hospitals to snag a doctor, and a receptionist makes plans to rope in a rich CEO. It's the same everywhere."

Resisting the urge to wrap her dish towel around his thick neck, she narrowed her gaze and leaned on the bar. "I'm surprised at you, Charles. You're cynical. Is this why you never married?"

"Ah, but that's about to change. I'm gonna propose to Marian."

Yeah, because Marian had money, and he wanted it. *Damn bastard*. "Well, good luck." She straightened and met his gaze. "It seems to me, women aren't the only ones looking for a rich spouse."

Chuckling, he raised his glass. "Touché."

Marian, you poor sucker. Now, the big question. Should Sky warn the woman? Even more important, would Marian believe her?

Chapter Eight

The following afternoon, under bright, sunny skies, Skylar stood on the boardwalk in front of the Whirlwind Casino, waiting for her lover boy to appear. "No more hiding," Monroe had said. "Make your relationship obvious." The man couldn't have said nicer words, and she almost laughed. If Academy Awards were given for undercover performance, she and Logan would win hands down. She turned toward the ocean.

Last summer, when the gang at the manor took her to the Jersey shore for a grand tour, Sky had expected to see spectacular beaches with beautiful waves crashing onto the sand. What she saw were four-foot-high sand dunes with some kind of weed growing from the top. Even now, as she leaned on the boardwalk's metal rail, she craned her neck just to see the water. Paths cut through the dunes to allow access to the beach, but a child's sandbox was more appealing.

White seagulls pecked at broken clamshells with the hope of a morsel left, just to add variety to their diet of french fries tossed by tourists. Despite a warm sun overhead, no one worked on a tan. Too early in the season, she supposed. Although, throwing down a blanket on sharp, pointy objects while seagulls flew overhead wasn't what she'd call a relaxing day at the beach.

Out on the ocean, a surfer in a wet suit sat on his

board. If he was waiting for the perfect wave, he might die of old age. From what she could see, waves looked no more than three feet high. Maybe the Atlantic Ocean was for beginners. When they perfected those minuscule waves, they could move on to something bigger.

A few people strolled on the beach close to the waterline with pants rolled up and shoes off. Sky shuddered at the possibility of seashells cutting into their skin and the cold water curling their toes. Not for her, thank you. Most people chose the wooden boardwalk to amble from place to place, whether checking out all the stores or heading to the next casino. For a sunny April afternoon, the air still had a bite that required a jacket, but some individuals were bundled with knit caps, scarves, and gloves, like the temps hovered at fifty below.

"Not very enticing, is it?"

At the sound of the familiar voice, Sky glanced over her shoulder and arched a brow. "Aren't you a little early for work?"

Valerie stepped alongside. "I'm meeting a friend for lunch, but she called to say she'd be twenty minutes late. It isn't often I come out onto the boardwalk and just be, you know? What are you doing here, waiting for Logan?"

Chuckling, Sky leaned her elbows onto the railing. "How did you know?"

Val joined her on the rail. "Honey, you practically glow when he walks in. It was simply a matter of time before you two got together."

Sky frowned at the dune in front of her. "I'm probably making a mistake. He's a nice guy, but he's hiding from an ex-wife."

"In other words, he won't make another commitment anytime soon." She sighed. "Men and their issues."

"True." She waved a hand toward the ocean. "Are all Jersey beaches like this?"

"You mean more dunes than beach?" She tucked a strand of pink hair behind her ear. "The dunes protect against flooding, but I think Atlantic City overdid it to appease the casinos. In my opinion, they look gross."

"There's hardly room to sunbathe."

"The casinos don't want people to notice the ocean. They offer amenities to keep their guests indoors. Serious beach lovers head north or south." She adjusted the purse strap on her left shoulder. "I like Cape May the best. It has the softest sand, and they use a machine that shifts out debris. But it's a family-friendly town and not a place for singles to hang. If I go clubbing, I head to Wildwood." She pushed up the sunglasses slipping down her nose. "Have you been down that way?"

Sky had no idea where Wildwood was, but she kept mum. "I'm not big on beaches." Which was the truth. She wasn't a sunbather or swimmer, either. Since her security clearance included what Monroe made available, Sky spoke little about her life in Chicago. He was thorough with this false-identity stuff, and she had to be careful about what flowed out of her mouth.

Val gripped the rail and leaned back. "You don't have to go to the beach. I'm talking dance clubs."

Sky snorted. "I don't dance."

Still with a grip on the rail, Val pulled forward and turned, brows high. "I'm surprised you said that. I kind of thought you were a dancer. Your movements are so graceful. You practically glide behind the bar, even in those heavy boots."

Well, yeah, martial arts training and all, but that was her secret. Maybe she should trip once in a while to show a bit of clumsiness. Smiling, Sky shook her head. "That's nice of you to say, Val. So, thanks. Do you live close by?"

"Galloway. Not too far."

For all Sky knew, Galloway could be on another planet.

Turning to put her back against the rail, Val cocked her head. "You never talk about yourself. Are you from around here?"

Uh-oh. Monroe said to keep all personal information vague. How vague should she be without sounding as if she was hiding something? She lifted a booted foot onto the bottom rail. "My roots are in the Midwest, but I drove east for something new. Being a bartender helps me get a job wherever I land."

"I take it you don't have family?"

"Nope. No family."

"That's rough." Val checked her watch. "Time to meet my friend. So you know, the little cubbyhole restaurant opposite our parking garage on Atlantic Avenue has great Italian food." Eyes going wide, she pushed away from the rail. "Hi, Mr. Grandal. I'm leaving." With an elbow, Val nudged Sky's arm, winked, then hurried away.

Logan stared at Val's back. "Learn anything interesting?"

"Yeah, good Italian food at the restaurant opposite the parking garage." She faced him.

Chuckling, he wrapped her in his arms and lowered his lips to meet hers.

She returned the kiss with a fervor that rose so quickly, she surprised herself. As usual, a kind of molding took place between their two bodies. In her mind, nothing felt better than his hard muscles pressing against her chest. He had suggested this public display in front of the Whirlwind Casino, but holy moly, she wanted more. With so many people passing, she couldn't strip him naked, could she?

After a few stimulating minutes, he slowed his kiss, and his lips moved across hers.

She had never before experienced such a display of tenderness. This wasn't the greedy CEO kissing her. This was Logan—her lover, confidant, and partner.

He lifted his head and smiled. "Hi."

"Hi, yourself." She barely verbalized the words. Her insides were jumping like crazy, and she had trouble keeping her knees locked. She cleared her throat. "You're pretty good at this acting stuff."

He kissed her nose. "I don't need to act with you in my arms. We're a natural fit."

Oh, God. She looped her arms around his neck to keep herself from sliding onto the boardwalk's splintered wood. She had to agree about the natural-fit part. From the moment they met, they clicked. She'd never met anyone like him and probably never would. If she wasn't careful, she'd ask him for a forever relationship.

After squeezing her torso, he loosened his arms and grinned. "I think we've put on an impressive act."

Oh, phoo. He was the undercover agent again. When would she learn how quickly he snapped from one role to the next? She pushed on his chest. "I wasn't acting."

He leaned close to her ear. "Neither was I." He released his arms but grabbed hold of her hand. "How about we head to my room and put that afterglow on my face?"

Rolling her eyes, she lightly punched his arm. "You're enjoying this, aren't you?"

He grinned. "Oh, yeah, babe. More than you know, and I wouldn't do this with anyone else."

Neither would she.

****

That evening, at his usual time, Logan stepped into the lounge feeling like a man on cloud nine. Nothing and no one could deflate this amazing high after a round of sex with Sky. He'd never met anyone like her. Nimble and quick, strong yet gentle. The list was endless, and never in his life had he used so many words to describe a woman.

What surprised him was the flash of vulnerability after their kiss on the boardwalk. The word wasn't something he associated with Sky. She had a quiet confidence he admired, but maybe the people walking by bothered her. When questioned, she shrugged off her answer. Yet, somehow, he got the gist of something bothering her. This brilliant revelation hit later after his brain cleared, and she went downstairs to work. She left with doubt clouding her gaze and, yes, even confusion. She couldn't possibly be concerned about his feelings, right? She insisted on the no-relationship rule, and he agreed because—hey—he was a guy, and relationships meant commitment.

Her confusion was his fault, of course. From the

beginning, he told her how he avoided an emotional bond with his cases—especially with women. The tactic was a means of keeping his distance. His wham-bam-thank-you-ma'am attitude served him well in his undercover work, but with Sky, he was fooling himself. He cared for this woman, and her being part of the assignment scared the hell out of him. Danger always hid in the shadows, and only a trained eye recognized the threat. Right now, her danger level hovered at the low end of the scale, but the shift could change. She might be a great bartender, but she wasn't a trained agent. Anything could happen, and the thought kept him awake at night.

Funny how he could face death with a chin held high and still be afraid to tell a woman how he felt. Looking back, from the moment he watched her hop off her motorcycle, he fell for that crystal-eyed beauty. He never told her, but beehive Jo was right. He and Sky were in a relationship. No other woman turned his head. As proof, when he walked into the lounge, he zeroed in on her behind the bar, caught one wink from her beautiful eyes, and blood pooled south. Tugging on his pants that were a tad too tight, he slipped onto his usual bar stool.

With her gaze bright, Sky placed a beer in front of him before moving on to serve others.

The bar was busy. Jason Carter sat at the other end, playing the video poker game. He rarely socialized and always sat alone, except for the occasional times when Charles, whether invited or not, took the stool next to him.

According to Sky's nightly reports, the security guy, Todd Daniels, hung around the bar whenever the floor wasn't busy. He always initiated a conversation with one of the regulars, but Sky's unwritten words told him Todd flirted whenever possible. How could he not? The man wasn't blind, but the name Todd Daniels wasn't on the missing Fed agent's suspect list. Had Todd entered the picture later, or did he make himself known because he couldn't stay away from Sky?

Harriet and Marian were becoming a steady twosome. Whenever possible, they sat at Logan's end of the bar always chatting or laughing between themselves. Tonight, Charles sat with them, and the chatter was more subdued. All three nodded in Logan's direction.

Like clockwork, Valerie hurried over to fill his peanut bowl. With a lip curling upward, she winked before nodding over her shoulder at Sky.

He took the gesture as an end to her flirting. While both Val and Carmela had some attractive assets, Sky was a stunner and the one who always drew his gaze. Her short-cropped black hair made her blue eyes pop. Add a smile, and she'd drop any man to his knees. He loved everything about her, even her big-ass motorcycle. Oddly enough, she had no idea how her beauty turned every man's head.

Johnny Dee approached and slipped onto the end stool near the bar opening. "Mr. Grandal, I'm Johnny Dee, the manager of this bar." He extended his right hand.

Logan cocked a brow. "You know me?" Come to think of it, this afternoon on the boardwalk, Val called him Mr. Grandal. Had Johnny already given her a heads-up to kiss his ass, or was she the elusive partner?

He took the man's hand. *Holy hell*! For a tall,

gangly fellow, his fingers felt like limp sausages, as if the guy never lifted anything heavier than a pencil. After releasing, Logan fought the urge to wipe his palm along his trouser leg.

Johnny grinned. "Yes, sir, I know you. The top brass always lets us know who's getting comped. The girls tell me you're a generous tipper, too."

After sipping his ice-cold beer, Logan grunted. "I'd give them every penny rather than give the money to my ex-wife."

Johnny bobbed his head. "You sound like you're talking about my ex. She was after everything I earned. Luckily, she died from a drug overdose before she could bleed me dry."

Monroe's research showed Johnny divorced two wives. Both were alive and happily remarried. Logan snorted. "Lucky you. My ex has a PI hunting for my ass."

"She after more money?"

"Oh, yeah. Probably all of it." He crunched on a few pretzels.

The memory of Sky with her favorite snack of beer and pretzels hit him. He spent many nights on her rear patio, enjoying the sounds of her crunching. She even saved the pretzel salt in a cute little jar.

He mentally shook himself. He should not be thinking of Sky while working a case. *Focus, man.*

Johnny leaned closer. "I can help you, Mr. Grandal, if that's what you want."

Logan turned halfway to study him. The little wisps of hair on the top of Johnny's head looked ready to fall out and float away. "How?"

"Maybe we should go into my office. I'll explain."

Standing, he nodded toward the three musketeers nearby.

Of the three, Marian sat closest to Logan. She had to hear Johnny's offer, but from the neutral look on her face, she was more interested in the olive in her martini. Logan stood.

Well, here it comes. Logan followed Johnny down the hall. He already studied the intel from Monroe. One of his operatives confirmed no cameras beyond the bar or in any of the side rooms. Johnny's desk contained a small lockbox to hold cash for the till, and he always kept the drawers locked, as per casino protocol. The service elevator at the rear of the hall also had no cameras. This last fact explained how Johnny left the premises with a client without anyone being the wiser.

Once inside the office, Johnny shut the door.

As offices went, the room was sparsely furnished and small. Enough space existed for a desk with a computer but no spare chair for a guest to sit. A two-drawer filing cabinet sat in one corner with an empty wire basket on top. Overall, not a personal touch could be found. He faced Johnny. "Okay, explain."

Crossing his arms over his chest, Johnny rested his butt on the front of his desk. "I have the means to give you a whole new identity and help you disappear."

"Is that so?" He had to put on an act here and not appear too eager. Skepticism was the keyword. He hadn't survived years of undercover assignments by being stupid. Peering through narrowed lids, he met Johnny's steady gaze. "Go on."

"I can get you anything you need. New passport, driver's license, car, airline tickets—anything, Mr. Grandal. Your disappearance can be temporary or permanent. The decision is yours. Most of my clients choose temporary because of investments. Like I advise everyone, set up online banking—if you haven't already. This enables access and transfer anywhere in the world." Unfolding his arms, he brushed a piece of lint from his trousers. "What I do is not illegal. I don't help criminals to disappear. I offer a service strictly for men, like yourself, who find themselves in a bind and almost always because of an ex."

Gaze steady, Logan stuffed his hands into his trouser pockets. "What's the bottom line? How much?"

"A cool two hundred and fifty grand."

Nodding like the money was simple pocket change, he fixed his gaze on Johnny. "What's the timeline to get everything together?"

"Depending on what you want and how fast you need to leave, no more than three to four days."

"That's quick." Yeah, before the client changed their mind. Pursing his lips, he strolled around the small space. "The whole idea of disappearing seems drastic. Yet, I can't find a way around the dilemma I'm in." He stopped before a small mirror hanging on the wall, then faced Johnny. "I'll think about it."

Johnny stood. "Take all the time you need, but try to make a decision before your PI comes sniffing around. Once the guy gets on your trail, he'll make it harder for me to help you." He strolled to the door and opened it. "Keep our conversation to yourself, Mr. Grandal. The fewer people who know, the better your success."

"Okay, thanks." He shook the limp hand. "I'll get back to you." The man made himself sound like a saint. Whether Johnny truly helped people remained to be seen. Frowning, Logan returned to the bar and signaled Sky.

She meandered over and smiled. "Another beer, Mr. Grandal?"

He grabbed the front of her T-shirt and tugged her close. "My room tonight after your shift." He kissed those luscious lips but didn't give her a chance to respond. After all, her stunned look created more gossip than a lingering lip-lock.

When she pulled back, she cleared her throat and smirked. "I'm surprised security doesn't rush in to question your actions."

"Don't sweat it, sweetheart. The kiss gives them a good idea, and your beautiful smile confirms it." Standing, he winked. "Don't be late."

She arched a brow. "Is that an order?"

"A plea, a request, I'll even beg." He grinned. "See you later."

Not surprising, everyone at the bar witnessed their exchange, Valerie and Carmela included. *Perfect.*

Chapter Nine

The following afternoon, Sky plodded into the bar, yawning. If her liaisons with Logan continued, she might need to pack a change of clothes. That would be the smart thing to do. Then, her day wouldn't start with a rush to her apartment, followed by a quick sprint back to clock in for her shift. Of course, she could eliminate the wake-up sex and breakfast in bed, or maybe the shower for two.

Oh, hell, who was she kidding? Time with Logan was a lot of fun. Sex aside, he was a great friend, and just talking forced her to forget all the nasty stuff about to come. She stayed all night wrapped in his arms because—well, why wouldn't she? They needed to convince Johnny, and with any luck, he wasn't persuaded yet. Then, she could continue her nightly dalliance for a while longer. *Fun, fun, fun*. And yes, Logan now kept an ample supply of condoms in his nightstand drawer. She entered the locker room and stifled another yawn.

In a way, if Monroe paired her with someone else, would the case have a chance of succeeding? *Unlikely*. She'd have a hard time showing an interest in a guy she barely knew. Besides, she and Logan had history, and Monroe used it to his advantage. Logan kept her calm and focused—two pluses to make the job so much easier.

Johnny popped into the doorway. "You slept with Grandal again?"

Well, golly gee. Why didn't the man just flag her down when she passed his office? Sighing, she hung her jacket. "Don't make me sound like such a tramp. He's a nice guy. If I'm not careful, I could fall for him." She already had strong feelings for Logan, but Johnny didn't need to know. She glanced at her wiry manager. "He told me about your offer."

Stepping in, he groaned. "I warned him to keep the offer to himself. The more people who know, the less he'll succeed." He stuffed his hands into his trouser pockets. "What else did he say?"

Well, here comes the bomb. She shot Johnny a smirk. "He asked me to go with him."

Stumbling back a step, Johnny stared. "He did? Why?"

She rolled her eyes. "What do you mean why? Think about it."

"Oh—yeah, right." Placing a hand near his mouth, he coughed. "And your answer?"

She closed her locker and faced him. "I have no reason to disappear."

"He offer to pay your way?"

"He'd have to. I don't have two hundred and fifty grand. I was half-tempted to tell him he can do a lot better with his money than hand it over to you." Folding her arms over her chest, she leaned against her locker. "Think about it. He won't need new IDs if a woman is with him. Hotels, planes, you name it. Everything can be placed in her name."

Monroe said to watch Johnny's reaction. If she could use the camera app on her phone, she'd show

Monroe the comment hit the mark. Johnny's face turned super red while his eyes blazed with fire. If he clenched his jaw any tighter, he might crack a few teeth. She wasn't sure if she imagined it or not, but the tiny wisps of hair on the top of his bald head stood on end and resembled antennas rising from a rooftop.

Lowering both hands to his sides, he curled his fists and hissed. "If he listens to you, then I'll be robbed of two hundred and fifty grand—double, if you go."

Yes, there was that. The poor guy looked downright venomous. Funny how she wasn't the least bit scared. And she should be. Johnny made people disappear. The question was how? She adjusted her T-shirt. "Relax, I said I was tempted."

"Then, make sure you keep your mouth shut. I'm offering him a new identity, which he'll need, regardless whether you're with him or not. I run a successful business and don't need your lousy input." Pausing, he twitched his jaw. Gaze narrowed, he scanned her from head to toe. "Maybe you should rethink his offer and go."

Cocking her head, she snorted. "Why? You trying to get rid of me?"

He shrugged. "The guy's got money to burn. You can live like a queen." He crossed his arms over his chest and leaned against the doorjamb. "So, why not? You have family or anyone who would track you down?"

"No. None." The perfect scenario to be put six feet in the ground. She inwardly shuddered.

"Then, what are you waiting for? You're free and clear to wander the globe with a rich man." Dropping his arms, he pushed away from the jamb. "And since I have a one hundred percent success rate, no one will ever find him."

Or me. The guy should be a salesman. He made disappearing sound so enticing. All the bastard wanted was to line his pocket with more cash. She huffed. "I didn't actually decline. You could say I kept him hanging." With a quick glance at the clock on the wall, she patted her back pocket to assure the presence of her phone. Monroe would tan her hide if she left the device in her locker. "It's time for my shift." Facing Johnny, she waggled a finger. "You know, if Logan's wife is as relentless as he claims, she'll hunt for him, no matter what the cost. I don't feel like going into hiding for any man." Approaching Johnny, she stopped. The damn man acted like a gatekeeper with his hands on his hips and eyes glaring. Really, what did he expect? He knew she spent time with his potential client. Logan was bound to talk, and she was bound to make suggestions. Smirking, she patted his arm. "Don't worry. I won't say a word to anyone about your side job. Nobody can blame you if you plan to retire early."

My, oh, my. His gaze zeroed straight to her soul. She could practically envision the wheels turning in his demonic brain. If she was a mind reader, she'd—no, never mind. She'd rather not know. Bad enough she handed him a reason to remove her from the surface of the earth. She'd rather not know how.

Finally, Johnny shook himself and forced a smile. "We could make a deal, Midnight. Accept Grandal's offer. I'll go through the process of making new IDs, and at the last minute, after the money exchange, you back out. I have a no-refund policy in place, which I will remind him at the first opportunity. His payment for you won't be rescinded." He met her gaze. "How's that sound?"

He gave her that damn forced smile again. *Ugh.* The man never had a sincere smile. His lips were always tight, as if the skin would hurt if stretched too much. Truthfully, he had no personality and, in her mind, was a piss-poor manager. Pursing her lips, she studied him. "Your offer sounds like I should get a cut of your profits, say twenty percent of the money paid for me. I'd earn a cool fifty grand." Whether he agreed to her terms or not, she felt the noose tightening around her neck. *Oh, the webs we weave.* "Look, Johnny. Grandal said he would make a decision and let you know later today. My part in this will be if you decide to cut me in at twenty percent." She cocked her head. "I am curious how you do what you promised. I've read stories of people falling off the grid, and I'd like to know how they're doing it."

He snarled. "How I run my business is privileged information, but play your cards right, and I'll think about cutting you in. Just be careful about what you say. People will come around and ask questions. We can't deny he was a steady customer, but the information stops there." Gaze glaring, he leaned close. "Got it?"

Her nose itched from his cologne. What the hell kind of cheap eau de puke did he buy? She rubbed her nose. "My lips are sealed." Slipping around him, she left the locker room and sneezed.

Holy moly. She had to fight like mad not to run straight out the front doors—wobbly knees and all. When she reached the bar, she grabbed the first clean mug and filled it with soda. She chugged the contents in four gulps, and her bone-dry throat thanked her. *Lord Almighty*. She wasn't cut out for this covert stuff. Where was Logan when she needed him? She could use his reassuring arms right about now. Sucking in a calming breath, she shook herself and sighed. Since she couldn't run and spoil Monroe's plans, she busied herself with cleaning the bar.

Generally speaking, crowds never filled the lounge until darkness covered the city. She never understood why, but she had to admit, working in a casino created some hefty tips. People won money and threw bills around like confetti. She should have wised up years ago and gotten a better-paying job at a nice tavern or dance hall. In Chicago, she worked in a corner bar because it was convenient. Her boss, Kevin, wouldn't make the ideal employer list, even if hyenas were his competition. He was fat and lazy and demanded the girls pool their tips so he could take a cut. Since she was the one the patrons came to see, she almost thumbed her nose when she gave her notice. She didn't, though. The old don't-burn-your-bridges scenario.

At around four o'clock, Marian strolled in and took a stool at the bar.

Sky searched for her companions, but finding none, she prepared Marian's usual. She slipped the martini onto a coaster. "It's rare to see you alone. Everything okay?"

Tossing her purse onto the bar, Marian grabbed her glass and sipped. "Sometimes, a gal needs to be alone, you know? I could go home and relax in front of the TV, but I have tickets to a show tonight. Charles is upstairs taking a nap, and Harriet took off this morning to get the guest room ready for a grandson she hasn't seen in ages."

"Where's home for you?"

"Lower Moyamensing."

Huh? Brows high, Sky backed up a step. "I have no idea where that is."

Marian chuckled. "Sorry, dear. It's a section in South Philadelphia. I've lived there since my second husband passed."

What was it with old cities that sectioned themselves to confuse people? Chicago was the same with this park, that park, and everything in between.

Jason wandered in and flopped onto his stool with a nod in her direction.

"Excuse me, Marian. I'll get his beer."

Jason, who looked to be in his late twenties, resembled a death-warmed-over cadaver. His hair stood on end, and dark circles surrounded a pair of tired eyes. Sky placed the beer in front of him. "You okay?"

With two hands, he scrubbed his face. "Yeah. Been at the craps table too long."

"You look like you can use a good twenty hours of sleep."

"Nah. I'll be fine after this break."

She should ask why he pushed himself so hard. Didn't playing the same games day after day bore him? Not like she had all the answers, but delving into the lives of bar patrons wasn't best for business. For one, Jason never came to the bar to talk, only to sulk.

She served another patron before returning to Marian and nodding at her empty glass. "Need a refill?"

"Yes, dear, one more. Then, I think I'll cheer myself up by visiting the jewelry store on the lower level. Ever been there?"

Sky shuddered. "I stopped in one day. I'd need a second mortgage to buy something. Let me get your drink." After mixing the martini, Sky slid the glass onto the coaster.

"That watch you're wearing is worth some coins." Marian pointed.

Sky extended her wrist. "My father gave me this before he passed. I'll treasure it, even when it breaks." She sighed. "Heart attack. While at work." When that phone call came, it turned into the worst day of her life. She still missed him. Although, Monroe said to keep things vague. *Oh, dear.* Maybe she told Marian too much.

Lips tight, Marian nodded. "My last three husbands succumbed to heart attacks. I don't know why men don't take better care of themselves."

"Well, maybe you'll have better luck with the next one." Grabbing a wet rag, she wiped the counter. "Charles seems devoted."

She grunted. "*Seems* is the keyword."

Brows high, she stopped wiping. "You don't think so?"

"Honey, when you get my age, you know when a man's playing a game. He latched onto me because of my money. I humor him because he can be fun…sometimes."

"And other times?"

Marian stared into her drink. "I'd say mysterious. I don't know what's going on in his head."

What woman understood a man's brain? Sky certainly didn't, and Logan was a good example. Sometimes, he acted like a lover, other times, as a friend, and still others, as an undercover agent. Her mind kept circling in the what-the-hell category. As for Marian, her suspicions should make her cautious with Charles. Sky liked Marian and wouldn't want to see her hurt. Of course, Marian could be the elusive partner. That fact sat like lead in Sky's gut. She rinsed her rag in the nearby sink. "Some women like mysterious."

Marian huffed. "Well, I'm not one of them. But I'll keep him around until someone better comes along." She sipped her martini. "And speaking of mysterious, take Jason over there. The man is like a clam. I wonder what drives him."

Sky glanced at Jason. He had his attention buried in the video poker game...again. "Personally, I don't think he can stop gambling."

"But where does he get his money?"

Sky shrugged. "What does Charles do?"

"Oh, he's retired, honey. I never asked how he made his money."

Yeah, too bad. One question remained pertaining to Jason and Charles. Where in the world did they get the money to gamble? No one uncovered any hidden stash—not the Feds nor Monroe. Sky refilled Marian's pretzel bowl. "Is Charles going to the show?"

"To placate me, yes, even though he hates country and western. After the show, we have reservations for dinner at one of the swanky restaurants on the pavilion. This time, he's paying!" She gulped the last of her drink, threw a twenty onto the counter with a wink, and left.

Two minutes later, Sky's cell phone chirped with a text message. With a quick glance at caller ID, she smiled.

—You'll get the twenty percent.—

****

An hour later than his usual time, Logan slid onto his stool.

With a soft smile, Sky placed a beer in front of him.

The one aspect he hated about this assignment was the lack of communication. With all the security in place inside the casino, he couldn't wear a wire, and cell phone usage was closely monitored, especially around the gaming tables. In order to keep suspicion to a minimum, he and Sky depended on signals, and her shirt tug told him their plan was in motion. Now, it was his turn to keep the ball rolling.

He shouldn't complain. After working as an undercover cop for the state police, he never had a partner. At times, situations turned scary, and on several occasions, he argued with his captain about lack of backup. Over the years, he managed to survive, but the experiences probably aged him a decade or two. His superior's lackadaisical attitude convinced him to accept a job with Monroe Security. He'd rather not wind up dead because his boss worked within the tight confines of a budget. Bob stressed safety above all else, and partners were the norm. What caused the nervousness was Skylar. She lacked the experience to know what was in store. Sure, he coached her and gave suggestions, but after today, anything could happen. The thought did not sit well in his gut. "Call Johnny for me, will you, honey?"

She shot him a side glare. "Right away, Mr. Grandal."

Chuckling softly, he sipped his beer. She'd ream his ass for calling her honey, but he'd take the punishment with a smile.

Sky used the buzzer under the bar to alert the manager, then continued down the bar to refill drinks.

As for regulars tonight, Jason sat in his usual seat at the other end, playing poker video. Several strangers occupied stools, but for a change, Logan sat alone at his end of the bar.

When Johnny emerged, he slipped onto the next stool and extended his hand. "What can I do for you, Mr. Grandal?"

As if the slimeball didn't know. Funny how he zeroed in on Logan without a glance toward Sky. Obviously, no one else warranted his attention. *But holy hell*! The man overdid his cologne. Was he trying to drive everyone out of the lounge? Resisting the urge to fan the air, Logan shook the limp hand. He'd like to squeeze until bones cracked, but hey, he was a professional. "I probably shouldn't have done it, but I told Midnight about your offer."

Grimacing, Johnny dropped his hand and shook his head. "You made a big mistake. You might have jeopardized your success."

"Yeah, look, I'm sorry, but I needed someone to talk to. During our discussion, she said something about a way to save two hundred and fifty grand, but she wouldn't explain. Instead, she said to ask you."

Johnny's posture stiffened, and he twitched his jaw, as if he chewed on marbles. As expected, his gaze shot daggers at Skylar's back. And to think, Johnny hadn't heard the worst part yet.

The manager cleared his throat. "I don't have any idea what she's talking about, Mr. Grandal. My terms are pretty straightforward and nonnegotiable." He nodded toward Sky. "She might be finagling to get some of your money. Women will do anything, you know."

"Like my ex?"

"Exactly. The next thing you'll tell me is you asked her to go with you."

Brows high, Logan straightened on the stool. "The notion never entered my mind, but that's a damn good idea. I wouldn't mind having a companion."

Johnny's jaw worked overtime, and again, the daggers flew toward Sky's back.

Any more teeth grinding, and Johnny might lose a few molars.

The man released a long breath. "Two people means two sets of IDs and another two hundred and fifty grand, Mr. Grandal. I also have a no-refund policy, in case anyone backs out at the last minute."

After taking a slow sip of his beer, Logan returned the mug to the coaster and frowned. "I'm not sure I should ask her. She shouldn't have to change her identity just to keep me company. I'm the one who's hiding."

"But by telling her, you decreased your odds of success. What are the chances of her keeping her mouth shut when your PI finds his way here and asks questions? You'd be better off taking Midnight with you. If the two of you don't work out, convince her to find a job in another city."

"She doesn't need a new name, though."

"Sure, she does. The PI will discover you and Midnight disappeared together. Without Midnight changing her name, suppose she uses her own credit card? That PI will find you faster than bees to a hive.

You'd be a sitting duck. Truthfully, Mr. Grandal, for anything to work, you and Midnight both need new IDs. It's the only way to succeed." He tapped on the bar. "When the time is right, you can go your separate ways, and she can resume her real identity."

Still frowning, Logan rotated his mug. "Makes sense." He sipped his beer, then stared into the liquid. Nodding, he turned to Johnny. "Tell you what. I'll talk to Midnight and get her to tell me what she meant by saving the money."

Johnny held up a finger. "Better watch yourself. She might be working her own scheme."

Of course, she was and doing very well, too. He coughed to hide his smile. "I don't get that vibe, but I'll keep it in mind."

"If you ask her to go with you, and she agrees, you must tell me as soon as you can. This stuff takes time."

"I understand. In the meantime, I'll talk to her tonight, but I can't wait around here forever." Since a show of nervousness would go a long way, he darted his gaze to the still-empty nearby stools. "Let's get started with my paperwork. What's the next step?"

Johnny glanced around the bar. "That's a wise move, sir. Come into my office, and I'll take some pictures for your documents." Standing, Johnny tugged on his ear. "The sooner we get everything ready, the better off you'll be."

Logan tensed. Could Johnny's ear tug be a signal? He'd caught the gesture many times on other cases and proved himself right. Under the pretense of sipping his beer, he scanned the lounge. Had Jason looked up from his poker game to catch the signal? Or how about Marion and Charles who stood just outside the lounge rails talking to Todd Daniels? And when had Valerie come in? Four others sat at the small tables, but they were complete strangers. If an ear tug was a signal, who received it?

Chapter Ten

With no answer to the ear-tug signal, Logan followed Johnny down the hall. As was his habit, he took a good look around to make sure no one popped from a side door, but Johnny would be stupid to try something without first getting the money. Regardless, Logan kept alert. He entered the small office.

"Shut the door, will you, Mr. Grandal?" Johnny walked round his desk, slipped a key into the center lock, and opened a side drawer. He rummaged. "This should work." He tossed Logan a blond wig.

Catching it, Logan frowned. "I could easily slip on a pair of eyeglasses."

"Nope. Facial recognition is a reality we live with these days. Since you're not a criminal, your best bet is a distraction by changing your hair color. We'll finalize your disguise at our safe house."

The Fed agent mentioned the safe house, but the notes didn't elaborate further. "Where's the safe house?" Logan turned toward the seven-by-ten mirror on the wall and tugged on the wig. In all the years undercover, he never once wore a disguise. Usually, a change of hair style and sometimes a beard did the trick. Grimacing, he stared into the mirror. "This looks terrible." The damn wig struck him as a cross between a mop and a mullet. Cheap, too, like Johnny bought it at a discount store.

Johnny chuckled. "Don't worry. I'll photo edit, but a hair stylist will be waiting at the safe house. She'll dye your hair to match the wig."

So, a *she* was involved. A noteworthy piece of news.

"Stand by the wall, and I'll snap some pics." After pointing toward the spot, Johnny took a digital camera from the desk drawer.

Logan stood where indicated and tried not to smirk at the camera. "You didn't answer my question about the safe house."

"You'll find out when you arrive. Hold still."

After a half-dozen photos, Logan removed the wig and tossed it to Johnny. Even after a few minutes, the damn rug made his scalp itch.

Johnny placed the camera and wig into the desk drawer and slammed it shut. "I'll start processing your passport and other paperwork, but let me know as soon as you can about Midnight. Her involvement might delay you a day or two, but I'll make it work." He crossed his arms over his chest. "Right now, we can't deny your being a steady patron at the bar. The security cameras will prove that. But when you disappear, only Midnight and myself will know. If she goes with you, then you'll have one less worry." Wincing, he rubbed the back of his neck. "I don't trust Midnight enough not to talk, and talking will make your disappearance troublesome. If she doesn't go with you, then I can only hope she keeps her mouth shut."

Dropping his arms, he stared at the large calendar covering the top of his desk and tapped on one of the squares. "We'll schedule your big day for Thursday. That gives you four days to get your affairs in order."

He looked up. "Acceptable?"

Logan glanced at the calendar filled with doodlings. He could read upside down but spotted nothing noteworthy. "Barring any problems with my banker, it sounds good."

"Great. On the morning of your departure, you'll check out of the hotel but have the concierge hold your luggage for pickup. I'll arrange for the transfer of your bags to our safe house, where I'll put them into a car trunk." He walked toward the front of the desk. "Have you decided whether to fly or drive?"

"I'll fly. Las Vegas."

Johnny grinned. "That might help convince Midnight. Where you go from Vegas is your own preference. I highly recommend flying to another destination afterward. Oh, and payment for my services is due the day of departure and is to be in cash. You should place the money in a backpack." He cocked his head. "Is that a problem?"

Pursing his lips, Logan whistled. "You're asking me to carry around an awful lot of money. Are you sure? A wire transfer would be easier."

"Cash or no deal."

Because money transfers could be traced. Face thoughtful, Logan scratched his ear. Then, he dropped his hand and met Johnny's gaze. "Okay. My banker might balk, but I'll make sure he doesn't drag his feet." He extended his hand. "I'll talk to Midnight on her dinner break, and let you know what she decides. This way, I can catch you before you leave for the night."

"Perfect." Johnny extended his right hand. "Be very cautious, Mr. Grandal. Women will do just about anything for money."

Logan didn't want to shake the limp sausages again, but left with little choice, he took Johnny's hand and gave it one pump. After dropping his hold, he headed for the door but stopped. He had to make this look good to be believable. So, he took an extra moment with his hand on the knob before turning toward Johnny. "You know what? You're right. Women can't be trusted, and I should have learned the lesson from my ex. I won't ask Midnight to go, and I won't ask her what she meant about saving the money. I'll do this journey alone." He wasn't sure what reaction to expect from Johnny. The man was a damn fine actor, and his face hadn't changed except for the slight wrinkling of the forehead.

With a nod, Johnny stepped forward. "We still have the problem of her knowing too much."

Yes, Sky was now a threat to Johnny's lucrative enterprise—just the way Monroe predicted. Frowning, Logan tightened his grip on the doorknob. "What are you suggesting?"

"She might need an incentive to keep her mouth shut." Lips pursed, he stared at his calendar. After a minute, he met Logan's gaze. "Fifty grand ought to do it. But the money has to come from you, Mr. Grandal."

Yeah, the fifty grand would cover Sky's twenty percent. *Shrewd, Johnny Boy.* "Why should I pay?"

He grinned. "Because, by telling her, you let the cat out of the bag."

Man, he would love to knock out a few of Johnny's coffee-stained teeth. Logan sighed. "All right. The amount is a hell of a lot cheaper than the cost of taking her." He squared his shoulders. "I'll arrange for the extra fifty when I talk to my banker." Hand still on the knob, he narrowed his gaze. "I don't want anything to happen to Midnight."

"Nothing will. You have my word."

Carved in stone, no doubt. Logan nearly ripped off the door knob on his way out.

****

"Did you meet with Grandal?"

Skylar jumped. Damn, this man always popped in behind her. Since he kept his office door open, he caught a glimpse of anyone who passed in the hall. Now, he once again had her cornered in the storeroom. She almost dropped the two whiskey bottles in her hands, and he'd probably take the loss out of her paycheck. Whirling, she sneered. "One of these days, I might drop something expensive. Make some noise, will you?"

He smirked. "Yeah, sorry. Call me anxious. Well?"

The word *devious* fit him better. Grabbing the bottle carrier, she slipped her stash into slots. Facing him, she huffed. "Well, what?"

"Did he change his mind and ask you to go?"

Jamming her hands onto her hips, she shot him a glare. "What do you mean *change his mind*? Did you expect him to?"

He cocked a shoulder. "When we talked earlier, he was having second thoughts."

Shuffling back a step, she stared. "About disappearing?"

"That and you."

"Oh…well." She shrugged. "We talked at dinner, but he acted a bit preoccupied." Turning back to the shelves, she pulled out a bottle of red wine and slid it into the carrier.

"So, you agreed to go?" After shifting from one foot to the other, he hissed. "Come on, Midnight. It's like pulling teeth getting information from you. If you want the twenty percent, you go. Period."

She loved yanking his chain, but Logan warned her not to overdo it...*darn*. She inwardly smiled and met his gaze. "I told him *no*. I wouldn't go, but for the right price, I'd keep my mouth shut."

Jerking, he peered. "And what's the right price?"

"A hundred grand. He said he'd think about it." Johnny's mouth moved like he was chewing tobacco. More than likely, he was swallowing the cuss words about to spew from his mouth. Yeah, she liked pulling his chain, all right.

He narrowed his gaze. "That's a bit greedy."

Greedy is as greedy does. Whatever the hell that meant. She probably heard the phrase on one of those stupid reality shows. "Look, Johnny. He's got the money. His hundred plus your fifty makes a nice chunk of change."

Leaning back and glancing up, then down the hall, he stepped from the doorway and growled. "The fifty grand from me is if you go, Midnight. As I see it, I don't owe you a dime."

"Except for what I know." Choosing a bottle of white wine, she held it to the light before placing it into the carrier. "Look, I'm being honest here, Johnny. I have no desire to disappear. I'll take the money and go on a nice vacation. I always fancied a long drive across country on my motorcycle but could never afford it."

Oh, my. She could envision the smoke coming out his ears as his brain cells exploded. The poor man should be swamped with indecision and hell-bent on an urgent consultation with his partner. She grabbed one more bottle of red wine.

With a gaze flashing fire, he glared. "Are you seeing him tonight?"

She glided the bottle into an empty slot. "Er, no. He said he had something important to do."

Johnny stepped forward, stopped, then turned on his heel and left the stockroom—but not without a side glance in her direction.

For a brief moment, she thought he might attack, but he'd be a fool to touch her at work. For one, he'd be flat on the ground and unconscious. And two, when security arrived, he'd have a lot of questions to answer. No, his logical choice would be to call his partner and discuss her demands.

Not to be cocky or anything, but all this lying was becoming easier with each passing day. For heaven's sake, she was Irish and raised by church-loving parents. Her mom and dad must be turning over in their graves. When she returned to the bar, she found the lounge deserted. Never one to miss an opportunity, she grabbed a wet rag and squirt bottle to wipe down the tables.

A middle-aged man tripped up the steps leading into the sitting area. Swaying, he grabbed onto the railing and then slumped onto the closest chair.

The walk must have taken all the wind out of his lungs. He was bleary-eyed and overweight with a double chin hiding his neck. He'd already had too much to drink, and she wasn't about to serve him more. She wandered over. "Can I get you a coffee?"

With a head rolling, he stared through bloodshot eyes and grinned.

Yuck. Even his teeth were tobacco-stained.

"Just what I need. A beautiful babe for the night. Come here." He clamped onto her arm and yanked her onto his lap. "The hotel said they're comping me with whatever I want, and I want you, babe."

Oh, good grief. If she wasn't holding the bottle in one hand and the rag in the other, she'd have intercepted his grip. Before she passed out from his bad breath, she attempted to stand.

The man held firm and squeezed her against his fat belly. "You ain't going anywhere, sweetie. You're mine for the night."

When donkeys fly. She was half-tempted to spray some cleaning solution into his face, but she'd play nice. Shifting the bottle and rag into one hand, she used her other hand to clamp onto the fingers inching up her thigh. Taking one of his fingers, she bent it backward. He yelped like a Chihuahua, his other arm loosened, and with one move, she slid from his lap. Spinning behind his chair, she placed her finger on a pressure point on his shoulder.

He yelped again.

She smiled. She could make him scream for mercy, but any further maneuver would cause a scene. Instead, she signaled to Todd Daniels. She never had trouble getting his attention. Every time he passed the lounge, he winked, and more often than not, she caught him staring, which was fine. Intoxicated patrons wandered in every night, and most, she handled without difficulty. Truth be told, she liked having Todd around.

Chuckling, he approached. "Another gentleman needing an escort to his room?" He nodded toward the squirt bottle in her hand. "I'm surprised he isn't drenched with that stuff."

"Trust me. It crossed my mind." She sighed. "This guy makes my third one this week, but he's the first to grab me like a freebie. I think the bartender on the lower level is spiking drinks."

Still chuckling, Todd helped the man to his feet. "Let's take a walk, sir."

The guy staggered. "She's coming with me."

Sky rolled her eyes. "I'm still working, sir."

"Oh-shay. You can come after your shift." He grinned.

Pul-lease. The least he could do was brush his teeth before opening his mouth. She smiled at the security guard. "Thank you, Todd."

"Anytime." He helped the man descend the steps.

With the tables clean, she returned to her position behind the bar.

Five minutes later, Johnny tapped on the counter. "I'm heading out." He scanned the lounge. "Quiet night."

Wandering over, she glanced at her wristwatch. "The auditorium will be letting out soon. Val's on break, but Carmela is still circling the tables." Grabbing a clean towel, she lifted a glass from the dishwasher and wiped.

Once again, he scanned the area, then leaned on the bar. "You know, Midnight, you'd make a great partner. I know you said you'd take the money and go for a long ride, but maybe you'd like to make a lot more."

She held her glass to the light, placed it on the shelf, and grabbed another. She met his gaze. "I'm listening."

"How about I give you a tour of what I do? You can get a better appreciation of why I'm successful with people like Grandal. What do you say we do the tour tomorrow, say around noon before your shift? We'll meet in my office."

A tour? Monroe would be thrilled. Logan would go ballistic, and she would have to fight not to throw up. Brows drawn, she cocked her head, as if contemplating his offer. *See*? She could act—a little. "That sounds intriguing, but what if I back out?"

"I guarantee you'll love it. If you don't, you take the money and skip town. No harm done."

Oh, sure. Johnny was such a trustworthy man. Before answering, she placed the polished glass onto the shelf, then turned to meet his gaze. "All right, I'll be in your office at noon."

"Great. See you then. Don't be late." Whistling, he left the lounge.

Gee-whiz. She could hardly wait. What fiendish plan did he have in store for tomorrow? Would she meet the partner, and then what? She had no idea what the tour entailed—maybe the house where the agent disappeared. Was there more? *Of course, there was more*. Either Johnny fulfilled his promise to the people paying for his service, or the bodies were buried in the basement. Tomorrow, she'd get her answer. A chill shot up her spine, and she inwardly shivered. *Oh, God, why am I doing this*? She could be home, watching some stupid reality show, instead of wondering whether she'd live through tomorrow. If her nerves didn't calm down, she'd need a sedative to sleep tonight, and the sedative better come with big muscles.

Finally, with her shift over, Skylar slipped on her jacket and clocked out.

"Midnight, wait up."

Sky turned before stepping onto the Down escalator.

Carmela hurried across the gaming floor.

Arching a brow, Sky waited for her coworker to approach. "I thought you left already."

"I need to talk to you. Let's walk together."

Well, this was a first. Since the three of them ended their shift at the same time, Carmela and Valerie usually took the service elevator to the parking garage while Sky headed for the escalator. Sky glanced over Carmela's shoulder. "Where's Val?"

"She's gone already."

They stepped onto the moving staircase.

Carmela touched Sky's arm. "Did Johnny ask you to check out Grandal?"

Of all conversations to have, Sky never expected this one. She arched a brow. "Yes. Why?"

"Because whenever a rich guy comes in and gripes about an ex, Johnny always asks one of us to find out as much info as possible." She bit her lower lip. "I tried it once. It made me too uncomfortable. Val did it twice, but she liked both those guys." She sighed. "A few years ago, we had a bartender, Caroline Blum. We were good friends. Johnny asked her to check out this guy named Stuart Holdcraft. They both disappeared."

The statement got her attention, but the escalator carried them to the first floor where the noise of too many slot machines assaulted her ears. Conversation became impossible without shouting. Sky hurried to the exit with Carmela close behind. Once on the sidewalk, Sky turned. "What do you mean *disappeared*?"

"Just that. I never heard from her again."

"Maybe it was true love or some such nonsense."

Carmela shrugged. "She told me she liked the guy, but I don't think she liked him enough to ditch her family." She nudged Sky. "Let's walk toward the garage." Once free from the front entrance, Carmela glanced over her shoulder.

Sky also looked but only saw people entering the casino. She touched Carmela's arm. "What's got your nerves in a dither?"

"Cameras. I really don't know what's going on, but I think Caroline envisioned a way to have a paid vacation. She agreed to a week in Aruba, but she never called her mom like she promised. Her dad even hired a PI, but the guy found no trace of Caroline or Holdcraft." Grabbing onto Sky's arm, she stopped her. "I'm worried about you. You planning on running away with Grandal?"

Warmth flooded Sky's chest at the sound of Carmela's concern. Of course, it could be an act. With so many uncertainties involved with the case, Carmela could be another ploy to get information. She studied the older woman. "At the moment, I'm not running away with anyone. Do you think something nefarious is going on?"

Cringing, she glanced right and left. "Yeah, I do, but it's a gut feeling. People come and go in our line of work, but I got Caroline the job. I feel responsible."

Luckily, the sidewalk had few people passing by. At this time of night, most visitors drove to a specific casino and parked in the casino's attached garage. Sky pointed down the street. "Let's keep walking." She was too nervous to stand still. Moving helped. Sky looked at her companion. "Does Val know how you feel?"

"Yeah, we talk. She knew Caroline."

"And you mentioned this to Johnny?"

She nodded. "All he said was Caroline quit. She wouldn't leave without telling me. Somewhere in the back of my mind, I know he's behind all this." She clutched Sky's arm. "Be careful, will you?"

"I will, but don't say another word to anyone else."

Gaze wide, Carmela dropped her hand. "Why not?"

Sky glanced in all directions. They were nearly to the opening for the parking garage. Taking hold of Carmela's arm, Sky stopped her. "For your own safety, stay quiet. Please, listen to me."

Mouth agape, Carmela blinked. "You're onto something."

"Maybe. Maybe not. That's all I can tell you right now." She shook Carmela's arm. "Promise me."

Carmela shifted her gaze from the hand on her arm to Sky's face. "All right, yeah, I promise, but nothing better happen to you."

Leaning close, Sky pointed a finger in Carmela's face. "Do not open your mouth nor ask any questions. If you believe something happened to me, you will remain silent. Got it?"

Carmela blinked again. "You're a cop!"

Dear Lord, that would be the day. "No, I am not. I'm Midnight Sky, bartender. Now, go home. And, Carmela—"

Carmela turned from the entrance to the parking garage and met Sky's gaze. "What?"

Sky smiled. "Thank you."

Nodding, Carmela hurried into the garage.

Oh, boy. Sky had some wonderful information for Monroe.

Chapter Eleven

After her talk with Carmela, Skylar felt all the tension in her body ease. If the drink server expressed concerns about her friend's disappearance, she couldn't possibly be involved in Johnny's enterprise, right? Now, all Sky had to do was clear Valerie, and the huge weight sitting on her shoulders would crash and burn. But how did one clear a person when asking questions raised suspicions? Suppose Val was the partner? Then, what? Sky would effectively tighten the noose around her own neck.

Yeah, Skylar Dawson wasn't cut out to be some secret agent.

As was her usual habit, Sky walked along Atlantic Avenue, which was the main thoroughfare running parallel to the boardwalk and beach. The night was clear and cool with a breeze full of salt air from the ocean. Naturally, she couldn't see any stars overhead because of all the street lights, and some cars spewed exhaust thick enough to make her wheeze. But hey, this was a city, and no city was a box of chocolates. Pollution, crime, and trash were three constants with urbanites.

After tonight's conversation with Johnny, she half-expected to be ambushed on her way home. Did he think she was so naive she couldn't see the writing on the wall? Johnny Dee wanted her by his side as much as he wanted head lice on his bald head. By now, he would have contacted his partner and, in all probability, devised plans for her elimination. The thought made her a bit jumpy. Every strand of released tension from earlier returned in full swing. Now, more than ever, she kept her instincts on full alert and gaze darting in all directions. Not like she was truly alone. Since ten at night was still early in a casino city, traffic on the main drag whizzed by. According to her relief bartender, the real parties started after midnight.

As she neared the old Victorian where the entire house was sectioned into rental units, Sky entered her second-floor room and released a long, shuddering breath. She arrived home without incident to see Monroe and Logan lounging on the threadbare sofa that came with the place. They had beers in their hands and a ballgame on the TV. Two large men in her small efficiency created a feeling of walking into a closet. Chuckling to herself, she closed the door. "Nice to see you gentlemen made yourself at home."

Naturally, they gave a mere nod in response.

Their gazes were riveted to the TV, as if the ball players were running around naked. After tossing her jacket onto her bed—well, hey, it was a one-room, cramped efficiency—she grabbed her own beer from the small, counter fridge, popped the tab, and swallowed several large gulps. She wasn't sure why her mouth turned into the Sahara. Nerves, maybe, or one too many pretzels. Of course, her conversation with Johnny kept rolling around in her brain, and a sense of dread followed her. With luck, Monroe had a few tricks up his sleeve, because all this walking-into-the-unknown was for the birds.

She collapsed onto a ratty side chair. "Tomorrow's my big day. Johnny's showing me the entire operation." She looked at Monroe. "I assume he talked to his partner?"

"He sure did." Using the remote, Monroe turned off the game and sat forward. He lifted his cell phone from his shirt pocket and punched a few buttons. "Pam recorded their conversation around seven fifteen this evening." He hit the Speaker button.

Unknown Caller: *"Two signals in one day. You think I'm made of gold?"*

Johnny: *"Don't bitch. You're the one who insists on a disposable phone. We have a big problem brewing. I don't know what the hell is going on. Midnight said she asked Grandal for a hundred grand to keep quiet, and she still expects the fifty grand from us."*

UC: *"Why, that greedy, little bitch."*

J: *"Not only that. I asked Grandal if he changed his mind about her going with him, and he said no. She hadn't met him for dinner, either, and he knew nothing about the hundred grand hush money. The woman's a damn liar."* A long pause. *"I'm getting a real bad feeling. Even though casino security cleared her, I'm not sure she's legit."*

UC: *"Or she has her own little game going on."* A brief pause. *"Is Grandal still forking over the fifty grand?"*

J: *"Yes, he's okay with that. So, what do you think we should do? Midnight is a hell of a lot smarter than I expected."*

UC: *"Well, she certainly surprised me tonight. She handled a drunk who was, at least, twice her weight.*

The guy grabbed her and yanked her onto his lap. In the blink of an eye, she was behind him and had him pinned down with a grip on his shoulder. The stupid bastard thought since the casino comped his stay, he had free rein with the employees. Too bad, you missed it. She impressed me."

J: *"I should have heard a commotion."*

UC: *"There was none. She moved like a flash of lightning. The guy didn't know what hit him. And another thing. On the boardwalk this afternoon, she and Grandal looked pretty chummy. If she's playing him, then she's a damn fine actress."*

J: *"She's got a brain inside that pretty head of hers, but we can't trust her."*

UC: *"I agree. I certainly don't want to lose our profitable business because of some conniving bitch."* A tapping sounded in the background. *"All right, here's what we do. Entice Midnight with a partnership. Give her the complete tour with the promise of more money to come. Play up the money angle. That should pique her curiosity."*

J: *"Do you think it's wise?"*

UC: *"If you have another option, then I'm all ears."*

J: *"I don't. I'll set her tour for tomorrow."* A heavy sigh. *"I almost hate to see her go. She's a great bartender and has the looks to draw in men. She'd be an asset."*

UC: *"We've been doing fine without a third partner. If she's playing her own game, then it's time she met a few pros to put her in her place."*

J: *"I just hope my bosses don't question why I lose so many bartenders."*

123

UC: *"That's okay, Johnny boy. I heard of one who's available."*

J: *"Good. Send him or her my way. I don't care what gender anymore. You know what will happen tomorrow, and I hate working behind the bar."*

UC: *"No, no, you need a female. We won't change our pattern. Women sucker in the men faster, and you know it."* A pause. *"I'm tossing this phone once we hang up. I'll be in touch tomorrow."*

Monroe stopped the recording. "I'd say the plan is progressing nicely." He glanced at Sky. "Who was around when you handled the drunk?"

Frowning, she chewed on her inner lip. "No one was in the bar. Todd Daniels saw me, of course. He escorted the guy to his room." While staring at the floor, she tapped her beer can. "The gaming tables were packed, and I never looked to see if any of our regulars were playing." Glancing at Monroe, she shrugged. "Sorry, Bob. The guy took me by surprise, and I reacted."

He waved aside the comment. "You did well, Sky, and your reaction helped push the case in the direction I want it to go. With your tour tomorrow, we can assume you'll follow the path of the other bartenders. We just don't know where the path leads."

Well, golly gee. He talked as if she was about to take a walk in the park. How could he act so casual? Her insides were jumping like crazy, and it would take more than a beer to calm her. Maybe she should practice how to say *no* to men like Monroe.

Gaze intense, Logan shifted his butt toward the edge of the cushion. "We assume they're dead. For all we know, his clients are basking on a beach somewhere."

"That's true." Monroe finished the last of his beer and placed the can onto the hardwood floor. "If it wasn't for the Feds being curious about the money and the missing agent, we wouldn't be sitting here." He nodded at Sky. "What did Johnny say?"

She slipped her can onto a side table with more water rings than a game at an amusement park. The apartment was old with scant furniture, but it was clean, and the bed wasn't lumpy and bedbug-infested. She met Monroe's gaze. "Johnny will show me what every client sees. I'm to meet him in his office at noon." The prospect of their meeting created a tightness in her chest that wouldn't be relieved by one beer. But a second beer was out of the question. Right now, her gut pushed the liquid through so fast, she wasn't sure if she should excuse herself and go sit on the toilet. How in the world did everyone do this job without having serious health problems? She'd like to live to a ripe old age, thank you very much.

Logan jumped to his feet and paced. "I don't like this, Bob. The plan hinged on me going first inside the house. Sky was supposed to stay behind the bar and eavesdrop." He stopped pacing and huffed. "We should have stuck to the original outline."

"I know, Logan, but nothing draws out a partner better than being double crossed, and that's the plan. Otherwise, the enterprise will continue. For all we know, they've been doing this for years. At the moment, Johnny is totally confused, and that's where I want him." Monroe shifted his gaze to Sky. "What do you think, Sky? You want to call it quits?"

She wasn't thrilled with the prospect of entering

their mystery house, especially alone. No one could tell her what to expect, and the fear of the unknown kept her nerves jumping. Hell, to this day, she couldn't watch horror movies, nor could she figure out the killer in a mystery novel. She hated surprises, and Johnny's house would be one big surprise. But she had street smarts. Somewhere along the way, she'd figure out what to do when the time came—she hoped. She released a long breath, then met Monroe's gaze. "I'm not a quitter, so I won't back out." Yeah, famous last words. She should tell Logan to engrave them on her headstone.

Logan jammed his fists on his hips and faced Monroe. "I have one question. If Johnny is truly providing this service, is it possible he involved Carmela or Valerie? They've worked there longer, and both women flirt with the customers. They can gather information as easily as a bartender."

Monroe leaned back and crossed one large leg over the other. "It's a possibility we can't ignore nor prove. Johnny mentioned *she* will be waiting at the safe house. Maybe it's one of them. Of the two, which one would you pick, Sky?"

She held up a finger. "I can't answer that, but I will tell you this." She relayed her conversation with Carmela. "In my mind, she's cleared."

"And how do you feel about Valerie?"

"Like I'm ratting on my friends." Jaw tight, she shifted on the seat. In her heart, she knew the thought was a dangerous one. At any moment, Sky could turn around and get stabbed in the back. Frowning, she played with the loose threads on the chair's armrest. "Carmela is Johnny's right hand whenever he leaves the bar, and on several occasions, she's expressed how she doesn't like doing his job without getting his salary." She plucked one of the threads. "Carmela said Valerie liked two of the men who disappeared. Luckily, she didn't vanish with them." She cringed. "I like them both."

Monroe wagged a finger. "You're letting emotions mar your judgment. Learn to separate the two. Otherwise, your opponents will uncover your weakness and defeat you."

When she pursued her third black belt, she listened to a similar speech from Grand Master Li. Of course, both men were right. She snorted. "I didn't want to do this is the first place. I'm not seasoned like you two."

Returning to the sofa, Logan lowered his butt onto the cushion. "Maybe the partner is Valerie. The fact she didn't wind up a victim might be significant." He turned toward Monroe. "We need to give Sky some advantage. Since we know the exterior of Johnny's house is covered with cameras, we can assume the same applies to the inside. And where the safe house is we have no idea." Frowning, he drummed his fingers on his knees. "We already track her cell phone. What if we wire her? She can avoid walking through the casino and reach the bar via the service elevator."

Monroe shook his head. "If Johnny finds a wire, it's an automatic death sentence. For all we know, the clients are searched before entering the house." He scrubbed a hand over his face, then met her gaze. "Sky, more than anything, I'm counting on your quick reflexes to get you through this. I'll have people outside to come to your assistance, but I won't kid you and say this isn't dangerous. If you want to back out, tell me.

I'll figure another way to draw out the partner."

Should she end it? The smart answer was yes, she should. She wasn't the bravest person in the world, but Monroe was right about her quick reflexes. She had speed over a bulky guy like Logan. If necessary, she'd take Johnny down. *Oh, God, the indecision.*

She grabbed her beer and gulped what remained. It was a little late in the evening for liquids. With her luck, she'd wake every hour to pee. After crushing the empty can—not to be macho, but the cans were paper thin these days—she nodded at Monroe. "I'll go in first."

Logan's jaw turned into granite.

At Logan's reaction, something hit deep inside her chest. The man had watched her back from the day she arrived in New Jersey, and the feeling created a warmth she never experienced with any man. She trusted him implicitly. But like it or not, tomorrow, she was on her own.

Leaning forward, Monroe withdrew a small notebook from his rear pocket and a pen from his breast pocket, then wet his thumb and flipped through the pages.

This simple habit was a carryover from his time as a state police lieutenant. One of these days, he might actually get himself a digital notepad.

He tapped the notebook. "Okay, Sky, give me some personal observations about the regulars at the bar."

She raised a brow. "You mean, more than what I put in my reports?"

"Yes. A gut feeling."

She hadn't quite gotten the hang of what to include

in her emails. When one day blended into the next, what could she say differently? The notes were like writing a diary about a boring life. "I don't know where to start." Frowning, she chewed her inner lip. "Jason Carter stands out as the most puzzling. He gambles for hours, comes to the bar and fidgets like crazy, plays video poker while he drinks two beers, then returns to the tables. He's polite but quiet."

"You told me hotel security has their eye on him."

"Yeah, he never stays overnight, even though the casino comps his room, and he occasionally takes advantage of his free meals. The guy must have a screw loose."

Monroe wrote in his notebook. "In other words, they suspect cheating. His finances aren't telling us much. In fact, we have no idea where he gets his money to gamble. Who's next?"

"Marian is a real trip. She flaunts her wealth with diamonds on every finger and pearls around her neck, but she makes a beeline for the penny slots while Charles plays the tables." She tugged on her ear. "Something about those two doesn't sit right. Charles dotes on Marian and pays her extravagant compliments, but he's pushing to be husband number four." She paused, then met Monroe's gaze. "On the other hand, Marian openly admits Charles will do until someone better comes along. Charles isn't wealthy like her other husbands. If they marry and he doesn't sign a pre-nup, he'll make out like a bandit."

Logan turned to Monroe. "You find out anything about Charles's finances?"

Monroe exhaled with a whoosh. "Pam dug pretty deep and found nothing out of the ordinary." He flipped through his little notebook. Stopping halfway through, he tapped the page. "Charles Dilly retired from a refinery seven years ago at the age of sixty-five, owns his home in South Philadelphia, and, basically, has no outstanding debts. His bank account is modest. He never married, has one sister living in Arizona, and two nieces and one nephew. The odd point Pam uncovered was a brother who mysteriously disappeared over thirty years ago." He flipped through more pages. "A Frank Dilly. He was married, but the wife died of cancer. They had one son, age eighteen, who also mysteriously disappeared. His name was Billy Dilly."

Sky groaned. "Frank named his kid Billy Dilly? My God, the teasing he must have endured."

Logan twitched his jaw. "Is Pam working on finding these two?"

"Yes, and so far, nothing. After five years with his brother's and nephew's no-shows, the City of Philadelphia seized the home as an abandoned property. The house was three blocks from Charles. From what Pam uncovered, no one profited from their disappearance." He puffed out a breath. "It seemed odd to have a father and son disappear around the same time, but no one suspected foul play. No official investigation was conducted." Flipping to a blank page, he poised his pen over the notebook. "Go on, Sky."

She stifled a yawn. "The one regular left is Harriet Jones. She sits with Marian most of the time and never drinks alone. She's nice, funny at times with her strange assortment of hats, but she always looks bored, like she'd rather be somewhere else."

"What about this security guy who comes in every night to say hello?"

She smiled. "Todd Daniels. Nice guy. Watches over me and the girls." Pausing, she stared at her boots. She wasn't sure why she still had them on. Usually, she stepped through the door and kicked them off. Of course, having two male visitors stopped her from stripping down to her underwear and heading to the shower. And boy, she desperately needed a nice, relaxing shower. She had a nagging suspicion that despite all Monroe's precautions, she'd meet a fate totally unexpected at the hands of Johnny Dee and his elusive partner.

****

Logan spent the night. Sky loved that about him. Somehow, he knew when she was nervous or undecided or just plain scared, and all she needed was to be wrapped in his strong arms. He was the only man she ever met who simply cuddled and expected nothing more. Naturally, sex with Logan created fireworks, but sometimes, the need to be held was the best therapy a man could provide. His tenderness helped her sleep, but by morning, the jitters returned.

How did one prepare for the unknown? Was that lesson number twelve in secret agent school? She had no idea what awaited her, and the anticipation twisted her gut into a tight knot. She couldn't eat. Logan managed to entice her with a piece of dry toast and a cup of tea, but everything tasted like dust. And yes, no coffee. She had enough jitters.

Before he left, Logan took her by the shoulders and lifted her chin to meet his gaze. His lips parted, but no words came out.

Over the past few days, she'd seen this expression appear, or she'd catch him watching her. If she had to put a word to the look, she'd say disturbed, which made no sense. Usually, he said what was on his mind, but he remained mum. She placed a palm against his stubbled cheek. "What is it?"

After shaking his head, he smiled. "If I've learned one fact about undercover operations, it's to expect the worst and never let your guard slip. Always go slow and move cautiously. I know you can take them with one hand tied behind your back, regardless of what weapon they use, but please, Sky, be careful. We'll be waiting outside for your signal, but I can tell you Monroe will need to tie me to the seat. Otherwise, I'll bust through the door faster than Johnny's next blink."

Sage advice from the master. She smiled at the warmth hitting her chest. From the first time they met, she always knew he cared, but she doubted his feelings expanded beyond the taking-care-of-his-partner stuff. If she judged by his actions, then yeah, she'd say he more than cared, but what would she know? He never admitted it. Just because her heart beat extra fast whenever he entered the room wasn't much to go on. And sex with Logan was so damn beautiful she couldn't even describe how she felt whenever they slept together. Was that love, or was the feeling a simple case of happiness? She had no past experience in matters of the heart, and Logan Greene definitely affected her more than any man.

Maybe somewhere in the not-too-distant future, she would figure it out, but she had to live through today first. With luck, death wasn't the worst to expect. But Monroe was right. The only way to sniff out a partner was to set out the bait, and the bait was her.

Chapter Twelve

At her prearranged time, Sky headed for the second-floor lounge feeling like a cow off to slaughter. The poor animal didn't know what waited at the end of the long chute, and neither did she. For sure, it wouldn't be pleasant.

She needed lessons on how to psych herself for an assignment. Monroe claimed she had the brains to get out of any situation. She wasn't so sure. Even Logan's words of encouragement disappeared as soon as she left her apartment. "Take careful steps," he'd said. "Keep your wits about you and don't rush." That was easy for him to say. She wanted to run in the opposite direction and never look back. Sighing, she arrived at the top of the escalator and stepped off.

As a rule, the bar was never busy from six in the morning until noon. Hot tea and coffee were the norm with the occasional soda on ice and sometimes water. If someone ordered an alcoholic drink, the servers mixed the concoction themselves. By early afternoon, bus groups arrived and stayed until dinnertime, but high rollers were noticeably absent until after three in the afternoon. For some reason, the dark of night brought more to the tables than any other time of day. By eleven p.m., the hard-core players planted their butts at the tables and one-armed bandits, and nothing short of a full-blown fire forced them to move.

When Sky entered the lounge, the day-shift servers stared like her head dangled from her shoulders. She gave a curt wave, as if coming in two hours before her shift was normal. Entering the hall, she hesitated. This was it. No turning back. Too many people depended on her role in this scheme. She either lived through the day, or she didn't. *Hell, what a thought.* Squaring her shoulders and throwing her chin high, she stepped into Johnny's office and knocked on the open door.

He glanced up from his paperwork and smiled. "Right on time." Tossing his pen onto the desk, he stood. "Once you see what I do, you'll be impressed. It's all completely aboveboard. Nothing illegal or dangerous."

Oh, sure. Like she had *gullible* tattooed to her forehead. The taped phone conversations pretty much confirmed his business wasn't what it seemed.

"Close the door, would you, Midnight?"

As she did so, she couldn't help feeling the closed door sealed her fate. Gad, she better not sweat. She couldn't dare show Johnny how nervous she was. She faced him.

Johnny tapped a knuckle on his desk. "You can make a lot of money, Midnight. After the tour, you can opt out and still work behind the bar. If you're smart, you will consider my offer."

If she was so damn smart, she wouldn't be standing in his office. Since her palms felt moist, she stuffed her hands into her jacket pockets. "Okay. Let's get this show on the road."

He smirked. "First of all, any change of plans with Grandal?"

She shook her head. "Haven't heard from him. So,

no change in plans."

"Well, that's a shame." He opened a desk drawer and slapped a resealable plastic bag onto his desk. "Put your valuables in here."

She arched a brow. "Why?"

"Standard procedure. Remember, you'll do precisely what my clients do."

Oh, dear. She swallowed. "Even my cell phone?"

"Especially your cell. Phones have a tracking feature. My clients are desperate not to be found, and most forget how their cells send out a signal. Don't worry. You'll get a new phone with a new number."

Oh, dear. Plan B already? So much for Monroe tracking her movements.

Johnny dangled the bag. "Turn your phone off first. I don't want it ringing in my drawer."

"How about I silence it?"

"No, a complete shutdown is necessary."

"All right." She followed his instructions, then emptied her pants pockets, and dropped everything into the bag.

"Watch, too."

The watch was a gift from her father. This one piece of jewelry with its tiny diamonds circling a crystal face never left her wrist...until now. Gritting her teeth, she released the clasp and dropped it into the bag. "That watch is more valuable to me than everything else in the bag, Johnny. Nothing better happen to it."

Smiling, he sealed the bag. "Don't worry. The bag stays in my desk drawer until you return. For our clients, it's the end of the life they've known."

Yeah, *if* she returned.

He slammed the drawer shut, then grabbed the desk

phone and punched in numbers. "I'm leaving the office. Carmela should be in shortly in case I'm detained. If you encounter any problems, call my cell." He hung up and walked toward the door. "Follow me." He grabbed his lightweight jacket from a hook and slipped it on. "We're going for a short walk. Since it's a little chilly today, you can wear your jacket."

Gee, isn't he nice. She didn't need the jacket. Her nerves generated far too much heat. At any moment, she might combust.

Leading the way, Johnny headed for the service elevator at the end of the hall. Once inside, he hit the button for the garage level.

She hardly took a breath before the elevator clunked to a stop. Gritting her teeth, she followed him around several delivery trucks and up a ramp until coming to the side street adjacent to the casino.

She searched for a familiar face. Monroe mentioned he would have eyes on her at all times, and even though he knew her destination, he arranged to have her followed. She hadn't expected to see anybody. After all, they were professionals. By now, Pam notified Monroe about the loss of her cell phone's signal, and Plan B was in effect. Smart man that he was, he suspected this might happen. She glanced at Johnny. "Aren't you concerned we're leaving the building together?"

"Not really. I've been here long enough to know the areas without cameras." Shooting her a glance, he winked. "Don't worry. I've been doing this for years."

Yeah, that's why the jitters wouldn't go away. Johnny made people disappear. She prayed she wasn't one of them.

Once they reached the corner, they crossed with the traffic light and continued for two-and-a-half blocks. One street resembled the next with each comprised of old bungalows separated by narrow driveways barely wide enough to fit modern-day cars. These were summer homes from eons ago when Atlantic City was the beach mecca on the East Coast. Since the majority of casinos stood along the boardwalk with all their opulent displays of wealth, the high-rise hotels created a striking contrast to the small houses one block away with their crumbling curbs and rut-infested asphalt. The entire city became a rich-versus-poor world.

According to Valerie, several blocks were leveled to allow the construction of shopping districts, but the stores were too high-end for local residents. Even along the boardwalk, stores hawked wares on overpriced goods, and feeding a family was a joke. Back home, she could buy a whole pizza fully loaded for the price of one slice here.

"How far are we going?" Hey, she had to act somewhat innocent, right?

"Almost there." Glancing her way, he smirked. "Don't be nervous."

She wasn't nervous. She was petrified. Was someone following her? She wanted to peek over her shoulder and get some reassurance, but Johnny watched her like she was ready to bolt. Since she couldn't look behind, she could definitely search ahead, but, of course, she spotted no one—just two old codgers across the street sitting on beach chairs.

She jerked. *No way*! Anthony Powers and Tyrone Houser sat in the shade created by a house, looking like they lived in the neighborhood all their lives. They had a small table and checkerboard between them, and their faces showed intense concentration on the game. *Well, I'll be damned.* What in the world were they doing here? But oh-my-God, did her heart soar.

"Here we are."

At the sound of Johnny's voice, she jerked again. *Dear Lord.* She was not cut out for this line of work.

Johnny chuckled. "Relax, Midnight. You won't disappear."

Famous last words. Damn good thing she made out a will.

He climbed the steps to a small bungalow.

A good coat of paint would do wonders to perk up this tiny house. Years of harsh weather stripped most of the original color to expose bare wood. The wooden porch wasn't any better. The boards sagged under her boots, and she swore she'd crash through with each step.

"To ensure secrecy, I have cameras everywhere." He pointed. "They have backup batteries in case the electricity goes out."

She followed his swinging hand. Cameras were mounted at opposite ends of the porch overhang, angled inward while a third camera aimed directly at the front door. *Kudos to Pam about the backup batteries.*

"I also have cameras on the sides and rear of the house." He grinned. "Can't be too careful these days."

Obviously, all his money went into security. He sure as hell spent nothing to improve the appearance of the house. "How about cameras on the inside?"

"No need." He took a set of keys from his trousers pocket and inserted one into the lock. "Clients spend about ten minutes here, mainly because I'm giving instructions." After unlocking the door, he kicked the bottom, and the door swung wide. "Come in."

Old house with an old door meant warped wood. If he kicked any harder, one of the window panes might come crashing onto the porch. Swallowing hard, she peered around the doorframe but couldn't see much with his lanky body in the way. She shot her gaze to the dilapidated building on the right, then to the more presentable one on the left. "Are any of these other houses occupied?"

He glanced over his shoulder. "Some, but most are seasonal residences. In another couple of weeks, people will come to open them up for the summer. Let's go."

Oh, boy. She either stepped over the threshold, or she backed away. Maybe men handled this stuff better. She certainly didn't. Her mouth had gone bone-dry, and a tingle ran the length of her spine that just wouldn't stop. No amount of pep talk from Logan or Monroe helped. She struggled with all her power not to turn around and run. But she had to do this, if anything, for the two bartenders who vanished. With luck, they were lying on a beach somewhere and not buried ten feet under a pile of dirt.

Sucking in a calming breath, she followed Johnny into a small foyer, and once the door closed behind her, she fought the rising sense of entrapment. Every muscle in her body tightened, and sweat dripped between her breasts. *Dear God, help me.* But she had to continue. Monroe would want a full report on the inside of the house. Forcing her jumping nerves to settle down, she scanned the interior.

A living room stood to the right. Two wingback chairs with stained upholstery were the only furniture, as if Johnny snatched them from someone's curbside trash. All the walls stood bare, with paint faded to indistinguishable colors. To the left stretched a wooden staircase leading to a second floor. The floors were bare wood and worn from years of traffic, and the front and side windows had bedsheets tacked to the frame. *Real classy.* The air in the house smelled stale, like Johnny never opened a window to let in a fresh breeze.

Trailing behind Johnny, she passed through the living room to what should be a dining room, except the main furnishing was a card table and one metal chair with a laptop plugged into the wall. The laptop lid was open and showing—she counted—eight camera squares, seven of which revealed exterior shots and all remarkably clear. One, however, focused on a safe somewhere in the house. Arching a brow, she pointed. "You have a safe here?" Without a second thought, she blurted the words. *Stupid, stupid.*

He eyed her through narrowed lids. "Upstairs. I can't walk around with two hundred and fifty grand in my pocket. So, yes, I keep a safe on the premises until I return with my car."

Well, he did say he wanted her as a partner, and potential partners asked questions. She studied the square. "That looks like a heavy-duty safe. I doubt anyone can walk out the door with it in their arms."

He snorted. "Trust me. I had a lot of trouble getting something so heavy up those old steps. The damn thing weighs a ton." He waved at the laptop. "FYI, all the cameras have motion sensors. They activate whenever someone or something comes near. That's why the computer's view screen was lit up like a Christmas tree when we walked inside."

"Nice, but you should have some sort of intruder notification, right?"

He tapped his breast pocket where he always kept his cell phone and grinned. "Can't live without it. My cell vibrates. Usually, a bird triggers the alarm, and sometimes, a person comes onto the porch to put a flyer in the door." Extracting the phone, he showed her the screen. "See? We set off the alarm. This way." After replacing his cell to his pocket, he led her into a small kitchen.

A tiny table and two ratty chairs sat against the wall and looked as old as the house. An ancient refrigerator—with a manufacturer's logo she didn't recognize—stood opposite a rusty sink, and every upper and lower cabinet had a door missing or dangling from its hinge. An unpainted kitchen door with no curtain opened to a yard full of sand and weeds, and directly opposite, another door, heavier and more ornate, shone with newness. *Odd.*

"Leave your jacket on the table, Midnight."

Jumping, she snapped her gaze to her boss. "Huh— what? Why?" Geez, could she sound more nervous?

Johnny snorted. "You won't need it."

Frowning, she unzipped the jacket and tossed it onto the table.

Johnny opened a kitchen drawer and took out a wand-like apparatus. "Arms up, please."

She stared at the black thing in his hand. "What are you doing?"

"To see if you're wired."

Well, what do you know? Logan wanted her wired, but Monroe said no. *Good call, Bob.* Folding her arms over her chest, she glared. "Why would I be wired?"

141

"Another precaution, Midnight. Get the arms up."

The damn man better not get too personal. Otherwise, she'd whop him one. Unfolding her arms, she elevated them like an airplane.

He hit a switch and passed it over her body.

Scowling, she followed his movements. "How come you didn't do this check in the office? If a person was wired, he'd reveal the location of your house."

Grinning, he winked. "I like the way you think. I have two reasons. Not all my clients follow me here. Some come directly from the airport or the bank. The second reason is casino security makes a periodic search for electronic devices. This wand would definitely raise a few eyebrows."

Yeah, no shit. "Okay, makes sense."

The wand beeped like crazy near her boots.

Oh, crap. She tensed.

Peering up from his crouched position, he narrowed his gaze. "What's in your boots?"

"They're steel-toed."

Brows high, he straightened. "You're kidding? Why?"

She shrugged. "I ride a motorcycle. They protect my feet."

"Then, take them off and let me see."

In other words, he wanted to inspect them more closely. "You can feel the steel toes, Johnny."

"Take them off, Midnight."

"Geez, okay." She slipped onto a wobbly kitchen chair and removed her boots.

He choked on a laugh. "You wear black socks, too?"

"Cushy black socks. They're comfortable." She

wiggled her toes. "They make me forget I'm wearing heavy shoes."

After shaking his head, he passed the wand over her boots. Again, it beeped like crazy. He stuck his hand inside each. "Okay, I don't feel anything. You're clean, but I can't let you wear these."

Well, hell. Shooting him a sneer, she waved a hand across the kitchen floor. "This house is filthy, and you expect me to walk around in my socks? Are you out of your mind?"

He muttered something under his breath.

Too bad, Johnny boy. She was *not* going barefoot and no way in hell would he win the argument.

Jaw tight, he hissed. "All right, put them on. We don't have time for you to run and grab another pair of shoes."

"Thank you." When necessary, she could be polite. She slipped her feet into the boots. "What's wrong with steel toes?"

"You'll find out soon enough."

"Oh? Am I passing through another metal detector?" Bending over, she tied the laces.

"Questions are for later, Midnight."

Yeah, if she survived long enough to ask. For a man giving her a tour, he was too damn secretive. Thankfully, he avoided her socks. She stood. "How about my jacket?"

He passed the wand over it and nodded. "You can put it on."

Oh, gee, thanks. She did so. "What's next?"

"From here, you'll get into the belly of my operation." He returned the wand to the drawer. Facing her, he held up a finger. "This house has one purpose. It connects to our safe house a block away."

The man must be pulling her leg. She arched a brow. "How?"

"A tunnel." Turning to the ornate door, he unlocked a heavy-duty latch and pulled the door inward. Grinning, he waved a hand. "Have a look."

She stared at a set of wooden steps going down into a black void. Complete darkness never frightened her, but the entire scenario felt akin to a horror movie where the audience shouted "Don't go down there!" And, of course, the actor never listened. As much as her nerves screamed to get the hell out and run, she had to play along. Sky tapped a knuckle on the wooden door. "This is a standard exterior door, and you're using a dead bolt to lock the cellar. Aren't you a bit extravagant?"

"Ah, but this is no ordinary basement. So, let me explain." He gripped the edge of the door and used his body to block her in the doorway. "You are to proceed down the steps. Once you reach the dirt floor, you are to hug the left wall, then follow the wall through a tunnel until you come to a similar set of wooden steps. Those steps lead into the kitchen of our safe house where someone will be waiting with all the necessary IDs to help you disappear."

"But I don't want to disappear."

He released an exasperated sigh. "I know that. We're going through the motions, and I'm giving you the speech I give every client. Go ahead. Get started."

She backed up a step, but of course, the damn man was in the way. "Really, Johnny, I've seen enough. I'm impressed."

"You've seen the tip of the iceberg, Midnight." He

narrowed his gaze. "If you don't experience the whole operation, how can you convince a prospective client?" After releasing his grip on the door, he crossed his arms over his chest and smiled. "Trust me when I say I can use someone like you. Not only are you a great bartender, but men flock to you because you're beautiful."

The man was so full of shit. And trust was not a word she associated with Johnny Dee.

"Go on. I'll call the safe house and tell them you're on the way."

Them? Did he have more than one partner, or was he using a figure of speech?

Sucking in a calming breath, Sky stepped onto a wooden landing and stared down as far as the sunlight in the kitchen allowed. She turned to Johnny. "No lights?"

He shook his head. "I can't take the chance of running wires and increasing the electric bill."

All the money he collected, and he worried about an electric bill? What a cheap bastard. She cleared her throat. "How about a flashlight?"

"Can't allow that, either. You'll see why."

"I doubt I'll see anything, Johnny. You can't tell me your clients go into the blackness willingly. Since everyone has to empty their pockets, that means no cigarette lighters, either."

"They're desperate people, Midnight. They'll do anything." He waved toward the steps. "Go ahead. Just remember to hug the left wall. Once you get to the tunnel, you'll feel a rope along the wall. Use it as your guide."

Cringing, she peered into the black void. "And

someone else will greet me at the safe house?"

"Yes. I avoid the place for security reasons. I'll be in my office later for any questions."

Heart racing, she hesitated. *This is not good.* She should have quit when she had the chance.

Nudging her, he grinned. "Don't dally too long. Your shift starts in another hour. Ready?"

Hell, no. She sucked in a long breath and descended the steps. When she stepped onto the dirt floor, she glanced over her shoulder as Johnny shut the door and threw the latch. With the thought of his ugly puss as the last image she'd ever see, she was plunged into complete darkness.

Chapter Thirteen

Skylar couldn't move. She was afraid to. Who in their right mind agreed to pay an exorbitant amount of money to be plunged into a black void? Did Johnny tell his clients what to expect, or was this basement of horrors for her benefit? Maybe—for argument's sake—he kept the lights off to scare her to death. But she wasn't afraid of the dark…technically. Although, she had to admit not seeing her hand in front of her face rattled her nerves.

Last night, Monroe listed a bunch of scenarios to expect—a knife at the back, a gun to her head, and maybe a fist or two thrown at her face. All those would trigger her ninja skills. If the partner waited within the house, she was to take down Johnny and the mystery partner. But no one came from the shadows. Nowhere on Monroe's list did he mention her being plunged into darkness. She shuddered.

Go through the tunnel.

Yes, she had to find the tunnel…in the dark. With Johnny turning the dead bolt, he forced his clients to proceed as instructed. How many times did someone say to hell with disappearing and return to the landing to pound on the door? Did Johnny bother to answer—if he hung around at all? He had his money and a no-refund policy in place. He left his clients with little choice but to bite the bullet and proceed…like her. She had to see this through. *Please, please, please, don't let me trip over any dead bodies.* Swallowing hard, she stood still to let her eyes adjust—for what good it accomplished. Not a shred of light hit her pupils. No basement windows to let in daylight, either. Nothing.

Hug the left wall.

The wooden staircase stood adjacent to the left wall, and she had no clue how far to the right wall. Judging from the size of the house, the basement couldn't be *too* big, right? Come to think of it, he never said how far to the tunnel. *Talk about going in blind.*

Left with no recourse, she took a long, slow breath to get her heart rate under control, released it just as slowly, and allowed her other senses to take over.

The basement smelled musty and damp. That in itself hadn't told her much. The house was only three blocks from the ocean, and for all she knew, basements in the entire city had a similar smell. She'd been in New Jersey short of a year, but one of the manor tenants explained how their state was a peninsula, and in some places, the water table rose as high as six feet from the surface. In her opinion, that's taking sea level a little too literally.

Not a sound hit her ears. If she discovered one important fact over the past several weeks, she'd label noise as an everyday constant in this casino city. Between delivery trucks bouncing over ruts in the street, combined with car horns and police sirens, she could hardly sleep at night. But here in this black void…zilch, like she had suddenly gone deaf.

Next came touch. Reaching her fingers toward the left wall, she brushed something bumpy and soft. Foam paneling? *How odd.* Who in their right mind used foam in a damp…she gasped, and a sudden coldness hit her core. *No way*! If she guessed right, she traced her fingers along soundproofing tiles and, in all likelihood, the same style Logan pinned her against after every weapons lesson. The only reason to go through the expense of soundproofing a basement was to mask the screams of his clients. Since no one had any idea what to expect, she could see it happening, and now, she understood the reason for the heavy-duty door. Johnny's clients were trapped, in the dark, with no way out but through the tunnel. *What a sadistic bastard.*

Hugging the wall as instructed, she slid her booted foot forward. Another slide, then another. She stopped to listen. Was that water splashing? More likely, Johnny flushed a toilet somewhere in the house, and the water rushed through a pipe to the sewer.

As much as she wanted to get the hell out of here, she fought the urge to hurry. With the wall as her guide, she continued at a snail's pace and never once lifted her foot. Around the seventh or eighth slide, her boot hit something metal.

A soft twang sounded above her head. A whoosh followed.

Her throat seized. *Well, I'll be damned*!

Skylar hit the dirt floor as something huge flew over her head. The breeze blew against her neck, and a shiver shot down her spine. Whatever it was swooped close and stopped with a loud thud that vibrated the overhead rafters.

Breathing hard, she remained frozen and listened while trying desperately not to sneeze from the stirred dust. Whatever sprung from the ceiling was triggered by her foot on…something. Should she move? Was another trap waiting to be released in case the first one failed, like maybe the ground would crack open and swallow her whole? *Oh, God, what a thought.* The overwhelming impulse to do something fought against the urge to remain in this position forever, but people depended on her.

Besides, Johnny might return at any moment to see if his booby trap worked.

Gritting her teeth, she rolled toward the wall and inched her shoulder against the foam. No way in hell would she sit up yet. Hugging the basement floor seemed like the safer course of action. Swinging her hand overhead, she touched a square metal object about a foot over her head. A battering ram? *Seriously?* With her fingers exploring more, she—*oh, shit*—it had spikes!

Crawling on her belly, she inched toward where her foot hit metal and fingered a smooth plate dug into the dirt about six inches wide and maybe a foot long. In the dark, no one could miss stepping on the trigger to release the trap. Clever, but the question was why?

She stilled. A sound overhead kicked her heart into her throat. Had she inadvertently triggered another trap? Whatever the sound was, she didn't like it. She flattened herself onto the dirt floor and listened. What the hell was that noise? A clanking…no, it sounded more like chains moving along a conveyor. Was the battering ram being lifted to spring another surprise? What the hell kind of sordid operation did Johnny and his partner have here? Swinging a hand over her head, she hit nothing but air. *Son of a bitch.* The ram had indeed returned to its perch.

She shuddered at how close she came to serious

injury. Yet, the spiked apparatus couldn't be the end to Johnny's madness. To prove anything, she needed light.

With the wall as her guide, she reverse-crawled to the wooden staircase. Despite the coolness in the basement, sweat tickled her back and dripped from her forehead. Monroe could argue all he wanted, but no way in hell would she proceed beyond the metal plate. *Call me a coward.* She didn't care, but she'd rather have light to see what else Johnny had in store.

When her fingers touched the bottom step, she exhaled a long sigh. She made it. Sucking in a calming breath for a heart beating a mile a minute, she crept to the landing. Even the heavy door had no light strip at the bottom.

Pressing her ear to the wood, she listened. Johnny's voice resonated from the—what?—maybe the dining room, and he said something about needing a bartender. *Well, no shit.* He assumed his trap worked. But she had no idea what happened after the ram struck. Were his clients destined to bleed to death from the spikes? But sharp points striking so low to the ground would impact the lower part of the legs. For what reason? To incapacitate them so they couldn't run?

All right, Skylar, think. Was there a tunnel? A booby trap with spikes told her the tunnel was a ruse. Yet, the trap wasn't meant to kill, either. If Johnny or his partner finished the job with a bullet, why not do so in the first place, like when the client reached the bottom of the steps, then bang-bang with a gun? Why go through the trouble and expense of a spiked battering ram when the soundproofing tiles would muffle the sounds of gunfire?

Beyond the door, the thump of footsteps echoed on

the wooden floors and headed her way.

Oh, crap. What should she do? But without knowing what happened after the trap, Monroe's plan would fall to pieces. Should she hide? *Oh, yeah, that was a big joke.* With the basement in darkness, she had no idea where. Was he coming to dispose of her body? No, that didn't make sense, either. She'd have leg injuries. He'd know she was still alive. Maybe she should lie on the dirt and moan. *Oh, hell, no.* She didn't like that idea one bit. Something else happened after the spikes incapacitated his clients, but what?

Uncertainty flooded her. *Damn you, Monroe.* She wasn't experienced enough for Johnny's little house of horrors.

All right, for now, she would hide and hope for the best. The big question, where? Without knowing anything else about the basement, then logically, she'd go under the staircase.

Relying on her ninja skills of light steps and swift movements, she descended while keeping a hand on the wooden rail as a guide. The rail was a lifeline to something solid and a means to keep track of her position in the darkness. She had no idea what waited under the steps, but she was about to find out. With luck, she'd find empty space, instead of a throw-all place for junk. Reaching the bottom as the dead bolt turned, she swung under the stairs in time to avoid the light in the doorway. Johnny's shadow formed an eerie silhouette on the dirt floor, but the open door gave her partial light to maneuver around some cardboard boxes.

Shit, shit, shit! The staircase was the open kind with no riser between the steps. If he searched the basement, he'd see her for sure. Ever so carefully, she squeezed between two boxes before a click snapped, and floodlights brightened the entire basement.

Squinting from the sudden brightness, she crouched lower. Within seconds, her eyes adjusted. Now that she could see, she wasn't hidden at all! She inched around more boxes half-eaten by mice. Hugging close to the wall, she crawled toward the corner of the bottom step.

Johnny descended with his shoes clomping loudly on the boards.

Moving closer to the wall, she caught a few spider webs in her face—*yuck*—and fought the urge to brush them away. Ever so carefully, she curled into a ball.

Johnny reached the bottom step and stopped.

For a change, her all-black attire was a godsend. She wished she could see the rest of the basement from her curled-up position, but she would wait. Her heart pounded, like it threatened to push right out of her chest. Damn, the organ beat so hard she swore Johnny would hear.

Monroe counted on her to use her brain and not panic, but she didn't do this covert stuff for a living. He never discussed a scenario where she was thrown into a pitch-black basement. If she bit her teeth any harder, she'd break a few molars. *What should I do?* Johnny could see she wasn't on the floor, bleeding. She'd have no choice but to take him down. Forcing herself not to freak out and give away her hiding spot, she ducked tighter into the corner.

Johnny remained stationary on the last step.

Why did he stop? Was he afraid of getting his loafers dusty? He was so close she could smell his cologne, and the brand reminded her of a thrown-together potpourri bought at a dollar store. She held her breath. *Please, don't make me sneeze.*

His cell phone rang.

A true saved-by-the-bell moment. With luck, the call would give her a few more minutes to think.

"Yeah, I'm checking the basement now. The trap sprung, so she's obviously in the pit."

Pit? What pit? She raised her head to see, but Johnny's legs were in the way.

"Hell, no, I won't look. I gave them enough time to drag her under, and you know damn well I won't come into the basement until after the fact. I don't want to see or hear anything. Look, I'm telling you. She's not in the basement. She had only one place to go. If you're so concerned, then get your ass over here." He slowly ascended the staircase. "I can't hang around. Carmela called and said the new bartender is waiting in the lounge. I've got to get back. Huh? Yeah, I raised the trap. Still works like a charm. Too bad, you killed the guy who installed it. If the mechanism ever breaks, we'll be stuck." A short pause. "Right. One problem eliminated. Grandal is next."

The door shut, the dead bolt latched, and the lights clicked off. She was once again plunged into darkness.

Okay, heart, take it easy. She released the breath she'd been holding and eased from her cramped hiding spot. Ever so slowly, she stood and brushed the cobwebs from her head and face with a silent prayer a spider hadn't hitched a ride.

Too bad, Johnny hadn't mentioned a name, like *Come see for yourself, Henry.* A name would help Monroe close the case faster, and she could return to her quiet life managing a boardinghouse. But what was the pit Johnny mentioned? And what did he mean by giving *them* enough time? "I need light, dammit."

With a grip on the wooden rail, she crept up the steps and listened at the door. *Nothing*. No footsteps and no voices.

A strange guttural growl rose from behind her.

Gasping, she whirled. What the hell was that? An animal? *Down here*? And she'd swear water splashed...again. Whatever growled sent a chill straight to her hair ends, and she was glad she stood at the top of the staircase.

All right, enough. Concentrate. Time to get out of here.

She pulled on the doorknob. Locked, of course. She took a moment to clear her mind of all thoughts, save one—the door. She fingered around the wood panel closest to the dead bolt. A heavy-duty door would take some effort, but wood could be busted. She hadn't a whole lot of room on the landing to use her legs, so she removed her jacket and wrapped it around her right hand. The cloth would make a nice cushion to protect her skin.

Returning her concentration to the panel, she positioned her stance for maximum impact and struck the wood with her covered knuckles. Once, twice, then on the third, the wood splintered. A fourth blow finished the job. Light seeped in, and she was never so grateful. Unwrapping her hand, she shook the jacket and slipped it on. Reaching around the panel, she found the lock and opened the door.

Whether it was her imagination or not, she sucked in a breath, as if her lungs were starved for air. The feeling was akin to taking a deep breath after being suffocated. She wasn't claustrophobic or afraid of the dark, but relief swept through her, anyway. She survived Johnny's plot. Now, she must uncover the full extent of his elaborate business, but first, she had to alert Monroe.

By now, Pamela picked up the phone conversation and relayed the information.

The words about her untimely demise would have Logan jumping from his seat, and if Logan watched Johnny leave, he'd break through the door and set off the cameras.

Stepping into the kitchen, she swung her gaze right and left and then checked the entire lower level of the house. She almost laughed. She just made enough noise to wake the dead. If Johnny wasn't standing by the door with a gun in his hand, then he truly left the house.

Sitting on the wobbly kitchen chair, she untied her left boot and slipped her hand into her sock to retrieve a small button taped under her ankle bone. She pressed it. This tiny device sent a signal to Monroe, telling him she was still in one piece and preparing to secure the house. After placing the button into her jacket pocket, she re-tied her shoe and stood.

Facing the basement door, she sucked in a calming breath and flipped on the lights. *All right, here I go*. She again descended the stairs and instantly froze on the bottom rung. Nearly the entire cellar floor was one gigantic hole! Every inch of the walls and ceiling were covered with soundproofing tiles, and as expected, no tunnel led to a safe house. Johnny's instructions to hug the left wall guaranteed a foot would trigger the overhead booby trap tucked between two rafters. *Dear Lord, how diabolical*. So, the trap swung down, stabbed a client with the spikes, and without question, propelled them into the pit. Instant disposal. *Ugh.* Did she dare look into the hole? How could she possibly avoid it just because she was afraid of what she'd see? Besides, dead bodies reeked of decay, right?

I gave them enough time.

She jerked. Johnny's words echoed in her mind. And he refused to look into the pit. Did it have something to do with the sound of splashing water and a low growl? What did he not want to see? Even more important, should she look? *Aw, hell.* She had to know. Avoiding the left side, she approached from the right and, ever so slowly, peeked over the edge. Her heart stopped.

Oh, dear God in Heaven, no!

Chapter Fourteen

Four beady eyes peered up from a murky pool of water. Just breaking the surface, long, bumpy shapes bobbed.

Sky muffled a string of curses. Johnny's clients disappeared, all right, straight into the bellies of two large alligators. His clients paid a small fortune to become a gator's meal. No wonder he soundproofed the basement. The screams of being torn apart would have sent chills scurrying up anyone's spine. She furled her fists. *That son of a bitch.*

Now, more than ever, she vowed to seek revenge for all the lives lost. For some strange reason, she glanced over her shoulder to make sure she was still alone in the basement. If she found Johnny behind her, she would have killed him on the spot, then tossed him into the pit. Recalling Monroe's words not to let emotions mar her judgment, Sky unfurled her fists, closed her eyes, and took a deep breath. When she opened her eyes, she shook her head. She still wanted to kill Johnny.

How could she not be angry? He nearly succeeded with his plan to feed her to his pets. If she hadn't hugged the wall while repeating Logan's words to move slowly, she would have been in an ideal position for the booby trap to do its deed.

Gathering the courage to finish her inspection, she

again peeked over the edge. Bits of clothing floated on the water's surface, but nothing attached to a body—*thank God*. The hole was about nine feet down with straight sides. Nothing to grab onto, either. The spikes on the ram and the damage it would inflict to a victim's legs guaranteed no easy escape. More likely, the taste of blood in the water activated the gators' appetites. She shuddered.

All right, enough time wasted. She ascended the steps two at a time to the dining room and plopped onto the chair in front of the laptop. This time, loosening the laces on her right boot, she slipped her hand into the sock to grab the thumb drive taped to her inner ankle. The steel-toed boots were a great diversion. Last night, as she, Monroe, and Logan brainstormed on how she could get past any type of body scan, she came up with the idea of taping the tiny devices to her ankles. And it worked. Johnny had concentrated on the steel toes and completely ignored her socks.

After retying the laces, she inserted the drive into a USB port. According to their tech expert, Pamela, the drive contained a program to freeze the cameras. This would allow Pam time to come in and do her magic while Monroe and Logan accessed the property.

The laptop beeped and prompted for a password—Pam's password, of course. Skylar typed *Sweetpea* and hit *Enter*. The screen flashed twice, and the cameras instantly froze. Breathing a sigh of relief, she headed for the front porch and waved to Anthony and Tyrone.

Anthony immediately talked into a small radio.

Within seconds, a white van pulled in front of the house. Monroe, Logan, and Pam exited through side and rear doors.

While she stood at the front door, Sky couldn't help scanning the neighboring houses, in case Johnny hired someone to act as a spy. Really, though, Johnny would be out of his mind to draw attention to his lucrative business. His spies would see a client going into the house and never coming out. But she searched for a fluttering curtain, anyway.

Logan flew onto the porch and wrapped her tight in a bear hug.

His arms felt wonderful, and all her tension melted away. No one else made her weak-kneed like Logan, and she could stay in his arms forever. But if he squeezed any harder, she'd need oxygen to reinflate her lungs. Sliding her hands to his neck, she tilted his head downward and connected with his worried gaze. She smiled. "I'm okay."

Releasing a long breath, he eased his hold and placed his forehead against hers. "I was scared half out of my mind. We saw Johnny leave, but you took a full fifteen minutes to send the signal. Monroe had to hold me down." After kissing her forehead, he dropped his arms. "Do I really want to see what's inside this house?"

"No, but you'll understand my delay soon enough." If she could stand outside for the rest of the day, she'd be happy. Maybe she could sit in the van and take a nap.

Monroe stepped onto the porch and squeezed her shoulder. "Good job. Johnny's phone conversation nearly had all of us charging in here. I'm glad you're all right. Now, we can finally get a look at this operation. Anything we should know?"

"Yeah, everything happens in the basement." She

gripped Monroe's arm. "I'll follow you inside the house, but I will not go down to the basement. You'll understand soon enough." Sighing, Sky led the way into the living room. "The cellar steps are in the kitchen. When you get to the basement, stay away from the left wall. You'll see a metal plate on the floor that releases a booby trap from the ceiling. I left the lights on."

Monroe and Logan exchanged wide-eyed glances and hurried toward the kitchen.

Their beautiful IT tech, Pamela O'Connor, with her gorgeous red hair pulled into a ponytail, patted Sky on the back, and headed toward the laptop. After studying the screen, she pointed to the squares. "This one is on a safe. Do you know where it is?"

"Johnny said upstairs."

Pam keyed a small radio. "You're on, Cracker."

Cracker? Sky hadn't met everyone on Monroe's payroll, but she'd definitely remember someone called Cracker. She stared at the front door.

Several minutes passed, and the buxom blonde from the state liquor board entered.

Sky gaped. "You?"

The blonde extended her hand. "Vanessa Moore. Nice to meet you. Here." She handed Sky a resealable plastic bag.

Wearing a big smile, Pam approached. "Vanessa is a phenomenal safecracker, Sky. She's also an ex-cop. When we lost your cell signal in Johnny's office, we took a calculated risk that the phone was either in your locker or his desk. So, we waited until our lookout spotted you and Johnny heading for the house, and Cracker slipped in via the service elevator. We couldn't take a chance of Johnny or his partner accessing the contents on your phone. We don't know which partner rigged the cameras, but one of them is tech savvy."

"Wow." Sky shook herself. "I'm impressed." She faced Vanessa. "But you posed as someone from the state liquor board."

Vanessa grinned. "What better way to inspect a place than to go in as a rep from the state board?"

My God, the woman had beautiful teeth, too.

Pam chuckled. "As unlikely as it sounds, we had to make sure Johnny wasn't hiding a safe somewhere in his apartment. Cracker also checked his condo. So, by process of elimination, the safe was here or wherever his partner lives." She returned to the laptop in the dining room.

Vanessa touched Sky's arm. "Where is it?"

After closing her gaping mouth, Sky shook herself. "Somewhere upstairs, but please, be careful. I haven't investigated the second floor. You might find a trap and possibly more cameras."

Vanessa nodded and lifted a small walkie-talkie to her mouth. "Tank, join me."

The man who walked through the door was the embodiment of big, black, and beautiful. Sky met him while he worked out with weights and discovered he easily lifted three hundred pounds with one arm. She hadn't had him on the martial arts mat yet, but something told her he wouldn't need any lessons.

With a nod in Sky's direction, Tank followed Cracker to the second floor.

Feeling stunned, Sky opened the plastic bag and placed the contents into her pockets. The diamond watch she handled with care. Every time she fastened the clasp, she thought of her father. God, how she missed him. *If he could see me now...* The daughter who never showed any ambition beyond high school was working for a security outfit as their martial arts instructor and, now, agent. Her dad was either jumping for joy or turning over in his grave.

A thump shook the house. The basement might be soundproofed, but no way in hell could they control the noise of the spiked ram. Sky caught Pam's puzzled gaze. "Johnny's booby trap. As much as I hate to admit it, the design's impressive."

"I gotta see." Pam ran toward the kitchen.

A moment later, Anthony and Tyrone entered the living room and hurried toward her.

My gosh. How she loved these guys. She hugged them. "I can't tell you how nice it is to see you." She stepped back. "I'm surprised, too."

Tyrone snickered. "Monroe recruited us to keep an eye on the place. Our orders were to watch for anyone who came or went."

"But geez, guys, I'd rather not put you in danger."

"Pah." Anthony waved his hand. "No one pays attention to two old men on lawn chairs. When you coming home? We miss you."

She choked up. She couldn't ask for a nicer bunch of tenants. "I miss you, too, especially Fay's cooking, but we still have work to do."

Tyrone took hold of her arm and squeezed. "You make sure you keep yourself safe. We want you back in one piece."

She couldn't agree more.

Monroe stepped from the kitchen and shook their hands. "Gentlemen, you did great. I can't thank you enough. You know what's next."

Anthony grunted. "Yeah, kill time until Joe's done."

What? Sky started and glanced from Anthony to Monroe. "Joe Ryan? You recruited Joe, too?"

Smiling, Monroe nodded. "He's sitting in your lounge, watching Johnny. We have a lot of work to do here, and we don't want interruptions."

"But what if his partner walks down the street and sees all your activity?"

"I've still got eyes on every corner, Sky, but I doubt he or she will show. No money was exchanged." He tugged on his ear. "Truthfully, I'd love for the partner to make an appearance. We can cuff him and close this case."

Wouldn't that be nice? But nothing was ever easy anymore. Monroe might be meticulous with his plans, but already, he'd had several deviations. Something told her more changes were yet to come. She sighed. "You have enough evidence to lock Johnny away. Can't you, you know, torture him to get the name of his partner?"

Monroe wagged a finger. "Yes, we can put Johnny away, but we have no guarantee he will talk. His partner can continue in another town with another poor sap to take the rap." He squeezed her shoulder. "No, Sky. We will proceed as planned."

Darn. She really wanted to go home.

Anthony patted her arm. "He's right, you know. These guys need to be put away for good." He turned to Tyrone. "What do you say we get going? Joe knows to meet us in the casino next door. Hopefully, we won't lose all our Social Security money waiting for him."

Chuckling, Monroe slapped Anthony on the back.

"Spend it, guys. I'm compensating you for today. You want a ride to the casino?"

"Hell, no." Tyrone rubbed his butt. "Those beach chairs were a little too hard for my bony ass." He threw a thumb over his shoulder. "We already put the chairs and table into the van, and we'll hitch a ride home in Joe's truck when we're done."

"It's going to be a long day, gentlemen. Just say the word, and I'll have one of my men drive you home."

"Nah, we'll wait for Joe." Anthony nudged Tyrone with an elbow. "Let's get going."

After the two men left, Monroe turned and wrapped her in a tight hug.

She might be five-foot-eight, but Monroe's six-foot-four made her feel like a little girl. Stepping back, she smiled. "What was that for?"

"Logan and I saw what was in the basement." He clenched his jaw, then stared at the ceiling before lowering his gaze to meet hers. "I've been a cop my whole life, and I have never seen anything like what we found. Ten to one, we'll discover a lot of bones on the bottom of the water hole." With his lips twitching at the corners, he peered through narrowed lids. "You did a number on the door."

She harrumphed. "I had a strong incentive to find light." She explained her journey from Johnny's office to her time in the dark basement. "The soundproof tiles are similar to yours in the shooting range. Those tiles were my biggest clue that all was not what it seemed."

"Thank God." He glanced over his shoulder. "I don't want Johnny to know about your special skills. So, I'll have the door repaired to look like new. We'll let him guess how you got out."

Cracker and Tank descended the steps and joined them in the living room.

With her lips stretched into a cocky smile, Vanessa held up a canvas bag. "Looks like a little over two mil, maybe more. Some of the Fed agent's marked bills are in here, too."

Monroe grimaced. "At least, we know for certain he didn't take off with the money." He jammed his hands onto his hips. "Good job, Vannie. You and Tank can head to the office. See how much of the money is from the Fed agent, then lock everything tight in the gun safe. We'll continue here for a few more hours."

After watching the two leave, Sky turned to Monroe. "You could have told me about Cracker."

Chuckling, he shook his head. "I keep her in the background as much as possible. Besides, you showed genuine surprise to see a state rep walk into the lounge." He withdrew his cell phone from his rear pocket. "Have a seat and rest, Sky. I need to make a few phone calls." He disappeared into the kitchen.

Feeling slightly lost, Sky stood in the middle of the living room and stared at the worn hardwood floor. Everyone had a job to do. While, technically, she had the hardest job of all, she still itched to do something, like punch a wall or wring Johnny's neck. She sighed and looked down at herself. Her clothes were covered with dirt. She probably still had spider webs in her hair. Her hands were filthy, and she'd bet dirt smudged one side of her face. She could use a nice, long shower, or better yet, a long soak in Logan's fabulous tub. And speaking of her lover boy...

Logan thumped toward her with a jaw like granite.

Dust covered his Italian loafers and echoed on the hardwood floors. His beautiful silk shirt showed signs he lifted something dirty against his chest.

The dirt probably came from hugging her. She should inspect his back for her handprints.

Clamping onto her arms, he wrapped her in another tight hug. "I'm ready to beat the bastard to a pulp." Easing his hold, he slipped his fingers into her hair and gazed into her eyes. "Those gators are both ten feet long. A victim might escape from one, but two would rip a body apart in seconds."

Oh, yuk. Thanks for the visual she didn't need. Tugging on his pants belt, she pecked his lips. "I followed your advice and moved slowly."

"Thank God." He placed his forehead against hers. "We found blood on the trap's spikes. Monroe called for his lab boys to get samples." He kissed her forehead and then held her at arm's length, his gaze gentle.

Something caught in her throat at the shine in his eyes. How could a man be so tough and yet so tender? Did he love her? Granted, he never said the words, but every action, every touch, and every look conveyed his feelings…like now. Maybe he'd rather she say the words first. If that was the case, the man might be waiting a long time. She wasn't sure how she felt.

Frowning, he searched her face. "You okay to continue?"

Shaking away the questions for which she had no answers, she patted his chest and smiled. "I'll enjoy this part, Logan." After what Johnny put her through? *Hell, yeah.* Nothing would please her more than to make that bastard squirm.

Chapter Fifteen

At his usual six p.m. time, Logan wandered around the gaming tables, looking like he couldn't make up his mind where to lose his money. After years of undercover operations, he found it easy to slip into his false persona and mingle with suspects. Usually, he played rougher characters and hung around in seedy bars, so this rich CEO role was a nice break. Still, even though this case was totally different from the past, he always waited for the knife in his back or the gun to his head. Not a pleasant picture.

The majority of Monroe's clients asked for protection, whether through Pam's technology expertise or an agent's bodyguard duties. Some cases required an undercover operative to stay in the background...like this one. A few months back, over beers, Monroe had talked about using Sky one day. She had the potential to become an outstanding agent, but Bob needed the perfect opportunity to convince her. When the missing Fed agent case fell into his lap, the big guy actually got giddy. Knowing Monroe, he'd find another way to use Sky. She was a hell of a lot smarter than she let on. In time, her confidence would grow and not be such a hindrance. Logan stopped by the roulette table and toyed with the chips in his hand.

Last night, Sky was an emotional wreck, but she surprised him at how easily she fell asleep in his arms.

Her trust shot an arrow into his heart and kept him awake all night. He was scared spitless at what she might face on her grand tour with Johnny, and his mind raced with all the worst scenarios. *Expect the unexpected.* How many times could he preach the phrase without sounding like a broken record? But this afternoon, because of quick reflexes, she survived without a scratch...*thank the Lord.* In another hour, Sky would be on her way to the casino from her apartment to continue with the next phase of Monroe's plan. Logan's job was to make sure the stage was set. He headed for the lounge.

Over the past week, while watching people gamble away their paychecks and the hoopla surrounding a big win, he could see how an addiction grabbed hold. To feed the craving, casinos comped people with freebies to keep them in the building, but these perks never enticed Jason Carter. He spent a fortune at the tables but never stayed the night and rarely took advantage of the free meals. In fact, the one comp he truly enjoyed was his unlimited drinks at the bar.

As for himself, the act of gambling bored him to tears. How could people sit for hours and throw their money away? He had better investments for his hard-earned bucks than to make a casino richer.

On the other hand, Marian and Charles grabbed onto every complimentary offer at their disposal. They practically lived in the hotel, ate all the free meals, and enjoyed nightly shows. Harriet, like Jason, went home, but she occasionally took the offer of a comped room. As for Todd Daniels, the security guard who flirted with Sky, nothing of importance emerged on his background check—not even a traffic ticket. At this point, Logan hadn't a clue who Johnny's partner could be. After climbing the two steps into the lounge, he paused in the center of the floor.

Jason was already perched on a stool, playing video poker and looking like he'd fall asleep any minute.

Another man sat at the bar, sipping a cocktail, and he, too, stared intensely at the video game in front of him.

Two women conversed over glasses of wine at one of the tables, but basically, it was a quiet night for the new bartender. He took his seat at the bar.

In the far corner, Joe Ryan lounged while reading a newspaper. Without so much as a glance, he folded his paper, threw a tip onto the table, and left.

Funny how three old guys, who never did anything covert in their lives, performed so well with minimal instructions. No eye contact and no acknowledgment were the keys to success. Monroe's idea to use some of the tenants from the manor turned into a good one. The majority of senior patrons stepping into the casinos arrived with a bus group, took the offered comp money, and spent it in the span of fifteen minutes. If they refused to open their wallets, they'd find a quiet place to sit until time to board their bus. No one would think twice when one of them lounged around for hours—like Too-Tall Joe.

The new bartender unloaded clean mugs from the dishwasher before reloading the bins with used glassware. She was a dark-skinned beauty, a little on the heavyset side, but she moved with efficiency.

While wiping her hands on a towel, she approached. "What can I get you?"

"A light ale would be nice."

"Coming right up."

According to Johnny's latest phone conversation, he didn't have the guts to listen to his victims screaming in the basement. The news hadn't surprised Logan one bit. He'd bet all the Fed money on the partner as the one in charge and, possibly, more sadistic. After all, the partner killed the person who installed the booby trap. Only a sick bastard would take pleasure in using alligators to dispose of the victims. The method of death was beyond cruel. Being torn apart while still alive was not a fun way to die. The visual turned his gut, and Logan silently vowed to put Johnny and his partner away for good.

Marian Masterson and Charles Dilly strolled in arm-in-arm and sat a stool away from Logan. Both exchanged huge smiles.

Coughing, Marian flashed a rock on her left hand the size of a boulder and grinned at Logan.

Well, what do you know? She hooked husband number four. Logan smiled. "Congratulations. Have you set a date?"

"Not yet." She patted Charles' hand. "We're checking our calendars. At our age, we don't feel the need to wait."

He'd like to make a bet on how long husband number four lasted. Marian was like a black widow spider—the species that ate their mate after a roll in the sack. In every one of her marriages, she was left a rich widow. Records showed all her other spouses died from heart attacks. That fact alone was suspicious. What puzzled him was Charles Dilly. He was just an ordinary man who retired as a pipe fitter at a refinery along the

Delaware River. He had a pension and some savings, but he hardly fell into the same category as Marian's prior spouses. Maybe Sky was right, and Charles was the pursuer.

The bartender slipped his ale onto a coaster.

He touched the cold mug. "Thanks. Where's Midnight?"

She raised a brow. "Who?"

Carmela came alongside and handed a drink list to the woman. "Midnight quit, Mr. Grandal."

He frowned. "Did she say why?"

After lugging her tray full of used glasses over to the dishwasher, Carmela shook her head. "Not to us. This is Anna."

"Hi, Anna." He waited for Anna to serve another customer before returning his attention to Carmela. "How did Johnny get a bartender so fast? Shouldn't he follow some kind of security protocol?"

She loaded the last of the glasses into the dishwasher and closed the door. "Anna's from the Treeline Casino up north. She already has state clearance." She nodded toward the other end of the bar. "She's a friend of Jason Carter." She hit the Start button on the washer.

At the sound of his name, Jason glanced up and raised his beer in salute.

Well, well. An interesting turn of events. On the recorded phone conversation, Johnny's partner mentioned the availability of a new bartender. In Logan's mind, Jason Carter just shot to the top of the suspect list.

Monroe's investigation into Carter's finances was sketchy at best. The guy gambled every day and dropped some big bucks. Where did he get the money? He had no disposable income, no viable job, and no noted inheritance. Bank records showed a checking account of twenty-three hundred bucks, all for automatic bill payments. He lived in a typical nondescript South Philadelphia neighborhood with his elderly parents, had no wife or girlfriend, and hardly any social life outside of the casino. In essence, he lived and breathed gambling. Did his very expensive addiction lead to a disappearing scam?

Logan sipped his beer. "I can't believe Midnight left me high and dry." Stretching against his seat's backrest, he peered down the hall. "Maybe Johnny can tell me where she went."

"He can't give you any details, Mr. Grandal. Casino policy." Carmela stepped behind the bar and grabbed the coffee carafe. "Is there anything special you need?"

Sadness tinged her voice. After hearing about Sky's conversation with Carmela, Logan felt more at ease with the Hispanic woman. If she were partnered with Johnny, Carmela would not have warned Sky nor told her about her missing friend. Carmela, along with everyone else, was still suspect until proven otherwise, but she, at least, fell to the bottom of the list. Process of elimination was the single most effective way to survive in this game of cat and mouse.

After sipping his cold beer, he frowned. "Last night, I asked her a question, and she said she'd give me an answer today." Lips tight, he shook his head. "Now, you tell me she quit. I'm not happy." Scowling, he tapped his fingernail against the mug. "I don't know what to do."

Marian cleared her throat. "I take it you had a bit of a lovers' spat?"

He snorted. "Not exactly." Sighing, he rubbed the nape of his neck. "Maybe I came on a little too strong."

Charles leaned forward. "What did you ask her?"

Marian slapped Charles' arm. "You're asking too personal a question, dear."

"Nonsense. The man's troubled. We're his friends." Winking at Logan, he raised his glass. "Cheers."

Chuckling, Logan lifted his mug. "Cheers." He sipped. After replacing his drink onto the coaster, he nodded. "Okay. I'll tell you. I asked her on a trip. She said the outcome of today will determine her answer. I have no idea what she meant."

Marian rotated her martini glass. "That is odd. Do you know, Carmela?"

After checking the drinks filling her clean tray, the dark-haired woman shot a glance from one face to the other, then hefted the load onto her shoulder. "No idea." She hurried to the gaming tables.

Charles signaled to Anna by raising his empty glass, then turned to Logan. "Where were you going?"

"Oh, you know, anywhere and everywhere. I'll wait a bit to see if she contacts me. Maybe quitting her job means she's tying up loose ends and, for some reason, can't get a hold of me."

"Or her answer is *no*, and she didn't have the heart to tell you. Right, Marian?"

Marian rolled her eyes, then patted her lover's arm. "Honey, Midnight's actions don't make sense. A woman can say no without quitting her job."

Logan spread his arms wide. "See? That's why I'll

wait." He guzzled a mouthful of beer, then skimmed his gaze over the busy gaming tables. Catching sight of a familiar strut, he locked his gaze on a man who just passed the blackjack tables. *Well, son of a bitch.* That cocky-ass strut had irked him from the day they met, and he definitely didn't like seeing it now—especially here. Monroe already talked to the jackass and told him how vital that he not return, but had he listened? *Hell, no, of course not.*

This was not good. Logan stole a glance at Marian and Charles, but they were busy looking all lovey-dovey. He slipped off the stool and hurried toward the lounge steps, just in time to stop Philip Santini from entering.

Pausing with one foot on a step, Philip gaped. "What the hell are you doing here?" He scanned Logan from head to toe. "You aren't dressed like a gardener, either." Snorting, he met Logan's gaze. "I suppose you're keeping Sky company while she works?"

Logan kept his voice to a low growl. "She doesn't work here anymore, Santini. So, you might as well turn around and go home."

"Is that so?" He craned his neck. "Oh." Taking a step back, he rocked his brows. "I don't know that woman."

Well, duh. Give the man a medal. "Yes, she's new. Why are you here? Monroe specifically asked—"

Waving a hand, Philip huffed. "I don't take orders from Monroe. You guys suckered Sky into this assignment, and that makes me mad as hell."

"Keep your damn voice down." Lips tight, he scanned the area to see if anyone overheard.

Todd Daniels, the security guard, stood nearby and

175

watched them.

With luck, he was too far to hear. Logan leaned close to Santini. "You can see she's not here."

The man narrowed his gaze. "Where is she?"

"She quit."

Santini laughed. "Do you take me for a fool? She didn't quit. You have her doing something else."

Desperately reining in a growing temper, Logan hissed. "Your presence endangers her more than you know. Even though she isn't here, we're not done. I'm warning you, Santini. Get the hell out. When all this is done, you can bitch all you want. And FYI, she wasn't forced into anything."

"Yeah, well, I'll get the truth from her."

Todd Daniels approached and placed himself alongside Santini. "Is there a problem, gentlemen?"

Philip shifted his gaze from Logan to the guard, then back. He gritted his teeth. "No problem. I'm leaving."

Logan made a mental note to punch the son of a bitch when no one was looking. On the other hand, Philip's protectiveness toward Sky was commendable—if misplaced. He waited until Philip stepped onto the Down escalator before turning to Todd. "Thanks."

The guard shrugged. "Just doing my job." He nodded toward the escalator. "Friend of yours?"

Logan snorted. "Hardly. Just a troublemaker."

While shaking his head, Todd wandered toward the gaming tables.

Forcing his muscles to relax, Logan returned to his stool at the bar.

Marian cocked her head. "Problems?"

Since his throat had gone bone-dry, he gulped a few swallows of beer. "That asshole thinks he's in love with Midnight. She warned me about him."

Marian clucked her tongue. "Seems every man is in love with the gal. I'm sorry she left."

"Me, too." Charles sipped his fresh glass of bourbon. "The lounge seems a little dull without her, and I'll admit, she's a sight for sore eyes."

"Hey!" Marian elbowed Charles in the side.

Swallowing the remainder of his beer in three gulps, Logan stood and tossed money onto the bar. "Yo, Anna, is Johnny in his office?"

Anna dipped a stirrer into a drink. "He should be. Want me to call him?"

"No, I'll go back."

Johnny's door was already open…naturally. How else would he overhear conversations?

The manager sat at his desk, staring at his computer screen.

Sending a woman to her death must be an everyday occurrence. Logan barely contained the urge to wring the man's skinny neck. He coughed.

Johnny glanced up. "Hey! What can I do for you, Mr. Grandal?"

Confess to hideous crimes would be a start. Logan pursed his lips. "I'm delaying my departure."

Eyes wide, Johnny shot to his feet and hurried to close the door. He faced Logan. "The process is already started, sir."

"Doesn't matter. I'm the one with the money."

"May I ask why the delay?" He returned to his desk but remained standing near his chair.

"Carmela told me Midnight quit."

He twitched his jaw. "That's right. She surprised all of us."

"Carmela also said it was against casino policy to give me her personal information."

"That's also correct. I can be fired." Gaze narrowed, he flopped into his chair and rocked. "Do you have a reason why you need to see her?"

Logan passed a hand through his hair and paced. "Last night, I called Midnight and asked her to come with me. She sounded interested, but she said she had somewhere to be in the morning, and she would give me her answer when I arrived at the bar."

Face draining of color, Johnny froze his chair mid-rock.

Logan loved how the he-said-she-said confusion flitted across his face. The man was torn on who to believe. *Prepare yourself, Johnny Boy. There's more to come.* Logan bit back his smile.

"But I thought you decided to let her be."

"I changed my mind." Logan almost laughed at the sound of panic in Johnny's voice. After all, with Sky's elimination, the man flushed an extra two hundred and fifty grand down the toilet.

Johnny pulled on his necktie. "That's a shame, Mr. Grandal, but I wouldn't delay your departure. You don't need her."

"True, but if you remember, she also requested a hundred grand to keep quiet." He rubbed the back of his neck, then met Johnny's gaze. "I can't believe she left before getting the money."

Swallowing hard, Johnny shrugged. "Be thankful. She saved you a hundred grand. But you do have to worry."

Logan shot him a one-eyed look. "Me?"

"Of course. You're the one who's going into hiding. You need all the secrecy you can get. It's no skin off my nose if she talks." He cocked his head. "Personally, you're better off without her. If you want, you can give me the hundred grand, and I'll see she gets it with the guarantee to keep her yap shut."

Yeah, he would say something stupid like that. What he wouldn't do to slap Johnny Dee senseless. Logan stuffed his hands into his trouser pockets, just to keep them to himself. "My agreement was fifty grand, Johnny. She told *you* about the hundred grand, not me. In my mind, you should fork over the other fifty." Hissing, he jiggled the chips in his pockets. "Either way, no woman walks away from easy money. My ex taught me that valuable lesson."

Johnny smirked. "Maybe her conscience got the best of her."

"Yeah, sorry, I don't believe that." Frowning, he shook his head. "Regardless, I'll wait a day or two to see if she contacts me." He chewed on his lower lip. "I've called her several times already, but all I get is voicemail."

Johnny shot his gaze toward the desk drawer.

Nervous much? Or were the wheels grinding in his conniving brain? With luck, Johnny was cussing out his partner for the suggestion to dispose of Sky before any money exchanged hands.

Standing, Johnny moved to the front of the desk. "Look, Mr. Grandal, I don't know why Midnight quit, so I can't help you. Maybe she's ignoring your calls because she's afraid to break your heart. In either case, she probably has her reasons." Johnny passed a hand over his nearly bald head, then stared at his palm.

He was nervous, all right, and the sweat on his head proved it. Losing the money because of Midnight's early demise was one factor. With Logan's delay, Johnny might have a few select words to say to his partner. Now, wouldn't that be an interesting conversation?

"Look, Mr. Grandal." He met Logan's gaze. "What about your ex? If you stay here any longer, you'll risk her PI finding you. Then, what?"

He waved aside the comment. "At this point, I don't give a damn." With a quick glance at his watch, he approached the desk. "Listen, Johnny, all I need is her home address. I'll go talk to her. If she says no, I'll live with it, then get the hell out of here."

Johnny bit his lower lip. "I can't give you any information, Mr. Grandal. I'm sorry."

Whirling, Logan grabbed the doorknob. With a glance over his shoulder, he sneered. "Then, I'll let you know if and when I'm ready."

Chapter Sixteen

Skylar didn't need a pep talk for this part of
Monroe's scheme. She loved every part of the
plan...sort of. She had a large role to play, and she
hoped she could pull it off. But as she walked toward
the casino, she threw aside her doubts and put a
determination into her steps. With her own eyes, she
witnessed how her greedy boss took money from
desperate people only to lure them into a pit of certain
death. A horrible death, too. The mental image of four
beady eyes breaking the water surface sent a chill
through her body. Combine the picture with the
soundproofing to mask the screams...damn, the chill
turned into a sliver of ice. One way or the other, she and
Logan would put away this bastard and his partner or—
what?

Lordy, I sound like a cop.

She almost laughed. Her as a cop? *No way in hell.*
From the beginning, she suspected Monroe planned to
indoctrinate her into his world of security stuff. This job
could have easily been handed over to Vannie as a
drink server or...oh, come to think of it, that wouldn't
work. Bartenders disappeared, not the servers. *Well, no
siree Bob*. No more after this. She would put her foot
down and refuse. Besides, how many more jobs
required the skills of a bartender?

At precisely seven thirty in the evening, Sky

strolled through the casino's main entrance, and the familiar sounds of coins dropping into bins blasted her ears. Slot machines had changed from metal currency to paper tickets eons ago, but the powers in the tower believed people would lose their money faster if the sound of coins hitting the bin filled the air. Whether they succeeded in brainwashing the public, she couldn't tell. They convinced their clientele with the penny machines, though. Nowhere on any casino floor could a patron find a penny machine less than forty cents a pull.

Relieved to step onto the escalator to the second floor, she ascended away from the ear-splitting noise of too many slot machines into the realm of subdued whispers—except for the craps tables, of course. With a quick glance at her watch, she meandered from section to section and purposely took her time. After weeks of working the bar, she memorized the habits of the regulars, and seven thirty was perfect to have all in the vicinity.

Like clockwork, Jason was at the blackjack table, fidgeting. He never removed his gaze from his cards, which wasn't a surprise. He never looked up from the video poker game at the bar, either.

Charles and Harriet Jones sat next to each other at the roulette table.

Catching Sky's movement, Charles met her gaze and cocked a brow.

Harriet followed his gaze, then smiled and waved.

Sky waved back and scanned for Marian. The older woman was probably on the lower level at the penny slots. She would be along later when her mouth watered for a martini.

Circling the poker tables with order pad and pen in

hand, Carmela glanced over her shoulder and froze. Eyes growing wide, she gaped.

Sky smiled, then gently shook her head with the hope the woman would take the hint and not say anything.

Carmela arched a brow but continued around the poker tables.

"Midnight."

Holy shit! At the sound of the male voice, she jumped. *Damn nerves*. Plastering on a smile, she turned. "Hey!"

Smiling, Todd approached. "Hey, yourself. Johnny said you quit. He already filled your position."

"Yes, I know, but I'm not here to work." *Just here to surprise people*. And Todd didn't appear the least bit surprised.

Todd's two-way radio crackled. He adjusted the volume. "What brought you back?"

"Oh, you know, to say hello to Val and Carmela...and you." She shot her gaze toward the lounge. Todd was a nice guy, but geez, she couldn't stand here and chitchat much longer. Johnny clocked out at eight, and time was short.

"Yo, Todd."

A male slot machine attendant hurried over. "We have a fight brewing at the bottom of the escalators."

"On my way." He touched Sky's forearm. "Later?"

"I'm not hanging around, Todd, but maybe another day?"

With a nod, he ran for the escalator.

Good. Now, she could get on with the show. Sucking in a calming breath, she entered the lounge.

Since the gaming tables were packed with a

standing-room-only crowd, Sky expected the bar to be the same, but the lounge wasn't busy. A couple of men and one woman occupied the center stools. A young couple sat near the hallway to Johnny's office while looking at each other like no one else existed in the universe. Sky chose a seat on the opposite end where Jason always perched his tired butt. She'd do him a favor and keep his stool warm.

A female bartender, with curly, dark hair pulled into a ponytail, approached. "What can I get you?"

"Your beer on tap, please."

"Local brand okay?"

"Absolutely."

"Coming up."

Valerie rushed to Sky's side and plunked a tray full of empty glasses onto the bar. "Wow, Midnight, what gives? Johnny said you quit."

Sky rolled her eyes. "Just like a man. He totally misunderstood. I'm contemplating a better offer."

"But he replaced you already. This is Anna."

The bartender slipped Sky's beer onto a coaster, gave a curt nod, then left to serve another man who plopped onto a stool.

Valerie nudged Sky's arm. "What's your better offer?"

Oh, wouldn't Val like to know. Sky waited for the beer foam to settle before taking a sip. She smiled at Val. "Would you tell Johnny I'm here?"

The woman's eyebrows rocked. "Sure." Frowning, Val grabbed her tray and carried it to the bar opening where she slid the heavy load onto the dishwasher. Then, she hurried down the hall.

A few seconds later, Johnny rushed out. Locking

his gaze onto Sky, he stopped dead.

Aw, the poor man. A vampire must have sucked every ounce of blood from his skin. Sky waved. "Surprise, surprise."

He practically fell against the bar and into the young couple nearby.

Valerie re-emerged, rolled her eyes at Sky, then set to work with her tray.

Hurrying over, Johnny gaped like a guppy.

Sky pointed toward the stool next to her own. "Better sit before you embarrass yourself."

He sank onto the cushion. "How did you—"

Interrupting, she waved her hand. "That's not important." She nodded toward Anna. "You found my replacement quick enough. I guess that's because you already knew my fate." She tsked.

He swallowed hard. "Why are you here?"

"You mean, why haven't I gone to the police?" She sipped her beer. *Not bad.* A hint of green apple lingered on her tongue. She met his gaze and smiled. "You have quite an operation going, Johnny boy. I don't know how you dug such a deep hole without using heavy equipment, but I noticed you have a nice backyard with more height than any of the neighbors."

He narrowed his gaze. "What do you want, Midnight?"

From the sharp tone of his voice, the man had a pretty good idea what she wanted. *Time for another surprise.* She ran a finger along the rim of her mug. "I see a lot of dollar signs flashing before my eyes." Cocking her head, she smirked. "I'm your new partner."

Gripping the edge of the bar, he went slack-jawed.

Geez. The man sure had a lot of molars missing from his back teeth. She pointed to his gaping orifice. "With the money you charge your clients, you can afford artificial implants. You'll chew a lot better."

He snapped his mouth shut.

To hide a smile, she took another sip of beer. "We'll do a fifty-fifty split. No negotiation."

Well, her comment returned the color to his face. Nothing like a little anger to raise the blood pressure.

Jaw tight, he slapped his hand on the bar and stood. "We'll discuss this in my office."

"Nope." She shook her head. "We'll discuss it right here." She turned slightly to face him. "The way I see it, you don't have a choice. It's my terms, or I go to the cops."

Hissing, he reclaimed his seat. "I already have a partner."

"Yes, I know. I overheard your phone conversation in the basement, and that's a damn shame. Your fifty percent must be split with your other partner while I get the other fifty. Like I said, no negotiation." She finished the last of her beer, slipped a ten dollar bill onto the bar, and stood. "You can, of course, dump your other partner."

Oh, my. The skin on his face turned to the color of ash. She actually expected him to barf all over the bar. Chuckling, she tapped his chin. "You have my phone number."

He shook himself. "Your phone is still in my desk."

"Is it?" She lifted her left arm to check the time on her diamond-studded watch.

Again, he showed his gaping orifice.

At this rate, every insect flying around would use his mouth like an airplane hangar.

He sputtered. "When—how?" Shaking himself, he clenched his jaw. "I don't know how you broke into my desk, but I haven't left the office since I returned."

"Must be magic." She winked. "I'm good, Johnny." She leaned close and stroked his arm. "Very, very good." Moving away, she smiled. "Don't wait too long to call me. I have the cops on speed dial." She turned to leave.

His cell phone chirped with a text message. Extracting the device from his shirt pocket, he glanced at the screen and quickly raised a hand. "Midnight, wait." He typed.

Instructions from the partner, no doubt. Under the pretense of giving him privacy, she faced the gaming tables. Not like she could see through the crowds. She spotted Valerie's colorful hair bobbing around the poker tables, but Carmela couldn't be seen.

Jason Carter rose from the blackjack table, stretched, and strolled to a super-crowded craps table. As he walked, he glanced down at something. A cell phone?

Harriet Jones with her pink hat full of daisies had left the roulette table and stood with her head down and back toward Sky. Harriet was like Valerie. Neither could be missed in a crowd.

Sky scanned for Charles and found him mingling with a group watching a big wheel spin. With his back to her, he could be discretely texting Johnny, but a phone too close to a gaming table would catch the eye of security.

Marian was still nowhere to be seen, and Todd

Daniels hadn't returned. Did any of them have murder in their eyes when Skylar walked in? *Why, no, of course not*. That would make her job too easy.

"Midnight."

And the final word is… She turned and smiled. "Did your partner relay his instructions?"

He bristled but gave her a strained smile. "We'll accept your terms, provided you do something to prove your worth."

Oh, sure, here it comes. "And what's that?"

A customer trudged in and slipped on one of the bar stools near Johnny.

Johnny touched her elbow and nodded toward the potted plants by the metal rail. "Let's move away from the bar."

Not like the lounge area was any better than the bar. The open-air design would enable anyone passing by to eavesdrop. She followed him to one of the vacant tables to the right of the lounge opening.

He glanced around. "Look, Midnight. Grandal canceled because he wants you with him. He told me he asked you to go."

"Aw, he's so sweet." She slipped her hands into her jacket pockets.

"He did ask you, right?"

"Yeah, he called last night."

Gaze blazing, he pressed his lips into a thin line. "Why didn't you tell me in the first place?"

She snorted. "Why? So you could collect an additional two hundred and fifty grand, then toss us both into the pit?" Leaning forward, she locked onto his gaze and hissed. "Now, though, I know what to expect."

Taking a step back, he frowned. "All right, let me lay it on the line. You're an excellent lure for guys like Grandal."

She rolled her eyes.

"No, really, think about it, Midnight. You can get rich working with us. My partner is bound to see what a great opportunity you present." With a crooked smile, he cocked his head. "What do you say?"

In other words, she'd whore herself in order to increase cash flow. Damn, she hated this man. He must think she was a total moron. What she wouldn't do to break Johnny's neck. The partner, too, whoever he or she might be. Clearing her thoughts before she smacked him, she nodded. "You already made me this offer, remember? So, yeah, I'm in, but on my terms. Fifty percent up front." She nodded toward his phone. "Tell your partner."

"I don't have to. It's a deal." He extended his right hand.

She looked at the hand, then met his gaze. "I don't trust you, Johnny. Your partner is the boss and the one who makes the decisions. I should be talking to him or her."

Sighing, he lowered his hand. "No can do, Midnight. My partner stays in the background at all times. You have to trust me."

She laughed. "Pul-lease. You and trust don't belong in the same sentence. But I'll tell you what." She folded her arms over her chest. "I'll talk to Grandal. You talk to your partner. I'm sure we can reach an amicable agreement."

"Deal." Right hand extended, he waited.

Glancing down, she could easily crush all his bones

and send him screaming to the hospital. The temptation to follow through on that thought made her hesitate. Forcing a smile, she took his hand and shook. "Okay. That's settled. I'll check to see if Grandal is upstairs." She slipped her cell phone from her jacket pocket and texted a quick message. The answer arrived seconds later, and she smiled. "He's in his room. I'll head up." She replaced the phone to her pocket. And because she had to make this look good, she leaned toward him while placing a palm on his chest. The man felt a little too bony for her liking, but Monroe said to linger. So, she did. She gave Johnny a slanted smile. "No time like the present to get the ball rolling, wouldn't you say?" With a wink, she tapped a finger under his chin, then stepped away.

Brows high, Johnny broke eye contact and shot his gaze everywhere. "Let me know what he says."

The man was a bundle of nerves, and she liked the look. *Serves him right.* Smiling, she shook her head. "The definitive answer comes from Grandal. *He'll* tell you whether he's going or not. He's the one with the money."

Grabbing onto her left arm, he tugged her close and sneered. "You better not double cross us, Midnight."

Oh, yeah, like he'd keep his word and make her a partner. She stared at the hand gripping her arm, then shot her gaze to his face.

Coughing, he released his grip and dropped his arm to his side.

He was damn lucky she didn't take a swing at his throat. Glaring, she leaned forward and growled. "I expect the same commitment, Johnny boy. And FYI, don't ever grab hold of me again, got it?" Turning on her heel, she left the bar.

She couldn't get away from the slimeball fast enough. Even breathing the same air annoyed the heck out of her. Stepping into the elevator, Sky hit the button for the fourteenth floor, then closed her eyes, and released a long breath. How in the hell did she stay so calm? On the surface, she might look cool, but underneath, her nerves were doing a number on her sweat glands. Opening her eyes, she sent a quick text message to tell Logan she was on her way—in case Johnny and his partner planned an ambush. They'd be fools to try something before their big payout, and a half mil in cash was a pretty big incentive to let her be. But hey, what did she know about the criminal mind? She could only keep alert and—as Logan preached— expect the unexpected.

Next, she sent her phone's voice recording to Monroe. This vital piece of evidence helped tighten the noose around Johnny's neck. The Feds had enough to lock Johnny Dee away for a long time, but the partner could go scot-free. Her job was to play her role and not lose her nerve. Surprisingly, her hands didn't shake, but her gut bounced around like she ate Mexican jumping beans. Keeping up a facade to fool Johnny and his partner took an effort far beyond her experience. With luck, she'd live through to the case conclusion. *Gee, what a thought*. When she arrived at Logan's door without incident, she released a huge breath, glanced right and left, then knocked.

Within seconds, the door swung open, and he wrapped her in an embrace—in the middle of the hall. Still holding her tight, he kissed her, then dragged her into his room.

Wow. He acted like a man desperate for sex. For show or not, he always had a way of calming her frazzled nerves. Truth be told, if he initiated sex, who was she to argue?

Once inside the room with the door shut, he dropped his arms and grinned. "How did it go?"

Well, okay, no dragging her to bed for a quick romp. *Mr. Professional, as usual.* Shaking away the disappointment, she patted his hard chest and smiled. "Perfectly." After giving him a peck on the lips, she dropped onto the sofa and untied her boots. "Has Pamela found anything useful with the laptop's camera footage?"

"Only Johnny and his victims entering the house."

"She placed her own cameras inside the house, right?"

"We're all set. Pam has a way to tap into their computer without anyone being the wiser."

Sky had to hand it to Pam. The woman was good. A tech graduate from MIT, she became a hacker for predators on the web and worked with several police departments. Monroe was lucky to grab onto her, and the salary he paid bordered on obscene. Truthfully, the woman was worth every penny.

With hands in his trouser pockets, Logan strolled over. "Pam found gaps in the footage where the cameras were turned off by remote access. We think it's when the partner comes to the house."

"Somehow, the news doesn't surprise me." She pulled off one boot and started on the other. "Johnny's face remains front and center with the partner always in the background."

"A shrewd move, for sure." Logan perched his butt

onto the edge of the sofa cushion. "We assume Johnny doesn't have remote access, or it's possible he doesn't know about the feature."

She finished with the second boot and pushed them both to the side. "Then, the partner must be the tech-savvy one." Who, though? And would tomorrow give her an answer?

Chapter Seventeen

With all the unanswered questions bouncing around inside her head, Sky felt a little queasy. In the blink of an eye, her assignment gravitated from a listen-and-observe to an active participant, and she was ill-prepared for the latter. Simply sitting near Logan on the suite's sofa was a prime example of a world where she didn't belong. He was surrounded by opulence and played a role for which he could win an Academy Award. Yes, he was good, and he knew what he was doing, but Monroe paired him with a novice who hadn't a clue for whatever lurked in the shadows. What if she failed Logan tomorrow? What if she did something so stupid, she endangered his life? She couldn't bear to live with such knowledge. Leaning back on the sofa cushions, she tucked her legs under her butt and faced him. "What happens if we can't uncover the partner?"

He stretched his arm over the sofa back and tickled her shoulder. "Then, Johnny takes the brunt of the charges, but he doesn't strike me as a man who will sacrifice himself to save his other half." He shrugged. "He might surprise us. For all we know, his partner could have a hold on him that will keep his lips sealed forever."

Raising a brow, she gaped. "Like blackmail?"

He snorted. "It wouldn't be the first time a person is forced into a life of crime because of a prior incident in his or her life. And by the way"— Dropping his arm, he sat forward—"Pam recorded the latest phone conversation." Reaching for the coffee table, he grabbed his phone, tapped a few buttons, then handed over the device.

Sky hit Play. The same muffled voice spoke first, and she raised her brows. "We can tell it's a man this time!"

He touched the hand holding his phone. "Not necessarily. All you hear is a deep voice. Don't forget about the app we talked about. It can make a woman sound like a man and vice versa. Listen carefully. You talk to our suspects more than I do."

But none of the suspects had a distinctive voice, no accents, nor unusual dialects. Even a subtle intonation would help, but the muffling made identification so much harder. Sighing, she restarted the recording.

Unknown Caller: *"We've been had, Johnny boy. I went to the house to transfer the money to my home safe only to find the inside empty."*

Johnny gasped. *"The house was empty?"*

UC: *"No, asshole, the safe."*

J: *"That's not possible."*

UC: *"I saw no damage on the safe's exterior door. So, our perp used the combination. You didn't give it to anyone, did you?"*

J: *"Do you take me for an idiot? Of course, I didn't. And you know damn well you're to tell me when you're transferring money."*

UC: *"Sorry, but given the time frame and Midnight's miraculous appearance, I figured I'd make some room for Grandal's contribution."* A heavy sigh. *"I checked the camera footage. Someone threw a black shroud over the lens covering the safe. It stayed that way for ten minutes. Then, it was whipped away. The outside cameras show our perp leaving while clutching a large canvas bag."*

J: *"Well, then, you saw who it was, and it sure as hell wasn't me."* A long pause. *"Are you going to tell me who this perp is or keep me in suspense?"*

UC: *"It's Midnight, Johnny. Got anything to say about that?"*

Sky smiled at the clattering sound coming through the phone's speaker, as if Johnny fumbled with his phone. *So far, so good.*

J: *"I don't know what to say."*

UC: *"You can tell me how she survived the basement. You said the trap sprung. No one can move fast enough to get out of the way. We paid good money to assure that fact. But somehow, she did. If she wasn't in the pit, then she hid somewhere in the basement. You had to see her."*

J: *"There's no place to hide, and you know it."*

UC: *"How about under the stairwell?"*

A long silence followed.

Poor Johnny. She'd love to see his face when he realized his partner was right.

Johnny cleared his throat. *"Look, I don't know how she survived, but our immediate problem is the money. How the hell did she get into the safe? It's burglarproof."*

UC: *"Not if she knows the combination. Sorry, boy, but she opened the safe and unloaded the stash in all of ten minutes. That's impossible unless she had the combo. I'm getting a real bad feeling here, like maybe you casually left the numbers on a sheet of paper in the center of your desk."*

J: *"I won't even comment on that stupid accusation."*

UC: *"You and her looked awful chummy at the bar tonight. She touched you like maybe you two have an intimate connection."*

J: *"What the hell are you talking about? You're hallucinating. There's nothing going on between us."*

UC: *"Well, after she stepped from the house carrying the bag full of money, she turned to lock the door with a key. You need to explain how she got hold of a key."*

A very long pause.

UC: *"You still there?"*

J: *"I don't know what to say. It was her first time to the house. Maybe you should check her apartment. She's upstairs with Grandal now."*

UC: *"And risk breaking and entering? Are you crazy? If I didn't know any better, I'd say you're setting me up. You and Midnight are in cahoots, aren't you?"*

J: *"Don't be ridiculous. And since you're throwing accusations, maybe you can explain why she called me Johnny boy. You're the only one who uses the phrase."*

UC: *"Get your head out of your ass and think about what you're saying. Women like her are a dime a dozen, but let's table this for now. We have some serious planning to do. She can bolt with our money along with Grandal's. That is one hefty payout."*

J: *"What should we do?"*

UC: *"The only thing we can do. We stop her. I'll give you details tomorrow."*

The conversation ended.

After hitting the Cancel button, Sky shuddered.

Johnny and his partner were planning her demise, and she struggled to control the chill shooting up and down her spine. They should have talked longer. Nothing would make her feel better than to know how they intended to stop her. She handed the phone to Logan. "I hope I don't blow it tomorrow."

Reaching behind him, he placed the phone on the end table. "You won't. They took the bait. We have the two partners at odds, and they're exactly where Monroe wants them. Nothing like a double cross to get the ball rolling."

With her confidence dwindling and nerves nearing a breaking point, she slid across the sofa and snuggled against his side. She needed his strong arms more than ever. "What happens next?"

He wrapped an arm around her shoulders and tugged her close. "Your apartment is under surveillance. Pam placed cameras on the inside, but it's all precautionary. We doubt they'll make a move until they get the half mil from me." He kissed her hair. "In the morning, I'll call Johnny and tell him you agreed to go, and I'm waiting for the money transfer from the bank. You'll meet Tank downstairs waiting in a gray-and-white cab. He'll drive you to your apartment under the pretense of you packing for our trip. You return here and settle in."

The details of the plan sounded so simple, but she couldn't help the shivers traversing over her skin. Logan's arm gave her some warmth, but she needed more. All this covert stuff was too new…too frightening. She wrapped an arm around his torso.

He squeezed her shoulder. "Don't be scared. You're doing great."

"I'm not scared." *Great*. Now, she was a liar. Maybe she should wear one of those adult diapers—in case she peed herself.

"Once this is over, the Feds can drain the pit and look for any remaining bones."

Egads. What a horrible vision. She shivered. "Do you think they'll find any?"

"Hard to say. Gators eat bones."

Oh, yuck. Lifting her head, she met his gaze. "How can you say that without getting angry? I can barely control the urge to kick Johnny and his partner to kingdom come."

He tapped her chin. "I've been around the block one too many times to show anger, Sky. Yes, the emotion is inside me, but I've seen worse. I can't let it get to me. You should do the same."

Easy words coming from a pro. How could she forget the image of the gators in the pit waiting for their next meal? When she worked in a bar, she watched people keel over from too much booze and, sometimes, vomit all over the place, but their arms and legs were still attached, and no blood squirted from their arteries. That was as gruesome as she got.

A knock rapped on the door. "Room service."

Before unwrapping his arms, Logan lifted her chin and kissed her lips. "I ordered dinner."

Ever the cautious cop, he peeked through the peephole.

Nodding to her, he opened the door.

Sky forced herself to her feet to allow the employee a chance to see her. Since no one could identify the partner, she and Logan had to play every angle.

After Logan tipped the guy and closed the door, he placed a finger against his lips. Retrieving his phone from the table, he activated a program, then scanned the entire cart twice. Straightening, he smiled. "Done."

Puzzled, she stepped toward him. "What was that about?"

"I'm checking for bugs. Here, look." He showed her the phone. "Pam gave me an app to detect hidden wires. She even forced me to practice by bugging Vicki's office. I found a tiny device buried in the bottom of a supply drawer. Whenever I return to my room, I give it a good sweep."

"Impressive. Have you found any?"

"No. Again, this is all precautionary." He tossed the phone onto the coffee table. "Let's eat."

She wasn't sure she had an appetite, but after lifting the covers on the plates, she sniffed in the enticing aromas of garlic sauce and mushrooms.

While they sat at the table by the window and enjoyed succulent pork chops, garlic mashed potatoes, and butter-soaked broccoli, Sky couldn't help the questions rambling around in her brain. She should be enjoying the food, the company, and even the view of the night sky.

"What are you thinking, Sky?"

The man could read her like a book. If she ever tried to hide something from him, she'd never succeed. Using the cloth napkin, she wiped her mouth and met his gaze. "I'm not a trained agent, Logan. What if I missed a clue during my conversation with Johnny?"

After swallowing, he sipped his wine. "Relax, Sky. If Johnny said anything on the voice recording, then Monroe and I would know. But these two are very good. We might get lucky with a slip, but I doubt it." Grabbing a roll from the bread basket, he slapped on a heaping portion of butter. "Frankly, I'm surprised Johnny didn't use a gun to dispose of his clients. The soundproofing was already in place, and a dirt floor made for easier burial."

"I'd rather die by a bullet than in the mouth of an alligator." She'd rather not die at all, but hey, the lesser of two evils. To hide a shiver, she stuffed a broccoli floret into her mouth.

After jabbing his fork into a piece of meat, he covered it with mushrooms. "I agree about the bullet." He met her gaze. "We never expected to see the pit. It's a cruel way to kill." He shoved the meat into his mouth.

She waved her fork. "And don't forget the booby trap. Someone is getting a big kick out of this elaborate setup." She sipped the perfectly-aged pinot noir. The subtle earthiness went well with the pork and mushrooms. Just what she needed to calm her nerves. Although, when she thought about it, how the hell could she eat with all the visuals flashing before her eyes? Hungry alligators, blood everywhere, limbs flying…*ugh*. But the food tasted too good to waste, and she devoured the garlic mashed potatoes like she hadn't eaten in years. So, maybe this was secret agent lesson number thirty-four—the one that taught to eat and be merry because tomorrow might be your last. With that revelation, the meal turned to dust.

****

After dinner, Logan had a personal plan to execute. His plan did not involve Monroe or anyone else from the firm nor did it include tactics, scenarios, or anything else related to the case. What's worse, he psyched himself like a gladiator facing ten opponents. All right, maybe the vision was a bit extreme, but he was new to this. He rehearsed a speech full of words Skylar wouldn't want to hear. They might make her shy away, but he couldn't afford to wait any longer.

Even though he ordered an expensive bottle of wine, he dumped the contents after they each drank one glass. Neither could afford any brain fog in the morning. For her, his words might produce a similar effect. He should have told her last night at her apartment. This afternoon, after what he discovered lurking in the pit, he and Sky were dealing with two vicious cons. To wait any longer would fill him with regret. God help him if anything happened to her.

Ordinarily, a man appreciated a woman like Skylar Dawson. She resisted any mention of a relationship, wasn't the least bit clingy, and never inquired about where or what he was doing. All she requested was honesty. She never demanded exclusiveness, but he knew she would not take him to her bed if he slept with another woman. In a way, he expected the same. So, yeah, they were exclusive, and whether she admitted it or not, they shared something special. In his mind, they had been in a relationship from the day they met—even though, he went incommunicado for several months. But the *R* word would be omitted from his prepared speech. No sense going hog wild and getting her all discombobulated.

He let her have time alone in the whirlpool. When she emerged from the bathroom wearing the hotel's fluffy, white robe, she smelled like some flower garden. Struggling not to bury his nose in her short hair, he took her hand and led her to the bed. As he nudged her onto the edge of the mattress, he smiled and fingered the collar on the robe. "Do you realize this is the first time I've seen you wear something other than black?"

Shrugging, she glided her palm along the sleeve. "It's too soft to pass up. Besides, the hotel doesn't offer a black robe."

Never in a million years would he believe he could fall for a woman with a one-color wardrobe or hair trimmed close to the neck. When seeking companionship, he preferred long-haired beauties so he could run his fingers through the strands. Like any man, he enjoyed a woman in a sexy dress and maybe high heels to showcase long legs. According to Fay, Sky owned a beautiful, off-the-shoulder black dress with killer heels, but a wise man would need to take a woman on a proper date to a classy place. Obviously, he was not a wise man.

One fact remained abundantly clear. Sky was a hell-raiser in bed. Her martial arts kept her body in great shape, yet not overly muscular. She was toned to perfection, which created some wild nights. Despite her tough image with her big-ass motorcycle and all-black attire, she was a gentle woman. He also loved that her soft skin wasn't marred by tattoos. In so many ways, the woman had a way of making him laugh. She was a contradiction and so damn cute.

Sky untied the sash to her robe.

"Not yet." He stopped her by lowering her to the sheets. Hovering, he gazed into her beautiful eyes. Every now and then, he liked slow and easy. Tonight would be one of the slowest on record.

Staring up, she arched a brow. "You're still fully clothed."

"For good reason. I want to talk." Yeah, like every man wasted time with small talk while a willing woman waited, but he had to say the words without distraction.

She slipped her fingers into his hair. "I'm glad you kept your cologne to be this big-shot CEO. The woodsy scent is so…you." Gaze twinkling, she bit her lower lip and smiled. "You know, I'm seriously thinking of expanding my master bathroom to put in a tub like the one you have here."

He laughed. "Honey, you'll need to knock out a wall or expand the side of the house to fit in that size tub." He tapped her nose. "It's doable on a smaller scale, though."

"And we're delaying the get-naked part." She toyed with his shirt collar. "What do you want to talk about?"

Even her touch tossed his thoughts in other directions. Her eyes, mouth—hell, it would be a miracle if he didn't weaken and just take her. He grabbed hold of one hand and kissed the palm. "It's rare for an undercover assignment to run smoothly, Sky. While we make every effort to anticipate each scenario, sometimes, something totally unexpected occurs. The pit, for example. How Johnny and his partner dug out so much dirt without anyone getting suspicious floored us. They must have done it over the winter months when most of the seasonal rentals were empty. The alligators were probably put in when they were babies."

Grinning, she tapped on his chest. "You need to work on your prelude-to-sex conversations."

He snickered. "I…er—" He cleared his throat. "I'm nervous."

Pouting, she stroked his jaw. "You shouldn't be.

It's just me."

"I know, but let me explain." He had practiced his speech and memorized word for word. Right now, he couldn't formulate one coherent thought. He released a long breath. "I don't want anything to happen to you, Skylar Dawson." He stroked her smooth cheek. "I love you, more than any woman I've ever known."

With her beautiful mouth agape, she stared.

He expected his confession to cause a reaction. At least, she hadn't jumped from the bed and bolted for the door. He traced a thumb along her lower lip. "You don't have to say it back, but you should know how I feel in case tomorrow—"

Pressing an index finger against his lips, she gave a soft smile. "I won't be naive and say nothing will happen. Truthfully, I'm scared and hope I don't blow it."

"You won't." He rested his forehead against hers. "I love you so much. From the moment I met you at the manor, I was a goner." He brushed his lips over hers, then stared into her incredible crystal-blue eyes. They always sparkled whenever their gazes met. Now was no exception. She had feelings for him—of that he was certain. Maybe it wasn't the *L* word, but something showed in her gaze. "Let me love you like there will be no tomorrow."

She blinked. "I—huh…okay."

No way in hell would she understand the depth of his feelings, but truth be told, he would gladly take a bullet for this woman and die a happy man.

Chapter Eighteen

After a night full of glorious sex that would live in his memories forever, Logan smiled down at his sleeping beauty. Slow and easy was perfect. He savored every inch of her skin and loved her like a man should. Surprisingly, she let him. Fast and furious was her speed, and slowing her took Herculean effort. But he held firm, and her surrender gripped his heart.

Despite every one of her tense muscles melting within his arms, he'd felt the doubt in her lips. Considering the danger ahead, she should understand why he said what he did. If anything happened to her, he would be devastated.

His four years undercover for the state police taught him every agent's days were numbered. One couldn't do the job believing they'd come out unscathed. For Sky, she was a complete novice and, in his opinion, not ready. If Monroe hadn't needed a bartender, he'd never have involved her so soon. Unfortunately, as with every case, events altered the course. Sky changed from simple observer to pivotal player and not because she mixed a great cocktail.

He checked his watch. Nearly ten. He had already showered and dressed without a peep coming from the bed. As much as he yearned to bend down and kiss her soft shoulder, Logan quietly left the room. Apprehension made his palms itch. He and Sky had a big day ahead, but right now, to get the ball rolling, he had a phone call to make. At this time in the morning, Johnny Dee should be at his desk and waiting. Logan would love to let the bastard sweat for another hour or two, but he had a plan to follow. He hopped on an elevator to the main floor. After stepping into the lobby, he searched for a quiet spot before hitting speed dial.

"Johnny Dee."

"She's in."

"Excellent. Passports and driver's licenses for both of you. Are you still heading to Vegas?"

"Yes."

"Got it. I can have everything ready by mid-afternoon."

Yeah, no shit. Since Johnny simply pushed his clients into an alligator pit, what more did the man have to do? Logan had met some vicious people over the years, but not once had he encountered death by animals. Johnny and his partner deserved to get a taste of their own medicine. Before his hand crushed the phone near his ear, he loosened his grip. "I'll meet a courier with the money around two and show at the bar afterward. Midnight needs an hour to pack a few bags, but she shouldn't take long." The phone vibrated in his hand. "Hold on a sec, Johnny. She's texting me." Glancing at the screen, he read the text message from Skylar.

—Thanks for a wonderful night. Once I get the signal from the cab driver, I'll head to my apartment to pack. Will let you know when I return.—

He fired off a quick reply.

—Talking to Johnny now. Be careful.—

A winking emoji followed.

Logan returned the phone to his ear. He could hear Johnny breathing with a slight wheeze. "Are you there?"

"Yeah. Was it her?"

"Yes. She'll be heading out soon. I arranged a taxi to pick her up and drive her back."

"And you have the backpack as instructed?"

"Midnight has one. She'll bring it."

"Great. Then, I'll see you later. By the way, is she meeting the cab out front?"

An odd question, but not totally unexpected. He cleared his throat. "Of course. Why?"

"No reason. Let me know when you get to the lounge."

After disconnecting, Logan stared at his phone. He had to hand it to Monroe. The boss man anticipated every angle, and one scenario had Johnny confronting Sky on the tarmac. Logan had every confidence in Sky's ability to get out of a situation, but he still worried. With all the cameras and valet attendants, Johnny would be an idiot to try something. But just in case, Tank would keep an eye on her. Logan replaced the phone to his pocket and sighed.

As expected, Sky never returned his declaration of love, and that's okay. She didn't run screaming from the room, either. Maybe one day, she'd surprise him. For now, he'd accept this confident, independent woman who could kick ass better than anyone. Someday, she'd realize he wasn't going anywhere...if they both lived through the day.

****

Skylar performed a lot of deep breathing these days. Luckily, Logan's suite had the room for some of

208

her tai chi stretching exercises. Being a beginner with all this secret agent stuff played on her nerves, and she thanked the Lord for all her martial arts training. Not knowing what would happen today kept her in a state of constant tension. Monroe could list every possible scenario, but nothing would take her mind off the alligator pit. *Stay focused, stay calm.* Those were famous last words from both Monroe and Logan. Every day aged her another year. If she wasn't careful, she'd return home with gray hair...*if* she returned home. She should ask Monroe for a gigantic raise. The man owed her big time for talking her into this. If she ever got him on her mat...

She shook away the thought. Who was she kidding? Robert Monroe had become a father figure to his employees—her included. He would never knowingly place her in danger. He depended on her quick thinking and ninja skills to get herself out of a jam. She'd already proven him right by surviving Johnny's booby trap, and today, she wouldn't be alone. She and Logan would face the odds together. That fact eased her mind a little. Logan might be strong, but he wasn't as fast, and that worried her, especially after last night's bombshell. He'd do something heroic, like jump in front of a bullet to save her. She extended her hands overhead, then bent to place her palms onto the rug.

How could he possibly love her? He wasn't supposed to fall in love, and all morning, she searched deep inside for a response. She couldn't find one. Although, last night, she had to admit his slow and easy sexual moves created sensations she never experienced. Sated? *Yes.* Confused? *Definitely.* She liked and trusted Logan, but what did love feel like? What if he said the words just to divert her mind from today's meeting? She wouldn't put the tactic past him. Truthfully, he succeeded. She faced danger today, and here, she was thinking of last night's glorious sex and when they could do a repeat performance.

Her phone chirped with a text message. Straightening from her stretch, she looked at the screen.

—*Here.*—

She chuckled. Tank was a man of few words. Taking a deep breath and adjusting her clothes, she threw on her jacket and left the room. *Showtime.*

After exiting the elevator at the lobby level, she glanced right and left. The lobby was crowded with people heading for checkout and porters pushing suitcase carts. No familiar faces caught her eye, but from working here, she witnessed the hustle and bustle at all hours. Even outside on the tarmac, valets rushed around to load and unload vehicles to earn a good tip. Johnny would be a complete moron to try something with so many witnesses. Lifting her chin and throwing her shoulders back, she headed for the main entrance.

Suitcases lined the curb as valet service loaded one trunk after another for departing guests. Several taxis crowded the curved driveway, waiting for a call to approach.

She scanned the drive for Monroe's own personal taxicab with the name *Carl's Transport Company* on the doors. The sedan was an older model with faded gray-and-white paint and looked slightly used and abused with tiny dents on the front bumper. She spotted it parked near the end of the long drive and away from all the other vehicles. Yes, the boss man had his own taxi. "Great for undercover work," he'd said. She wouldn't be surprised if he had a limo stored somewhere and maybe even a hearse. Following the sidewalk, she maneuvered around luggage and people and made a concerted effort to take her time. She really wanted to run like hell, just to get away, but hey, she had to follow Monroe's well-constructed plan.

The cab driver's door opened. Tank unfolded his large frame from behind the steering wheel and stepped onto the tarmac.

He was older than the other agents. Retired from the marines after a twenty-year career, he caught Monroe's attention with his explosives expertise. If ever a time came to blow up something, Tank Davenport was the man to make it happen.

"Midnight!"

At the sound of her name, she glanced over her shoulder and stopped.

With fire in his eyes, Johnny Dee hurried down the sidewalk.

Since valet attendants and guests crowded the area, she had no need to feel threatened, but she tensed, anyway. The man's expression was akin to a stone mask, and his body posture was as if a board immobilized his spine. Obviously, he wasn't here to congratulate her on snagging Logan Grandal. She pivoted to face him and braced herself.

Growling, he grabbed onto her left arm and pushed her closer to the building.

The move surprised her. Ordinarily, he'd be flat on the ground by now, but Monroe wouldn't get his answers from Johnny if he was unconscious. She tugged against his grip and glared. "What did I tell you about grabbing me?"

Tightening his grip, he hissed. "What the hell are you trying to pull?"

"I don't know what you're talking about." *See*? She could play dumb.

"You know perfectly well what I mean. My *real* partner thinks we're in cahoots. Do you know how dangerous that is?" He yanked her arm. "How'd you get into the safe?"

She could easily snap every finger circling her bicep, but she had to act all innocent-like. Just to make some sort of effort, she twisted. The man might be wiry, but wow, he had a good grip. "Look, my cab is waiting." She nodded toward Tank.

The big man stood like some bull ready to charge.

"You aren't going anywhere, honey, not until I get some answers. Tell me how you broke into the safe."

Something pinched the back of her legs. She glanced down at an evergreen bush. One more backward step, and she might break a few branches. She glared at Johnny. "What safe?"

"Don't play dumb. We have you on camera."

"Oh. Yeah…well, I couldn't figure out how to turn them off."

Sneering, he leaned close. "I'd also like to know how you got a key to lock the door. Who the hell are you?"

Oh, wouldn't he like to know. She smirked. "I said I was good. I took the money away from your partner. We can do a fifty-fifty split."

Jerking back, he shot his brows halfway into his scalp. "He'll kill me!"

He, huh? Johnny confirmed the gender. The fact should please Monroe. She peered at the hand on her arm. "You're hurting me, you know. If you leave bruises, Grandal will see them."

"Like I give a damn. Grandal won't live long enough to see them."

Yeah, if Johnny had his way, neither would she.

Tank strode over. "Is there a problem, miss?"

Johnny turned to him and glared. "Go grab another passenger. She isn't leaving yet."

Sky sighed. "Grandal ordered the cab, Johnny. The driver's taking me to my apartment, then returning me here."

Tank furled his fists into tight balls.

Uh-oh. At any second, Tank could swing and break Johnny's neck. She gave her co-worker what she hoped was a reassuring smile. "Wait for me by the cab, driver. I'll take care of this."

The big man narrowed his gaze but returned to the opened car door.

Everyone in the firm knew she could handle five men at once without breaking a sweat. One man would be like a walk in the park. But she had to play the role of a street-smart female without going too far. She shot Johnny a one-eyed glare. "Loosen your hold, or I will break your arm."

"I doubt you can do that."

"I fooled you, so far. Would you like a demonstration?" *My, my.* From the look on his face, he clearly debated whether she was lying or not. "I can also scream and cause a real scene. You've already caught the attention of several valets." Truthfully, the valets were too damn busy rushing around for their tips. For them to notice, she'd need blood squirting out her ears.

Snarling, he dropped his hand. "Where's our money?"

Ouch. She rubbed the sore spot. "In a safe place. I needed an insurance policy—in case, you and your partner reneged on our agreement and tossed me into the pit." She cocked her head. "Maybe you should throw your partner in. Then, you and I can go into business."

"Damn you, Midnight." Cringing, he ran a hand over his wispy strands. "I can't cut him out."

"Why not? Say adios and give him a push." She grinned.

"It's not that simple."

She waggled a finger. "Ah, I get it. You're the puppet on a string."

Face muscles twitching, he bristled.

Gotcha. Monroe suspected the partner as the brains behind the operation. The phone recordings confirmed it. Johnny's reaction sealed the deal. "Look, Johnny, I'm not some naive kid. I'll hold onto the money until you prove you're trustworthy. Like I said, it's an insurance policy. You want your money returned, you gotta let me live to retrieve it. Now, if you'll excuse me, I've some packing to do. Grandal is expecting me to return at a reasonable time."

Leaning forward, he glowered. "I don't trust you to blow our chance with Grandal."

Grimacing, she fanned her hand in front of her face. "You have bad coffee breath, Johnny boy. A mint after every cup should help."

"Look, Midnight—"

"No, you look." She jammed a finger into his chest. "We're talking a half mil here, Johnny. I won't do anything to jeopardize our big payoff. Just make sure you and your *other* partner are on the same page." Turning on her heel, she headed for the taxi and stepped inside. As soon as the cab door closed behind her, she sank into the back cushion.

Once he eased the vehicle into traffic, Tank eyed her from the rearview mirror. "Are you okay?"

Bending forward, she buried her face in her hands. "I'm a bundle of nerves."

"You didn't look it. Monroe would be proud."

"I'd rather be fired." Dropping her hands, she flopped back onto the seat. "I hope I don't screw up everything."

"You won't. You're better than you think, and Monroe knows it."

She harrumphed.

Chuckling with a deep, throaty voice, he maneuvered the car through traffic.

Tank might be older than the rest of the guys, but he hid his age well. One way was to shave his head to destroy any evidence of gray hair. She met his gaze in the rearview mirror. "You don't do undercover stuff, do you?"

"Not if I can help it. Bodyguard duties mostly. Like now." He grinned.

Yeah, the man was built. He had more muscles than Logan. She didn't know his real first name, but because of his size, everyone called him Tank.

"I'm sure the day will come when Monroe needs a big guy to work some undercover operation." He shot a glance over his shoulder. "I am hard to hide, though."

"Yeah, lucky you." She slipped her cell phone from her pocket and sent the latest recording to

Monroe. *Poor Johnny*. The noose around his neck got tighter every day.

Tank glided the cab to a stop in front of the old Victorian and cut the engine. "I'm coming in with you."

"Yes, I know." She opened the door and exited onto the sidewalk. Since this was the last time she'd step into the place, she had orders to clean out her apartment and pack everything into the trunk. She wouldn't miss the little cubbyhole. It was okay as far as a vacation rental, but to live in it full-time? *No*. Too cramped and too old. Winter would be downright drafty, and without air conditioners, summers would be torture. Even though smoking wasn't allowed in the building, she often caught a whiff of cigarette smoke, which was a dangerous violation of the rules. One false move, and this old Victorian would ignite like a match.

Tank popped the trunk and extracted a canvas tote. After slipping the strap onto his left shoulder, he joined her at the curb.

She slid her gaze from the house to him and glanced up...and up. The man was a giant. He'd be a match for Too-Tall Joe. "I hope Pam told you where she hid the cameras."

"Yup. Three total. She even gave me the boxes to pack them in." He tapped the tote. "Ready?"

More than ready. After today, the case would close or totally blow up in her face.

Chapter Nineteen

After receiving word that all aspects of Monroe's plan were in place, Logan wandered into the lounge. For some reason, he felt a little jumpy, and the emotion wasn't like him. He had a reputation for having nerves of steel, and nothing or no one rattled him. When he acted alone, he went with the flow and usually caught the bad guy in the act. If he had to sniff out an associate, he waited and kept his eyes and ears open. But Monroe gave Sky an integral role. She was the bait to get the partner to surface. So far, she'd done well, and today, she had a command performance. He prayed like hell everything went according to plan.

In the far corner, Joe Ryan sat at a table to watch the hall to Johnny's office. The old guy read a newspaper and nursed a beer, like he had all the time in the world. As before, the ex-Navy vet gave no recognition.

According to Sky's nightly email reports, she mentioned who sat where, what time they arrived, and the time they left. She often complained about writing such inane information, but whether she realized it or not, she included important facts. So, here, at three thirty in the afternoon, he wasn't surprised to see Marian Masterson and Harriet Jones perched a few stools from his usual spot.

The two ladies were becoming quite the pair. They

even giggled like schoolgirls once a few rounds of hard liquor hit their bellies. As usual, Harriet wore a colorful hat. Today, she sported a purple fedora with dangling plums. Every time she turned her head, the three little pieces of fruit danced. Slipping onto his stool, he smiled. "How are you ladies doing today?"

Marian huffed. "Losing, of course. We're taking our afternoon break." With a quick glance at her watch, she raised a brow. "You're early."

"I'm trying my luck before the crowds arrive. Where's Charles?"

"Taking a nap." She released a heavy sigh. "I hope naps aren't standard procedure for him. He takes them a lot."

Harriet chuckled. "If you joined him, you might change your mind."

"Ha! I've more important things to do besides sleeping my life away." She sipped her martini.

Thanks to Sky's confrontation with Johnny by the cab, they knew for certain the partner was male. This information eliminated all the female suspects and, of the regulars at the bar, left Jason Carter, Charles Dilly, and possibly Todd Daniels. The fact Johnny mentioned a *she* waiting at the safe house was discarded.

Could the partner be totally disconnected from the bar? Any number of people would have clear views of the activity in the lounge—like a pit boss wandering around the gaming tables or another security guard. Hell, the personnel watching the overhead cameras were in an ideal position. They, along with a pit boss or guard, wouldn't be questioned if they whipped out a cell phone. Dealers were eliminated. No way would they be allowed to use a phone while on the casino floor. Regardless who or where the associate stood in the picture, Logan and Sky had to keep on their toes.

Jason Carter stumbled in, looking his usual disheveled self with hair askew and scruff on his chin. He collapsed onto a stool at the other end of the bar, yawned with a gaping orifice, then nodded at Logan and the ladies.

Did the man ever sleep long enough to ease the dark circles under his eyes? What pushed him so hard? Of all possible suspects hanging around the bar, Jason and Todd were at the top of Logan's list. Who else appeared strong enough to help Johnny dig a pit and haul dirt up a flight of steps? The other suspect, Charles Dilly, had age and weight against him. Digging a hole and hauling dirt would strain an older man's heart. However and whoever helped, the endeavor must have taken months. On the other hand, if Johnny and his partner hired people to excavate the basement, their bones could be in the pit alongside the guy who installed the booby trap. The idea of such a thought caused Logan's gut to clench. He raised a hand to catch Anna's attention and then pointed to the coaster on the bar.

Johnny's fear of his partner was another factor to consider. Of the three suspects, which one would cause such a reaction? Todd Daniels? He had the build and strength to break Johnny in two and also had equal height. Monroe's research into Todd's life hadn't uncovered anything unusual. He lived alone in a Pleasantville apartment—just outside of Atlantic City. He had a modest bank account, no outstanding debts, and worked casino security for the past seven years— three years at the Whirlwind.

Jason didn't look strong enough to crush a pretzel. He was also a foot shorter than Johnny with hardly any muscle mass. But looks could be deceiving.

Anna, the bartender, slipped a light ale onto the coaster and winked at Logan before heading over to Jason.

According to Monroe, Anna still worked at the Treeline Casino on the midnight to eight a.m. shift. She took the temporary job at the Whirlwind until a replacement could be found. She was doing Johnny a big favor by working two full-time jobs. The fact that Anna was Jason's friend and showed hours after Sky supposedly quit reinforced Jason as a prime suspect.

Logan sipped his cold beer, then leaned toward the ladies. "How's the new bartender doing?"

Marian twisted her red lips to the side. "I miss Midnight. She made a mean martini." She popped a pretzel into her mouth and chewed. "Maybe I should do like that spy-guy in the movies. You know, shaken, not stirred."

Using the mirrors behind the bar's liquor bottles, Harriet adjusted her hat. "Anna makes a good grasshopper. I order that when I don't feel like wine."

Logan chuckled, then raised a hand to catch Anna's attention. "Buzz Johnny for me, will you, Anna?"

"Sure thing." She reached under the bar counter and pressed a button.

Several minutes later, Johnny wandered from the back hall and caught Anna's gaze.

Anna pointed toward Logan.

Plastering on a smile, Johnny sat beside Logan and nodded to the women. "Nice to see everyone."

Like he hadn't heard me talking to the ladies. To

maintain some sense of control, Logan wanted Johnny to come out to him, but the man had the same idea and kept Logan waiting.

"We're discussing bartenders," Harriet said.

"Ah, well." Johnny toyed with one of the coasters on the bar. "They come and go. A better offer, usually." He slapped the bar and stood. "Did you want to see me, Mr. Grandal? We can talk privately in my office."

"Sure." *Well, here we go.* After a quick sip of his beer, Logan set the mug on the coaster and followed Johnny down the hall.

Once inside the office, the bar manager shut the door. "I take it the money has arrived?"

"Yes, we're all set. Midnight is in my room, waiting for my call."

Jerking, Johnny narrowed his gaze. "You left her alone with a half million in cold cash? Is that wise, Mr. Grandal?"

The poor guy got a little too pale. Logan loved the look, but he had to play his part. He raised his brows. "Why? You think she'll take it and run?"

"It's a strong possibility." After passing a hand over his bald head, Johnny crossed his arms over his chest. "Look, I've worked here a long time, and I've seen all sorts of schemes. Both men and women wait around, pick their target, then strike like vultures. Some people operate under the pretense of looking for a relationship, but no matter what story, their primary purpose is to get their hands on the money."

"Like Charles with Marian?"

Brows high, Johnny grinned. "Yeah, like him. He's pretty obvious, isn't he?"

"I want to puke every time I see them together. But

they're engaged now." He shrugged.

"Well, look. About Midnight." Dropping his arms, he cleared his throat. "You gave her the perfect opportunity to leave you high and dry. I can tell you for a fact she is not what she seems."

He could say that again. Every word was true. Logan squinted. "Explain."

"I can't—not yet." He walked to the door and grabbed the knob. "For your own peace of mind, why don't we take a ride to your room and see if I'm right?"

My peace of mind? The man must think himself a comedian. Logan shook his head. "I trust her."

"But you shouldn't." Staring down at the floor, he twitched his jaw, then lifted his head to meet Logan's gaze. "How long has she been alone?"

Logan checked his watch. "Maybe forty minutes. Why don't I call and have her come down?"

"After forty minutes, she could answer from anywhere in the city. We should make sure she hasn't bolted."

Logan felt a surge of excitement to see Johnny sweat, but he had to play his skepticism right. While chewing on his inner lip, he eyed Johnny with the hope of conveying his disbelief about Sky's intentions. After Johnny's one fidget too many, Logan took him out of his misery and nodded. "All right, you're the expert. Let's go."

On the way through the bar, Logan gave the discrete finger signal to Joe Ryan.

****

With every step, Skylar couldn't shake the itch from nerves that vibrated like loose strings on a guitar. She paced Logan's spacious suite, unable to sit still.

Her mouth had gone bone-dry an hour ago. Yet, she didn't want to drink. Filling her bladder with fluids wouldn't be conducive for today's success. What in the world compelled her to do this? She wasn't an actress or anything remotely resembling a spy. Johnny would see right through her, and she'd spoil all of Monroe's plans. The boss man gave her an opportunity to opt out, but did she take it? No, of course, not. *Idiot.*

Her jacket should hide wet armpits, right?

All her life, nothing bothered her. As far back as she could remember, she was always the cool gal. Not cool-cool as in everyone hung around her. She was more like the laid-back and uninterested type. But now...*whew.* Forcing herself to stand still, she took a moment to do a few breathing exercises. This, at least, stopped her from wearing out the carpet.

Don't think about the impending danger. Think about Logan.

Yes, good idea. Last night, he'd thrown her for a loop, but deep down, she sensed his feelings simply from the look in his eyes. She never expected Mr. Commitment-Phobe to say the words, though. From the beginning, he gave her his no-relationship speech. He worked undercover for the state police and couldn't afford any attachments—which was fine. No relationship meant no commitment. At the time, she considered him a bit presumptuous, but after they formed a partnership to uncover the killer at the manor, they couldn't deny the attraction building between them. She slept with him, and they've been warming each other's beds ever since.

As fate would have it, she wound up working for Monroe, and their no-relationship status turned into friends with benefits. On occasion, she'd stay at his place, and the same applied to him staying with her. No fussing, clinging, or expecting a hot meal upon arrival. She was no domestic goddess in the kitchen, so she had to throw in that last tidbit. After a few months, they fell into an easy pattern. Now, though, what did he expect after dropping his bomb? Love meant commitment, right? *What the hell does he want from me?* The pacing resumed.

When she delved deep, she wasn't sure what emotions Logan elicited. A fondness, maybe. Definitely friendship. But love? Sleeping together and enjoying great sex wasn't her definition of love. She never experienced the breathless feeling so common in romance novels, but she had to admit her chest acted a little funny whenever he walked into the room. She should have asked her parents. They were deeply in love. When her husband died of a heart attack, Mom suffered from depression for years. Would Sky feel the same for Logan should he die before his time?

She shook herself. She wasn't ready to think along those lines. Stopping in the middle of the room, she closed her eyes and sucked in a deep breath.

Well, so much for deep breathing.

Thinking of Logan didn't help her nervousness one bit. How could people do this kind of stuff for a living and not develop ulcers? If she survived, she'd tell Monroe no more. Stand firm. Martial arts only. She'd put her foot down. *No, no, no, and no*! She resumed her pacing around the suite.

Her cell phone chirped. Damn, she jumped six inches off the floor. Whipping out her cell, she read.

—*You're on.*—

The message came from Joe Ryan. Logan and Johnny were on the way.

Aw, crap. She wasn't ready, might never be ready, but she had to do this. She couldn't back out. Too much depended on her role.

Yeah, some role. She never tried out for school plays and never had any desire to put herself front and center for people to notice. In grade school spelling bees, she purposely misspelled an easy word just to be eliminated. When high school rolled around, she wore black to blend into shadows and not to call attention to herself. Monroe better appreciate how much she put aside for this damn case.

She checked her watch. *Time to get the ball rolling.* After sucking in a calming breath, she grabbed the backpack, stepped into the hall, and glanced right and left. No one was about except for a maid's service cart and a room service tray on the floor with a half-eaten sandwich. *Yuck.*

Hurrying toward the center of the hall, she turned into the large alcove where several people waited for one of four elevators.

Seconds later, the ding of an approaching car prompted the small crowd toward its doors. Another ding followed, indicating a second car arriving.

Since Skylar had no idea which elevator Logan was on, she hung back.

When the first car opened its doors, no one stepped out, and the waiting people filed in.

Okay, here we go. Ordering her stomach to stay calm, she positioned herself near the other elevator and kept her gaze averted.

The doors opened.

Logan and Johnny emerged into the hall and stopped.

Oh, boy. She prayed she could pull this off. If not… *No, don't think like that.* After rubbing a moist palm against her thigh, she took a step forward, as if in a hurry to get onto the elevator when she glanced up and froze.

Gaze glaring, Logan entered her space. "Going somewhere, Midnight?"

Wow. He looked ready to tear her head from her shoulders. If she didn't know him, she'd back away or, at least, get ready to defend herself, but the man had more experience acting a part.

Damn, he was good. She lifted her chin and forced a smile. "Hey, guys. I was just coming down."

Johnny's face had an I-told-you-so smirk she would love to smack off his lips, but his glare floored her. Pure hatred exploded from his gaze, and she swallowed hard. Damn, she hadn't a drop of moisture in her throat. She coughed and shot them a nervous smile—which was probably more of a grimace.

Glowering, Logan stepped closer. "You were supposed to wait in the room until I called."

Johnny sneered. "Do I know women or what? She was skipping out on you, Grandal."

With a growl, Logan yanked the pack from her shoulder and then grabbed her arm. "Let's go to the room."

Well, hell. Could he pull her arm any harder? Maybe he'd like to pop her shoulder out of joint for good measure? She flashed Logan a glare.

"Hold on, Mr. Grandal." Johnny took a few steps from the alcove and swung his gaze right and left down each hall. "Follow me. We'll head to the service elevator. It will take us to my office. Housekeeping will be working in some of the rooms, so let's be quiet." He narrowed his gaze. "And you will be quiet, right, Midnight?"

Logan squeezed her arm.

"Ow! All right, yes."

Following Johnny, Logan yanked her down the left hall.

Her lover boy never warned her to expect all this roughness. Sure, he needed to look good, but geez, if the abuse kept up, she might take a swing at his handsome face. After shooting Logan another glare, she followed Johnny.

Before starting the case, Monroe provided an awful lot of intel—like how the main elevators had cameras, but the service elevators did not. Cameras also covered every hall within the hotel and...*hey*! With so much security, why weren't guards rushing to her rescue? Wasn't anyone looking at the monitors, or had Monroe arranged another of his many machinations?

Reaching the service elevator, Johnny hit the Down button. Within seconds, the car arrived—empty. Johnny inserted his pass key and punched the button for the ground floor—the truck unloading zone.

Oh, joy. So much for a ride to the office.

Since Logan still had a hold on her arm, she tugged. "He's taking us to the garage, Logan."

"I don't care where we go, Midnight." Once the elevator doors closed, Logan tightened his grip and whirled her to face him. "How can you do this to me? I trusted you."

"Look, I said I was coming down."

"No, you were skipping out, because I sure as hell didn't call you." He dropped his hold.

While rubbing her bicep, she jerked her head toward Johnny. "I'm sorry, but this man makes his clients permanently disappear."

Logan huffed. "That's the whole idea."

"No, I mean really permanent—like death."

Logan shot his gaze to Johnny. "What's she talking about?"

Johnny shrugged. "Like I said, Mr. Grandal, she can't be trusted. At this stage, she'll say anything to save her ass. Maybe we should discuss our problem away from the casino's prying eyes." He glanced up at the floor indicators. "Almost there."

Shifting the backpack, Logan adjusted the shoulder strap. Then, snarling at Sky, he again grabbed her arm. "I'm holding onto you, in case you plan on bolting once the doors open."

Yeah, I'm tempted.

The elevator clunked to a stop.

Ground zero in her opinion, and her heart took off like a rocket. If Logan wasn't alongside, she'd be hell-bent in the midst of an escape plan. When the doors opened, she fully expected to see someone holding a submachine gun—Valentine's Day Massacre style.

What she saw was even worse.

Chapter Twenty

Valerie stood on the other side of the elevator, slack-jawed and wide-eyed.

Potential partner or innocent bystander? Considering Val's expression, Sky went with bystander. Val showed as much surprise to see them as they to see her. But the perky co-worker inadvertently put herself in a dangerous position, and Logan's slight squeeze on Sky's arm told of similar conclusions. Now, what to do about it…

Val shook her mouth shut. "Hi. I just came to get something from my car." She shifted her gaze between Logan and Sky, then focused on Johnny. "Are you leaving?"

Lips tight, Johnny hissed. "For a little while. Maybe you should come with us."

Sky shot a glance at Logan. No way in hell would she let Johnny hurt Val, but the drink server was a witness to the three of them together. *Not good.* Sky slapped the wiry man's arm. "Val can't leave Carmela all alone, Johnny."

While glaring at Val, Johnny twitched his jaw.

The man was clearly torn, but if he didn't take care of Val now, he would do the deed later. *Monroe, you better be listening.* Someone needed to keep Val safe. Sky shot another look at Logan, hoping like hell he was a good mind reader.

Logan gave a slight nod, then turned to the manager. "Yo, Johnny. Did you tell Carmela you were leaving?"

Johnny snapped his gaze to Logan. "No." Baring his teeth, he shifted his gaze from one face to the other, then turned to Val. "Tell Carmela I'll be about thirty minutes. I need to show these two something." He leaned close and pointed a finger in Val's face. "You should never have left the floor without telling me."

"Sorry, but you weren't around. I told Carmela I'd be five minutes, but you're turning it into ten." Val stepped to the side to allow the three of them to exit the elevator. She locked her gaze on Logan's grip on Sky's arm and arched a brow. "Is everything okay?"

Logan nudged Sky through the open doors. "Everything's fine, Val. Go back to work."

The woman had questions shooting from her gaze, but she hit the button to move the elevator, and the doors closed.

Sky released a long breath. Val was safe—for now.

Logan yanked Sky's arm. "We had an agreement."

Wow, nothing like getting back on track. She had to figure out where they were in their little charade. Forgetting to watch her footing, she half-tripped off the concrete ramp. Logan's hold on her arm righted her. *So embarrassing.* She was supposed to be sure-footed. She gave him what she hoped was an appreciative nod. "I don't know what you're talking about. I don't want to disappear."

"But you agreed to go and waited until I got the extra cash. You planned all along to steal me blind, didn't you?"

Glancing around the garage, Johnny coughed.

"Why don't we get in my car and go to my house? It isn't far. We'll settle this in private." He pointed to a blue sedan. "I'm parked right over here."

Sky glared at Johnny. "I've seen your private place, remember?" She turned to Logan. "You don't want to go."

"Why should I believe you?" Logan jerked her toward the car. "You were about to walk out with my money. Come on. Get inside."

Geez, must he be so rough?

Waiting by the open rear door, Johnny again smirked.

Approaching, she sneered at Johnny. "We can walk."

"And take a chance of you bolting? No way." Once again glancing around, Johnny hissed. "Get a move on before a delivery truck comes in. We don't want anyone else to see us." While leaning on the open door, Johnny nodded at Logan. "Sit in the back with her, Mr. Grandal, and make sure she doesn't take a flying leap out the other side."

Logan practically shoved her into the car.

She was getting a little annoyed with all this pushing and shoving. Good thing she had some restraint—although, she'd never hurt Logan…much.

The car barely had a chance to warm up before Johnny parked in front of his little house of horrors. Like yesterday, Skylar scanned the area for familiar faces. No Anthony or Tyrone this time. She and Logan were destined to walk into the house while backup waited somewhere down the street. A shiver shot through her at the vision of what the house contained. Did Monroe need her here? Couldn't Logan go alone?

Sky just wanted to get the hell out of the car and run.

Without looking at her, Logan squeezed her knee.

The damn man read her mind again. But truthfully, she wouldn't let Logan face danger alone. If anything happened to him, she'd feel terrible. Sex aside, he was a good friend, and those were rare.

After turning off the ignition, Johnny glanced over his shoulder. "Hold onto her, Mr. Grandal. I'll get the door." Gaze narrowed, he pointed a finger at Sky. "No funny stuff, hear?"

Resisting the urge to grab onto his finger and break it, she nodded. Monroe better appreciate her restraint, because she sure as hell would love to kick Johnny in the balls and change his voice to soprano.

When the door opened, Logan nudged her. "Let's go."

She slid across the seat, then felt another hand grab hold.

Johnny clamped onto her upper arm and practically hoisted her from the car.

His grip was a hell of a lot tighter. She almost swung at his ugly face but bit down the urge.

"I got her, Johnny." Logan grabbed her arm.

Yeah, ouch. With all this manhandling, she might sport some ugly bruises real soon.

Logan pushed her forward. "Move."

"You guys are getting a bit rough, you know." She tripped up the steps. Turning her head, she glared at Logan. "Stop pushing me."

Logan hissed. "If you'd stop dragging your feet, then I wouldn't have to push. Keep moving."

Okay. This was it. They either lured the partner, or they failed. With the house under constant surveillance,

Monroe would know. Where the hell was his signal? She met Logan's gaze.

He gave a discrete nod toward a telephone pole by the curb.

Tacked to the wood was a flyer for *Martin's Excellent Cleaning Services*—their clue. The partner had arrived.

Well, hell, why didn't Monroe move in and arrest the culprit? Why must she and Logan continue their— *Oh yeah, proof.* Monroe wanted undeniable evidence to convict Johnny and his partner. She almost laughed—as if alligators weren't enough.

Still with that smug look, Johnny held open the front door and waved them in.

With his grip on her arm, Logan pulled her back a little.

Damn him. He wanted to go in first—in case bullets flew. *Too bad, lover boy.* She'd make sure he didn't. No sooner had she stepped beyond the foyer when a shadow moved from the far corner of the dining room.

She froze.

With a broad grin on his face, Charles Dilly sauntered across the sparsely furnished living room. In his right hand, he held a nine-millimeter automatic.

Well, golly gee. Because of Logan's gun education, she could now identify the weapon about to blow out her brains. Her heart sank. She hoped to meet a stranger, that it wasn't one of the regulars, and Monroe and Logan were totally wrong about everyone. But she could see with her own eyes how everything fell into place.

Logan tightened his grip on her arm. With flaring

nostrils and a gaze like ice, he stared at Charles.

My, oh my, if looks could kill. Then, like flipping a switch, his expression morphed into the client again, and his fingers loosened on her arm. *Dear Lord.* The man could act. On the other hand, she was about to pee her pants.

Dropping his hold on her arm, Logan stepped in front of her. "What the hell is going on?"

At this point, Monroe should barge in and arrest everyone, but no, that wasn't the plan. To put Johnny and his partner away for life, Monroe and the Feds demanded hard evidence—as if a gun pointed at her head wasn't hard enough. They also needed to know how many victims had fallen into the pit. Couldn't they uncover this information during an interrogation, you know, like give them a shot of truth serum?

After securing the front door, Johnny shoved them both into the living room. "Midnight stole two million from us, Mr. Grandal, and we'd like to get it back."

Oh, yeah. She forgot about that little tidbit.

Mouth agape, Logan faced her. "You took their money?"

"Pah. They're delusional." She waved a hand in the air. "Would I have waited for your half mil if I took twice that from them? I'd be on a plane to Tahiti."

Johnny yanked the backpack from Logan's shoulder. Jerking, he raised both brows. "This feels awful light for a half mil in cash." He unzipped the main compartment and rummaged. Growling, he dumped the contents onto the floor.

Pieces of cut-up newspaper covered Logan's feet.

Face red, Logan kicked the paper. "What the hell?" He whirled, gaze blazing. "Where's my money,

Midnight?"

"I don't know what you're talking about." Did she sound convincing enough? To her ears, her voice shook.

Stepping forward, Charles sneered. "She's a damn good actress, Grandal, and probably the best I've seen in a long time. Look, Midnight, we have you on camera leaving this house with a large canvas bag. Somehow, you got into our safe."

Johnny walked to the wingback chair, lifted the cushion, and extracted a thirty-eight special.

She was getting good at this gun identification stuff.

He pointed the gun at her chest. "Where's our money?"

Still facing her, Logan spread his arms wide. "And mine. You played me."

"She played all of us, Grandal."

Damn you, Logan. By keeping himself in front of her, he acted like a human shield. *Totally unacceptable.* Partners did this shit together, and she wasn't thrilled with him giving his life so she might continue. Her nerves were already taut enough to snap, and he wasn't helping matters. For Pete's sake, she could hardly catch her breath. Fear gripped her like never before, and her knees threatened to buckle. What good would she do if she passed out? Willing herself to stay calm, she purposely stepped alongside Logan and patted his thick arm. "These guys have a nice little enterprise going, Logan. They make a lot of money from people desperate to disappear. As insurance, I hid the money."

Glancing quickly at her feet, he shot her a warning look and, again, positioned himself in front of her.

"Insurance against what? I still don't understand what the hell is going on."

She couldn't let Logan sacrifice himself for her. Squeezing his bicep, Sky took one step to the side. "Tell him, Johnny, or I will."

Johnny frowned. "I suppose he deserves an explanation. What do you say, Uncle Chuck?"

Uncle Chuck? They were related? Sky shifted her gaze from Charles to Johnny.

The two men didn't look anything alike. Johnny had about six inches more in height, and compared to Charles's beer-barrel belly, his lanky frame gave him a malnourished look. She spotted no familial resemblance—unless she compared their lack of hair on the tops of their heads. Charles was completely bald with trimmed sides. Johnny still had wisps coming from his scalp. If they were truly blood-related, in another few years, his head would look like his uncle's. Their straight noses looked similar…somewhat.

Narrowing his gaze, Logan sneered. "You guys can't possibly be family."

Charles snickered. "Ah, but we are, Mr. Grandal. Tell them the story, Billy. It's damn funny."

Billy, eh? Hadn't Monroe mentioned a Billy something? *Holy crap!* She gasped and received another warning look from Logan. *Oh, right. Keep it cool.* But damn, Billy Dilly! The missing nephew.

Johnny scowled at his uncle. "Another time."

"No, no, tell them now." Charles cocked his head. "They can use a good laugh."

Oh, sure, before the inevitable dive into the deep pit. Charles's sense of humor needed improvement.

Johnny deepened his scowl but faced Logan.

"Yeah, we're related. We have different last names because I changed mine. Move toward the dining room, please." He waved his gun.

Following instructions, Logan placed his hand on the small of her back and nudged her toward the wall opposite the card table.

He must see an advantage to this position, but slap her on the side of the head, she hadn't a clue why.

"Don't move." Johnny growled the two words. "You see, Grandal, I had an asshole father with a weird sense of humor. Despite the objections of my mother, I was christened Billy Dilly. Now, I ask you. Can a kid survive adolescence with that kind of name? It was sheer torture."

Sky shrugged. "You could have told everyone to call you Bill."

"I did. Then, instead of chanting Billy Dilly, they sang Bill Dill."

Charles grinned. "I loved it." Catching Johnny's glare, he coughed. "That was all my brother's doing."

So, where was Johnny's father? Did Charles make him disappear, too?

"Anyway"—Johnny twitched his jaw—"as soon as I graduated high school, I changed my name. A friend of mine created false IDs for college kids. I've been Johnny Dee ever since."

Jamming his hands on his hips, Logan glared. "And I suppose your friend taught you everything he knew about the process?"

Wow. Logan, like the pro he was, stayed in character. How much evidence did Monroe need? Her nerves weren't used to all this excitement. She'd like to drop this charade and get the hell out of here.

"It's time we showed Grandal the basement. How about it, Uncle Chuck?" Johnny motioned with his gun. "Lead the way, Midnight."

Oh, holy hell, no! Why me, dammit? She clenched her fists. "I'd rather not."

Logan shifted his gaze from Sky to Johnny. "What's in the basement?"

She huffed. "You don't want to know."

Charles laughed. "Sure, he does. He's the one who legitimately wants to disappear." He waved his gun. "Move it, darling. Let's head to the kitchen."

She had to bite her lip. She could so easily disarm both of them.

Logan grabbed hold of her arm and shot her a look.

The damn man suspected she was on the verge of swinging, and he was right. She sighed. Mister Undercover Cop was no fun at all. She stepped into the kitchen. When she reached the basement door, she turned to Charles. "You played Marian, didn't you? You don't love her. You want her money."

Charles winked. "Yeah, she's a catch with a hefty bank account. A bit too prudish for my liking, but I'll overlook her attitude for the sake of love." Chuckling, he shook his head. "Can you believe she hates pre-nups? What idiot in this day and age gets married without protecting their bankroll? Tell me, how can I possibly pass up that?" He nodded toward his nephew. "My meeting Marian wasn't by chance. Billy called and said she was hanging around. So"—he shrugged—"I hung around, too. Turns out she's the dumbest broad I've ever met."

Poor Marian. Charles was a slick SOB, and Sky was right all along. Charles pursued Marian with the hopes of making himself husband number four. Before the honeymoon was over, the woman would wind up in the pit—assuming she hadn't an ironclad will in place. More than ever, this murderous enterprise needed to stop.

Johnny tapped on the rickety kitchen table. "Both of you, empty your pockets."

Well, so much for recording on their cell phones. She shot a glance at Logan.

Jaw tight, Logan narrowed his gaze. "Why?"

"Sorry, Grandal. No electronics beyond this door. You'll understand in a minute."

Yeah, mustn't give the gators indigestion.

"Turn them off first."

Frowning, Logan followed instructions and slipped his cell phone onto the table.

When she caught Johnny's glare, she complied. Déjà vu all over again.

Snarling, Johnny pointed the gun at her feet. "I see you're still wearing those steel-toed boots. Take them off."

"No. I hate walking barefoot."

"What the hell do steel-toed boots have to do with anything?" Logan threw his hands into the air and shook his head. "I don't understand any of this shit."

Charles snorted. "You will in a moment. And, Billy, let her be. She's not going far." Pointing his gun at Logan, he jerked his head to the side. "Open the door, Grandal. You're about to see why our little enterprise is so successful."

More than anything, Sky wanted to avoid the basement. *See?* She didn't have the stomach to do all this secret agent stuff. *Dear God in heaven. Help me.*

Chapter Twenty-One

Clamping onto his right arm, Sky stopped Logan from turning the dead bolt on the cellar door. "We've reached the point of no return."

Yanking his arm from her grip, he sneered. "Sorry, honey, you lost all credibility. Why should I believe anything you say?"

"Oh, I don't know. Maybe because I'm good in bed?" His expression morphed between annoyance and pissed, which looked kinda cute. She had to force back a smile.

He stepped into her space and put his face close. "You took my money, Midnight. If these two are right, you took their money, too. I'd like to know where you stashed it."

Fighting the urge to kiss him, she leaned back and cleared her throat. "I told you. It's insurance. If they kill us, the money stays hidden forever. And I won't tell you while these two goons can hear." She jerked a thumb over her shoulder.

Charles tugged on his ear. "I gotta hand it to you, Midnight. You had guts pulling off your heist, but we'll discuss your options in the basement. Go on, Grandal." He nodded toward the door.

Pressing his lips into a thin line, Logan turned the bolt and swung open the door. After staring into the black void, he cocked a brow at Charles. "Are you turning on a light?"

After a quick glance at his nephew, Charles sighed. "I suppose. I would have preferred you be surprised, but Midnight knows what to expect."

"Yeah, death." Passing a hand through her hair, she grunted. "Like I truly believed you and Johnny wanted me as a partner. You must think I'm stupid."

Charles held up a finger. "Foolish, maybe, but not stupid." He flipped the light switch. "Go on, Grandal. Have a look."

With a glance over his shoulder, Logan stepped onto the platform and leaned forward.

One might think he stood on a ship's plank and peered over into the water below. She had to hand it to Logan. He was a good actor.

Jamming the gun barrel into her spine, Johnny nudged Sky to follow. "We can avoid all this if you tell us where you hid the money."

"Ha! Not a chance."

He nudged her again, a little harder this time. "Then, I suggest you follow Grandal. And by the way, Midnight, how did you get out? I know I locked the door."

"Did you?" She shot her gaze at Charles.

Snapping a glare toward his nephew's back, Charles pressed his lips into a thin line.

Funny how the implication of a little double cross worked wonders.

Descending the steps behind Logan, she swallowed hard. The familiar mustiness of the basement hit her nose. Was she afraid? *Well, hell, yeah*. She'd rather not see the pit again, and the closer the bottom of the steps came, the tighter her stomach knotted. Sucking in a deep breath, she stepped onto the dirt floor behind Logan and stopped. Yup, there was the pit, exactly as she left it. She shivered.

Couldn't they call it quits now? How much more intel did Monroe need? For heaven's sake, Johnny and Charles were right behind her, chuckling like this entire scene was hilarious.

Whirling, Logan glared at the two men. "What the hell is this?"

Charles snickered. "Welcome to our very profitable enterprise." He nudged Sky with the barrel of his gun. "Move near Grandal, sweetheart. We can't have you standing by the steps all day."

If it weren't for Logan ordering her to follow his lead, she'd take down Charles in a heartbeat. Glowering at the older man, she stepped toward Logan.

Like yesterday, Johnny reached the bottom step and stopped.

Billy Dilly didn't want to get near the pit earlier, and he sure avoided getting near it now. His face was a little too pale, and his gaze darted from one end of the pit to the other, as if the gators would climb out and attack him. On the other hand, Charles looked cool as a cucumber. He struck her as a man who would stare over the edge to cheer for the alligators.

"Before we begin…" Charles strolled away from the staircase and positioned himself about ten feet away. "I'm sorry you didn't get the big speech, Grandal, but Midnight can clue you in."

Logan glared at Sky.

After faking a cough, she waved a hand toward the pit. "This is your journey into oblivion, Logan. For two hundred and fifty grand, you can fall into the pit and never come out. And don't think for one minute I'm part of their business. Yesterday, in their attempt to get rid of me, I received the hundred dollar tour and managed to escape their trap."

"I'd still like to know how." Johnny growled the words as he joined his uncle.

Well, what do you know? Billy Dilly actually stepped onto the dirt floor.

Shifting his glare to Johnny, Logan clenched his hands. "What trap are we talking about?"

"Take a look, Grandal." Johnny jerked his head toward the pit.

Sky patted Logan's arm. "Stay away from the left side. They have an overhead booby trap that guarantees a little shove on their clients' legs." She pointed.

Logan glanced up, frowned, then peered over the edge of the pit. He gasped. "Son of a bitch!" With the veins popping in his neck, he spun to face Johnny. "Are you shitting me?"

Johnny grinned. "Just a few pets we keep."

"But holy hell, alligators?"

Shrugging his thin shoulders, Johnny laughed. "What can I say? It was Uncle Chuck's idea."

Confirmation of the sadistic one. Sky shuddered and stepped closer to Logan. No way in hell would she look over the edge. "Nice, eh? See? Permanent disappearance. You'll notice the sides are straight with no possibility of climbing out." She tugged on his shirt sleeve. "I suggest we move away from the pit before they decide to give us a little push."

Hissing through bared teeth, Logan moved toward the right side of the basement.

She surprised herself at how calm she stayed.

Would she be tearing her short hair out if Logan wasn't nearby? *Probably*. But Monroe told her what he accomplished here, and last night over dinner, Logan discussed a few possible scenarios. One major concern was guns. Charles and Johnny would have no way to force them into the hole without a weapon as a threat. So, Logan suggested, once they were in the basement, they inch away from each other, and she agreed. For one, the maneuver would guarantee Logan saving his own life instead of hers. The basement wasn't large. The pit stretched from the back end of the house to about ten feet from the staircase and from one side of the house to the other. The water table remained constant because of the close proximity to the ocean.

Charles raised his gun. "Stay where you are, Grandal. I want you both near the edge. You, too, Midnight. Get alongside him." He waved his free hand at his nephew. "Act like a herding dog, boy. Keep Grandal still."

Snapping a glare at his uncle, Johnny moved toward Logan.

Ordinarily, she'd tell Charles to go stuff an egg, but Logan said to follow their demands until he gave the signal. Ever so slowly, she took her position alongside Logan.

Growling, Logan shot a cutting glare at Johnny. "You murder everyone for money? How can you live with yourself?" He took a small step to the right.

With a smile, Johnny pointed his gun at Logan's chest. "It's the perfect setup, don't you think? People, like you, want to disappear, so we make sure they do."

"But, shit—alligators?"

Skylar slid her feet to the left.

Charles grinned. "Gators don't need to eat all the time. In fact, they can go for months without food. By the time a client falls into the pit, he—or she—becomes a meal ticket, and those gators act like hungry bastards. The spikes on the booby trap put a little blood into the water to ensure them a nice, tasty meal."

Dear Lord. Without question, the man was a pure sadist. Sky wanted to break his neck so bad. How could Logan stand there and listen, as if feeding humans to animals was a common thing? Even his face looked calm—no anger or expression to reveal his thoughts. Meanwhile, she forced herself not to scream about injustice and greed.

Charles waved the gun. "Go on, Grandal. Jump in."

Logan snorted. "Yeah, right." While glancing over the edge, he stepped to the right, then turned to face Johnny. "You'll have to shoot me first, because I will not jump in willingly. But guns make too much noise. Your neighbors will hear."

Chuckling, Johnny waved his gun. "Look around, Grandal. This basement is soundproofed. No one hears anything, not even screams." Gaze narrowed, he leveled his pistol at Logan but swung his gaze to Sky. "One more time, Midnight. Where's our money? If you tell us, we'll spare Grandal."

Oh, sure. Like her former boss was so trustworthy. She stuffed her hands into her jacket pockets. "I have all the money hidden in a special place. If I don't retrieve it in the next day or two, then a letter will be sent to the Atlantic City Police Department with details about your entire operation."

Cocking a brow, Johnny shot a glance at his uncle.

Well, that got their attention, or maybe, she signed

her death warrant. She couldn't tell which. While forcing a smile, she moved two steps to the left. "If you want your money, you have to let us go." She held up a finger. "Both of us."

Charles sighed. "I'm getting too old for this game." He turned toward his nephew. "We have enough money, don't we, Johnny boy?"

Still with his gun pointed at Logan, Johnny turned to his uncle. "*You* have the money, not me. I'm still waiting for my share, but it was your idea to hide it in your home safe. When were you passing a few bucks my way, Uncle Chuck?"

Charles waved a dismissive hand. "Be thankful I take charge of the money. Otherwise, Midnight could have walked away with a lot more."

Come on, Logan. Johnny and Charles were focused on each other. Wouldn't this be the best time to attack? She wanted to get these bastards. Why the hell was he waiting?

"Hold on a sec." Logan took a step to the right. "While you two discuss your share of the profits, I want to know how many people you suckered into this hellhole?"

Oh, yeah. Evidence. She sighed.

After a nod from Charles, Johnny puffed his chest and grinned. "So far, sixteen. You'd be surprised how many desperate rich people we meet."

Sky grimaced. "Sixteen unlucky souls. Sixteen times two hundred and fifty grand would be…hmm, four mil." She shifted her gaze from one man to the other. "You killed for a hefty chunk of change, gentlemen." She was always good at math. Some of her high school counselors pushed her to go to college to be a mathematician. She laughed at them.

Turning to face her, Charles pointed his gun directly at her heart. "For the last time, Midnight, who gave you the combination to the safe?"

The first time a man aimed a gun at her, she avoided the shot because of her speed. She sure hoped her luck held for this bastard's bullet. Dropping her hands to her sides, she gaped. "No one." Did she sound innocent enough? Did either of them notice how far apart she and Logan drifted?

"You expect me to believe you're an expert safecracker?" Charles huffed out a laugh. "I don't think so, honey." He narrowed his gaze. "Tell me who gave you a key for the front door."

Sky glanced at Johnny.

Charles shot a blazing gaze at his nephew.

My, oh my. If looks could kill, Johnny would be on the floor by now, dead.

Sneering at his nephew, Charles took a step back and shifted to look at Johnny. "I knew you two were working together. There's no other way she could have survived the basement unless she never went down in the first place."

Brows high, Johnny also stepped back. "What the hell are you talking about? No way I'd screw you." He snarled at Sky. "Who gave you the key?"

With their attention diverted, Logan took another slow step to the right, which put him in close proximity to take down Johnny.

Charles snorted. "Don't pretend, Billy Dilly. Everything makes sense. While you left to tend to the new bartender, Midnight opened the safe using the combination, then locked the front door on the way out.

But you forgot about the cameras, didn't you? You couldn't turn them off without an alert hitting my phone." Sighing, he shook his head. "You never were a bright boy, Billy. Maybe you're the one holding the money because you're cutting me out." He raised his gun hand and pointed at Johnny.

Johnny swung his own weapon toward his uncle. "What the hell are you talking about? I don't know who Midnight is, but it's obvious she's turning us against each other. Can't you see this is a setup?"

"An elaborate one of which you are incapable of planning." Charles glanced at Sky. "Midnight must be the brains."

Aw, how nice. Charles just paid her a compliment. If she was so smart, she wouldn't need to look at Logan for reassurance. But hey, she had to stay cool—even if her heart beat halfway into her throat.

Johnny hissed. "So, what now, Uncle Chuck? Do we throw away years of success because of her? Maybe she's waiting for us to shoot each other."

Yeah, not a bad idea. She moved another step to the left, which put her closer to Charles and within striking distance.

Charles chuckled softly. "You can fire away all you want, Billy. I took the bullets out of your gun."

Gasping, Johnny slapped open the cylinder and cursed. "I can't believe you'd do this. I don't know who Midnight is working for, but it isn't me. Maybe it's her and Grandal."

"Regardless, it's time to put an end to any questions." Charles turned toward Sky.

Well, having one gun to deal with was certainly safer than two. Unfortunately, the one with the bullets was aimed at her chest. She forced a grin. "Ask away, Charles. It doesn't mean I have any answers."

Frowning, Charles passed a hand over his bald head. "Yeah, you're right. I'll eliminate Marian sooner." He waved his gun at Johnny. "You go first."

Brows high, Johnny jerked. "Where?"

"Into the pit, of course. Don't look so shocked. It was coming to this. Marian's death will make me very comfortable. I won't need to do our disappearing business anymore. It's time to retire."

Cursing up a storm, Johnny flung his gun at his uncle.

Ducking, Charles fired and missed Johnny by a mile.

Logan nodded at Sky.

Well, it's about time.

With the speed that earned her three black belts, Sky swung her leg at Charles, kicked the gun from his hand, then caught the weapon in midair. Before her quarry had a chance to react, she latched onto his still-outstretched arm, flipped him over her shoulder, and threw him straight into the pit. A loud splash followed.

The man screamed like a banshee.

At the same time, Logan grabbed ahold of Johnny and struck the bar manager with a fist straight to his long nose.

The guy staggered. Within seconds, blood poured from his nostrils.

Logan clamped onto Johnny's shirt and growled into the man's face. "This is for all the people you killed for money." He threw a second fist into Johnny's face and, with little effort, tossed him into the pit.

They now had two banshees screaming bloody

murder.

A beep echoed from somewhere in the overhead rafters. "Great job, you two! We have everything recorded. On our way."

Since the basement had so many shadowed corners, Pamela had installed cameras with microphones. The cameras were also infrared-capable, in case the two partners left them in the dark. Sky had to hand it to Monroe. When it came to the latest technology, he spared no expense.

Logan approached and wrapped her tight in his strong arms.

Her nerves still vibrated like crazy. Even her knees wobbled, and she sucked in his strength.

He kissed her hair. "Damn, that was scary." He tipped up her chin. "You did very well."

"For a newbie, you mean." Not in the least ready to be released, she wrapped her arms around his waist and rested her head on his thick shoulder. "I'm not cut out for this line of work."

"You're better than you think. You followed my lead all the way, and that was important." He squeezed her tight. "Except for upstairs." Loosening his arms, he used a finger to lift her chin. "You kept moving away."

"That's because you were using your big body as a shield. I don't want you to ever sacrifice yourself for me, Logan. We're partners. Equality and all that."

He smiled. "I would welcome you by my side any day."

With a brow arched, she tilted her head. "Really?"

"Yes, really." He kissed her nose. "Partner."

Footsteps pounded overhead and sounded like a herd of elephants storming through the house.

Chuckling, she took Logan's face in her hands and kissed him, then stepped back. Glancing at the pit, she covered her ears with her hands. "You might think those two idiots would recognize plastic replicas in the water with them."

Logan laughed. "I won't tell them if you don't. They deserve to be scared spitless."

She couldn't agree more.

Chapter Twenty-Two

"I'm home!" Skylar Dawson stood inside the back door to the kitchen at Ginger's Manor, not in the least concerned if anyone heard her or not. Her heart felt light, her mind clear, and yes, she wanted to kick up her heels. After closing her eyes, she sucked in a deep breath through her nose and savored the wonderful aromas of good cooking. Today's meal smelled like Italian, maybe spaghetti and meatballs with tomato and basil sauce—a crowd favorite. Gad, how she missed this.

At the stove, Fay Bartleson stood, stirring a huge pot. Glancing over her shoulder, the housekeeper hurriedly hooked her big spoon onto the pot handle and turned with a wide smile. "Come here, girl."

Sky slid easily into Fay's arms. Yesterday, after the Feds arrested Johnny and Charles, the thought of going home to sleep alone in her own bed hadn't an iota of appeal. Logan, in his infinite wisdom, had presented an offer she couldn't refuse. Since hotel checkout was at eleven in the morning, the charge for another night had automatically been billed. He suggested they spend one more night in his suite. They made love in that glorious tub, then afterward, in his spacious bed. They ordered room service and, this time, drank the entire bottle of wine. In the morning, he joined her in the shower. He'd never said the *L* word again, but she felt his love with every touch and kiss. She still couldn't open her mouth to tell him how her heart exploded whenever he walked into the room. Someday…maybe.

After breakfast in the suite, Sky joined Logan in his black sports car for a ten o'clock meeting at Monroe Security. This would be her first debriefing—whatever the hell it meant. But she gathered with the others in the conference room and almost fell asleep. The whole process consisted of a bunch of questions that made her wonder why she wrote daily reports.

Now, she was home and did a happy little dance to be surrounded by everything familiar. It felt good. Tonight, she'd sleep in her own bed and, by morning, drink her own coffee at her kitchen table while watching the birds fly around the gazebo outside her windows. For the first time in weeks, she could breathe without shuddering. The stress levels alone nearly destroyed her, and she truly expected to develop a nervous tic. Living in an Atlantic City apartment too cramped to be comfortable didn't help. And yes, she missed the tenants and couldn't wait to see them. As soon as she'd parked her motorcycle in the garage and threw her duffel bag inside the rancher, she hightailed it to the manor. She wouldn't waste another moment to announce her arrival.

Anthony, Tyrone, and Too-Tall Joe ambled in with big smiles.

She hugged all three, and her heart soared.

Since it was still too early for dinner, Fay brewed a fresh pot of coffee and cut slices of chocolate cake. She placed each piece on a plate and passed them around as everyone took a seat at the kitchen table.

The questions flowed. Sky hadn't all the answers,

but she shared what she knew. "Johnny pled guilty, but Charles held off until his lawyer advised him otherwise. Neither man had a choice since everything was recorded via our cell phones and the cameras in the basement. Search warrants confiscated the safe in Charles's Philly home where the Feds found more money stashed. A million was already missing, so they followed a paper trail to find out where it went." She bit into the gooey chocolate cake and sighed. "I missed this, Fay."

Anthony tapped the table. "Stop stuffing your face and get on with it, woman. Where did the paper trail lead?"

Yeah, nice to be back with these guys. She chuckled. "Charles opened an account at a bank in the Cayman Islands. Needless to say, Johnny had no idea his uncle already screwed him out of his share of the million bucks." She sipped her coffee. "Anyway, most of us had our own suspect in mind as the likely partner. Neither Charles nor Johnny had a police record. In fact, none of the suspects had so much as a parking ticket. The overall consensus, though, was Marian because three of her husbands died suddenly and left her rich. No one suspected Charles. He was just a regular guy who hung around Marian to make himself husband number four."

Tyrone slapped the table and grinned. "You knew it was Charles, didn't you?"

Lowering her cup to the table, she shook her head. "I had no clue. My only complaint with Charles was the way he doted on Marian. All his gushing and fussing became downright sickening. He admitted he would toss her into the pit after getting his name on some of her accounts, but he had to be careful. Marian's will had four children named as beneficiaries, and throughout all her marriages, she never once changed the will."

Fay shuddered. "In other words, he had to filch her money from the accounts until he was satisfied he had enough. What a heartless man."

Sky wiped her mouth with a paper napkin. "I liked Marian. So, I'm glad we saved her from certain death."

Joe finished the last of his cake and pushed the plate to the side. "I had my money on that Jason guy. There was something really wrong with that boy."

Sky merely nodded. At the debriefing, Monroe told her that casino management hired his firm to investigate Carter. They suspected him of cheating but couldn't prove it. As it happened, the personnel watching the security cameras had centered their concentration on Jason and totally ignored Johnny's many conversations with the wealthy patrons.

Since Pam had compiled dossiers on all the suspects, she dug a little deeper into Jason's personal life, and within a day, Monroe presented a report to the casino along with a hefty bill. Jason wasn't cheating at all, but his gambling was an addiction he couldn't control. Somehow, he managed to win whatever he lost and always came out even. He never stayed overnight in a comped room because he lived with his elderly parents and refused to let them worry. As for declining the free meals, he had food allergies and rarely ate out.

The one aspect that worked well involved Carmela. She was immediately promoted to bar manager, which she richly deserved. In a way, Sky was glad to be home, but in another way, she missed the comradery of working at the bar. She wouldn't tell Monroe, of course. He'd only put her in another bar on another case.

After clearing his throat, Joe wagged his left finger. " 'The path of the just is as the shining light, that shineth more and more unto the perfect day.' "

Yup, another saying that made absolutely no sense. Where in the world did Joe find these quotes? Thank God, he hadn't gone into his preacher mode while at the casino. Security might have tossed him onto the street.

Tyrone leaned forward. "What happened to the gators?"

After taking a sip of her coffee, she lowered the mug to the table and sighed. "They had to be killed and stomach contents inspected. The last known victim was the Fed agent. Since gators eat bones, and they take time to digest, the Feds expect to find his bones within their bellies." She took another bite of cake and swallowed it with the coffee.

Everyone sat back and stared.

She shifted her gaze from one shocked face to the other. "What?"

Fay pointed to her cake. "How can you eat after a visual image of a gator tearing a man apart?"

Sky glanced at her dish and shrugged. "I…don't know." Was she conditioned already? Logan had mentioned how sights, sounds, and smells wouldn't faze her. But geez, this was her first case. She couldn't possibly have adapted so soon, right?

Tyrone cleared his throat. "All right, tell us about the pit. How deep was it?"

"A little over thirteen feet. Johnny said it took them five months to remove the dirt. They installed some kind of conveyor system to haul the sandy soil up to the kitchen and out the back door." She sipped her coffee. "Since the house was so close to the ocean, the deeper they dug, the higher the water level rose, and everything turned to wet sand." She shook herself at the memory of those beady eyes staring up.

"Did the Feds go in it?"

"Yeah." She rotated her cup. "They couldn't drain the pit completely, so they used a diver to retrieve the bones along with shoes and belt buckles." She shivered. "I told Monroe the next time he needs a bartender, *don't* call me."

Fay stood and leaned over to give Sky another hug. "I'm so glad you're back safe and sound. Will you join us for supper?"

"Gosh, yes. I don't have anything in my fridge."

"How about Logan? Is he coming?"

"He's still tying up loose ends. He'll be along in a day or two." Like any man who had a stomach for the gruesome aspects of a case, he drove back to the house and stuck around to see everything coming out of the pit. For her, she couldn't get away fast enough. *Ugh.*

She made no secret Logan frequented her bed. Even though he had his own place near Monroe Security, he spent his nights in her bed several times a week—unless he worked a case. Then, she'd miss him like crazy. Was that love? Last night, she almost talked about her feelings, but he hardly gave her a chance. This morning, she tried again, but for some reason, the words stuck in her throat, which was just as well. She wasn't sure what to say.

Maybe she was being a coward. Ever since he mentioned the *L* word, she wondered what it would be like to spend a lifetime with a man and have children. Marriage had never been on her radar, and she wasn't even sure she would be a good mom. What would she do if she had a little girl? Dress her in black, too? That would be cruel.

Four nights later, a knock sounded on the rancher's back door.

Logan had a key but never used it unless he arrived very late. Those late-night visits were her favorite when he slipped into her bed and made love while she was still half asleep. Sometimes, he felt like a dream coming to life. There again, the question of love came to mind, but great sex was…well, great sex, not love. She kept telling herself that, anyway.

Grabbing the remote to lower the volume on the TV, she jumped from the sofa to answer the door. He looked rested—and very handsome. Gone was the executive with the tailored trousers and silk shirts. He returned to his blue jeans that hugged his thick thighs and T-shirts that emphasized his strong chest and arm muscles. In another few weeks, his hair would be at the length she preferred. She smiled. "Hi."

Crap. She hadn't meant for the word to come out breathy, but he affected her in ways no other man ever had. She liked him…a lot, but those words sounded too weak, even in her mind.

Stepping inside, he returned the smile. "Hi, yourself." He closed and locked the door.

"Did you eat?" Since Monroe told her to stay home for two weeks and relax, she had time to shop and refill the fridge. Of course, after her mini vacation, she would continue with her original job as martial arts instructor.

"I'm good. What I want is to hold you."

Oh, well, sure. He couldn't have said nicer words. She slipped into his arms and lifted her face for a kiss. He was such a marvelous kisser, but right now, something troubled him. His lips told her so.

He guided her to the sofa and sat while tugging her close to his side.

She knew Logan well enough not to push, but he was unusually quiet. She placed a palm on his stubbled cheek and turned his head toward her. "Talk to me."

Grabbing her hand, he kissed her fingers, then rested her palm against his chest. "The Feds identified five victims from the bones at the bottom of the pit. One was female."

"Oh." So, the assumption that the female bartenders met their fate came true for one. She shuddered. "Go on."

"They're testing the DNA on the booby trap. So far, it's mixed results. Johnny admitted telling the female bartenders to stay close to their man, and holding hands would be best. This way, when the ram hit, they fell in simultaneously."

Her gut roiled. If those two men were here, she would inflict bodily harm to make them believe their life was over. "That is so sick. Which one came up with this gruesome enterprise?"

With his arm wrapped around her shoulders, he rubbed his fingers up and down her arm. "Johnny got everything off his chest. He admitted to accidentally killing his father when he was eighteen. His classmates relentlessly teased him about his name, and he'd had enough. He arrived home, determined to drop out of school, but when he entered the house, the first words from his father's mouth were *Billy Dilly, do this* and

Billy Dilly, do that. Johnny snapped. He hit his father with his heavy backpack loaded with books and broke his neck. Sad to say, I sympathize with Johnny. With such a name I, too, might have lashed out."

"But Johnny killing his father was an accident."

"True. In a panic, instead of reporting the accident, he called his uncle. Charles helped dispose of the body, then with Charles's suggestion, Johnny finished high school, then took on a new identity and skipped town. Johnny's mother had died years before from cancer, and as an only child, Johnny had no one else to call." He fussed with a piece of lint on his pant leg.

"As we suspected, Charles was the brains behind the operation. When he found out his nephew became manager at the casino bar, he blackmailed Johnny into participating. Charles also bought the Atlantic City house and the gators. With both purchases, he used Johnny's name." He released a long sigh. "Whether Johnny realized it or not, his uncle set him up to take the fall." He shook his head. "I expected Johnny to show some remorse, but neither man flinched when the judge read the charges. Monroe called them two peas in the pod—truly sadistic."

"I really wanted to hurt them."

Smiling, he tapped her nose. "I know. I saw it in your face. But the evidence is conclusive. They are going away for a long time."

"Yeah, big deal. They'll get three square meals a day and free medical care. I don't call that justice."

"Neither do I, but the system is what it is." He squeezed her shoulders. "You proved you could do this type of work, Sky. I'm proud of you."

She grunted. "Never again. I worked my first and

last case. Most of the time, my nerves were near breaking point."

He kissed her hair. "Not all cases are gruesome. You'll feel more confident on the next one."

"Nope. No next one." She toyed with the front of his T-shirt.

"You say it now, but admit it. We make a great team."

"I admit nothing." *Oh, my God.* He was trying to convince her to continue. Could she develop nerves of steel? *No, no, and no.* Why would she even ask herself such a stupid question when she had no desire to become a full-fledged agent? *Well, hell.* Only one activity would divert this conversation toward something more pleasurable. She stroked a finger along his stubbled chin. "Are you tired?"

"For you, never." Giving her a one-eyed stare, he cocked a brow. "Why?"

Why, indeed. She slid off the sofa and held out her hand. "I don't want to talk shop anymore. Let's go to the bedroom."

"Did you—"

"Yes, as ordered. I bought a fresh box of condoms."

Large size…for her man.

A word about the author...

With a growing backlist of books, Jane Drager writes about heroines who are strong-willed, independent, and comfortable in their own skin. She keeps the sex scenes to a minimum, focusing instead on the mystery that draws the two main characters together.

Jane has lived her life as diverse as her stories but retired from her long career as a Respiratory Therapist and instructor. She's married to a wonderful organic farmer who keeps her busy with canning and freezing.

Visit janedrager.com

Other Titles by Jane Drager
All Chocolate, Extra Cherries
Ask Nothing in Return
Ice Cream Dreams, anthology
Infinite Choices
Memories for a Lifetime
No Place for Tomorrow
Secrets and Assumptions
Secrets by Necessity
Testing Midnight
The Riddle Key
Until We Say Goodbye

Thank you for purchasing
this publication of The Wild Rose Press, Inc.

For questions or more information
contact us at
info@thewildrosepress.com.

The Wild Rose Press, Inc.
www.thewildrosepress.com

www.ingramcontent.com/pod-product-compliance
Lightning Source LLC
Chambersburg PA
CBHW052024020726
47501CB00004B/1225